BEAUTIFUL
MONSTER

USA TODAY BESTSELLING AUTHOR

SARA CATE

Cover design: Opulent Swag & Designs

You have no place being in my thoughts, and yet, you own every single one.

Chapter 1
Sunny

The fine blue tip of the pen bleeds ink into my pores as I color in the azalea on my inner thigh. It'll wash off in the water, so I snap a pic of the flower before I slide into the pool. The backs of my legs are scorched from the hot stone deck, and the cool water soothes the burn as I sink beneath the surface. I've been avoiding the water because I know my sister's friends will only start harassing me once I'm at arm's length.

"Aww...Sunny's come to play," Fischer drawls as he swims over. I splash him in the face to keep him away, but it doesn't last long. His hands wind around my waist, pulling me deeper into the water.

Fischer is the worst one. He has warm honey-colored hair and crystalline blue eyes that make it a crying shame he doesn't put that pretty face to good use by being a decent human being. Why my sister keeps him around, I have no idea.

I know she sleeps with him from time to time, but she won't admit it—not that anyone would brag about letting

Fischer Huntley get between their legs. It's hardly an accomplishment.

"Fischer, leave her alone," my sister Cadence calls from the patio. She's mixing herself another margarita while her other friend, Liam, flirts with her from the other side of the bar.

My sister, recently on the splits from her long-term, disloyal boyfriend has always preferred the company of boys over girls. Very rarely, she'll have a girlfriend over, but then Cadence will complain to me nonstop afterward about how annoying she is.

"I'm just playing with her," Fischer says as he tries to dunk me in the middle of the deep end. I use the opportunity to swim away, making it clear across the pool before coming up for air. When I resurface, I hear him shouting to my sister. "Why doesn't your little sister like to have any fun?"

"She's just not as immature as you," Cadence answers as she saunters over with her margarita and vape pen.

"You have any fun friends, Sunny?" he asks as he takes the cig from my sister and pulls a long drag from it. The strawberry-scented cloud wafts my way so I have to hide behind the waterfall feature to avoid it.

"Do you have any friends at all?" I ask.

"Ohhh…" Liam howls from the side of the pool. I like Liam. He's a stoner and isn't the most reliable guy my sister hangs out with, but at least he's nice and understands boundaries.

I know for a fact Cadence hasn't slept with Liam. With the exception of Fischer, she tells me about every guy she sleeps with, and there have been more than a few. She shares her stories with me, so I can live vicariously through her, or so she says.

Cadence is hell-bent on keeping me as virginal as possible, like my own personal chastity belt. Not that I want to get naked with any of the guys in Pineridge anyway. Most of them are immature, self-absorbed, creeps anyway. I see the way they look at me, letting their hungry eyes travel my body like a violation. I've yet to meet anyone in this town that actually gives a damn about getting to know me first.

"Hey, kids," Mom calls as she steps outside with more margarita mix in a big clear pitcher. "Who needs a refill?"

The boys rush forward to get their red solo cups replenished, and I catch my mother's eyes drift toward Fischer's bare chest as he climbs out of the pool.

It's so humiliating, I have to look away.

Ever since Dad left, my mom has been acting like she's Cadence's age. It's a desperate attempt to siphon some of her youth. Like if she appears young and fun, she'll be able to shed the twenty years of life she'd rather forget.

And she is fun...until the tequila drunk turns stale and vicious.

I wish she'd go back inside. I wish for one moment she'd act like a normal mom and go do something on her own while her kids hang out with their friends...even if neither of these guys is my friend.

But she doesn't, of course. Instead, she pours herself a glass and walks toward the pool in her two-piece suit and sheer coverall that ends just below her tush.

Cadence throws me a cautious glare, and I swim toward the opposite side of the pool. I don't want to be too obvious as I evade my mother's presence. But I also don't want to be around when she starts firing unanswerable questions at me: *when are you going to get a boyfriend? Why don't you ever have friends over? Why can't you just be normal?*

My mother and I are just too different. If I were more like my sister, she might be more inclined to love me. She used to be confused by me, maybe even a little annoyed,

3

but since my dad left, it's morphed into an obvious hatred. It's clear to me now that he was the buffer between us.

Climbing out of the pool, I forgo the towel and air-dry on the lounge chair. It's been an unusually hot spring in Pineridge, and while roasting in the sun is easy to do everywhere else in California, here in Northern California, it's a luxury we don't waste.

Picking up the blue pen next to my water bottle, I try to fix the azalea tattoo, but now it's just a stain, smeared and too fuzzy to repair. So, I move to the other leg and start to sketch the roots of a Sycamore tree.

A hushed gasp steals my attention. My head snaps up to see my mother gawking at the yard behind ours, hiding her face with her giant margarita glass filled to the brim with tequila, lime juice, and sugar.

"Oh my god."

"Is that...?" My sister jumps into the pool, swimming closer to my mom. The boys don't seem the least bit interested; both are now elbow deep in a bag of chips on the patio table.

"Alexander Caldwell," my mother whispers loud enough for everyone within a square mile to hear.

My eyes dance back and forth from the pen in my hand to the yard behind ours. I try to pretend I don't care, but still, I look.

Our yard is gradually sloped downward beyond the pool, and between our yard and the great big white house behind us is a row of leafy trees that almost hides the deck, pool, and pool house of what was, until now, a vacant home.

I can make out movement on the wide deck, and I notice dark blue pants, tightly fit and tapered above the ankle. He's walking around the large yard, quiet and alone. I can't make out his face yet to confirm my mother's original claim. She's been claiming for weeks that there was a rumor the house was purchased by Pineridge's richest and most elusive bachelor.

"No way," Cadence breathes, her lips parting as she tries to watch him from the corner of her eye. She swims across the pool, attempting to look as normal as possible just to steal a glance, and when she does, she sucks her lips in between her teeth and swims back with a stifled smile and wide eyes. "Oh my god, it is!"

My mother practically squeals, but Cadence hushes her with her hands over her mouth.

"What is he doing in a big house like that?" Cadence whispers.

"Who cares? He's loaded. He can live wherever he wants."

"Is he still single?" Cadence continues, fishing another look over Mom's shoulder.

"Single enough. That man will never get married."

Cadence starts fixing her hair. Even after a day in the pool without makeup and a blow dryer she still looks like someone you'd see in a perfume commercial. My sister has that natural beauty that draws men in like bees to honey, and that attention has been her lifeblood since she was fifteen.

"Well, he hasn't met me yet."

They break out in a tittered laugh as I steal another look at the man across the yard. I've seen Alexander Caldwell online, mostly when he did charity benefits or when he started dating a supermodel in the valley, showing up on Buzzfeed and making Pineridge proud.

But I've never seen him in person.

He's walking in the grass now, seemingly inspecting his new property and unaware of the two hyenas behind him, ready to pounce. With his back to me, I can't make out his face, but somehow, just by his walk, I recognize him.

"Oh my god, he's coming this way," Cadence mouths quietly.

"Hey neighbor!" my mom shouts in a sing-song tone as she stands up and waves at the man standing down by the low hedges that separate our yards. My sister and I watch in mortification as he hesitantly waves back.

"Jesus, Mom," Cadence mutters.

"Can I interest you in a margarita?"

He walks up to the yard now, resting his broad forearms on the aluminum fence, and even with the Ray-bans covering his eyes, I recognize him. That's him. Alexander Caldwell, practically in my backyard.

It takes him a moment to respond, and with that almost-hidden scowl on his face, I imagine he's trying to find a reason to decline my overeager mother's invitation. With her energy, I wouldn't doubt she could tie him up and chain him to the porch if given the chance.

I can see the war he's waging with himself from here.

"What the hell…" he says as he heads toward the open area between the trees.

My eyes nearly bug out of my head when he climbs the slope toward the pool deck. My sister jumps out of the pool to greet him while my mother pours his drink.

I hope he likes tequila.

Cadence stands less than a foot away from him, wearing no more than a square foot of fabric on her whole body. I watch as she shakes his hand. He holds onto it a second too long, smiling with teeth brighter than the sun.

My sister looks like someone has just sat her in front of a buffet after weeks without eating. Her eyes are trained on him as they exchange greetings. He makes some remarks about her name, asking if her parents played the drums in a marching band, at which she laughs. I bet if he didn't have those glasses on, we would all see his direct gaze at her full breasts. With the way they're hanging out of her bikini, I have a hard time not staring at them too.

For a moment, I think I should get up. Maybe I'm expected to greet him or something, but I can't seem to move. From the corner of my eye, I notice my sister's friends scatter, going inside or leaving for all I know. And I understand why. Alexander has a presence. If I were a man, I wouldn't want to be around him either. He's not even on our porch yet, and already everyone and everything dwarfs in comparison. My mom calls him up to the bar where she has his drink waiting, but in order to get there, he has to pass me, still sitting in my lounge chair.

At first, he regards me with a lazy glance, but just as he's completely blocked the sun, his eyes on my face, he stops.

"And who are you?" he asks.

My name falls out of my mouth on its own as if summoned by his request. "Sunny."

"What's that?" he mumbles, nodding toward the intricate blue design on my inner thigh. I feel myself gulp as I look down at the now-faint azalea.

Somehow, I've forgotten how to speak. When I look up at him, his smile is gone, and his sobering gaze is on me.

After a moment, when it's clear I won't answer his question about the ink on my leg, he lets out a sexy chuckle.

"Nice to meet you, Sunny."

He closes the distance to the bar where he shares a drink with my mom. I can do nothing but relive the moment when he stood, towering above me, his eyes on my inner leg, somehow as intimate as if it had been his touch.

My finger traces the blue flower while I try to pretend

he had no effect on me. And every so often, I glance up toward where he stands, flirting with my mother and sister.

Almost every time I look, he's staring at me.

* * *

The ring echoes through the phone five times before the voicemail picks up.

This is Daniel Thorn of Thorn Talent Management. I'm sorry I missed your call. Please contact my assistant, Ilsa Levi at ilevi@ttm.com if you can't reach me. Thank you.

I let the silence settle for a moment before I start speaking. "Hey, Dad. Me again. Wondering if you wanted to meet this weekend. Maybe do lunch. Ilsa can come. I'm not going to email her though, like your voicemail message said. I'm not a client. I'm your daughter. So maybe just pick up when I call. Just once would be fine. Or you know...call me back. Whatever."

Instead of hanging up, I let the call run in silence while I sit alone in my room. It takes a long two minutes before the voicemail beeps and the call ends. Staring at the black screen, I pick it up and scroll through my recent calls, counting the outgoing ones never answered.

Seven. Seven since he last answered, and that was a month ago.

Tossing it back on my bed, I pick up my sketchbook and finish the dark tree sketch, adding detail to the leaves the way they look out my window against the cool sunset.

Cadence lands on my bed with a crash, totally fucking

8

up the sketch I was working on. It was just a doodle, but still...it pisses me off when she does that.

"Cadie! Dammit."

"Can you believe Alexander-fucking-Caldwell was here?" She grabs a pillow from my bed and starts doing vulgar movements with it. "I can't wait until he wrecks me. I bet he has a massive cock."

"You're disgusting," I laugh, taking the pillow from her before she can hump it anymore.

"You're just jealous." She plants a margarita-scented kiss on my cheek.

The sudden reminder of alcohol prompts my next question. "Where's Mom?"

"Out cold. Let's hope she stays that way." Her voice is only slightly slurred. My sister can drink as much as our mother without the mean and nasty side effects. Cadence is funny, loud, and overtly sexual when she's drunk. Mom is almost exactly the opposite.

Hence why Dad left six months ago.

Well, that and his twenty-two-year-old secretary.

"Yeah, forever," I mumble, not even feeling bad for it. Some days I wish she was dead because then at least I could miss her. At least that way time and death could conjure up positive feelings about my mother while I forget the bad parts.

"Don't say that, Sun. You don't mean it."

"I know. Did Fischer and Liam leave?" I ask.

"Yeah, they didn't like me flirting with the rich guy so much. Seriously, Sunny. Think about how nice it would be if I could land a guy like Alexander Caldwell." Flipping onto her back, my sister fans out her gorgeous black hair against the bright white comforter on my bed. It almost looks like the roots of a tree or ink spilled into the ocean.

"Don't move," I mumble as I sketch each strand onto a

9

blank white page. My sister is used to it, so she continues on like I said nothing.

"And I don't mean just fucking him, Sunny. Imagine if I could settle down with a guy like him. We could *both* get out of this house."

"I'm not living with you and your rich husband." Concentrating on my sketch, I think about it anyway. How nice it would be to have a fresh, happy home to live in, instead of one filled with so much spite that we eat hate for breakfast each morning. I don't want to live with my sister, but if my dad doesn't start answering my calls, I might be out of options.

After dropping out of art school last semester, I don't have any real opportunities, and no one is replying to my job applications—even though I put out about a hundred last month alone.

"Besides," I continue. "I don't think Alexander Caldwell is really the settling down kind of guy."

"You don't know that. I mean, he bought a house in the suburbs. Plus, he's what...thirty?" she says, screwing up her face.

"Forty." Yeah, I looked him up on my phone while my mom was trying to get him to drink a second margarita.

"See? I bet he's looking for a nice young woman to give him lots of orgasms and babies."

"Gross," I mutter, as I finish the sketch with the curls at the top of the page.

"You're almost twenty, Sunny. You'll be horny for guys like Alexander Caldwell soon enough. It's weird that you're not already."

What my sister doesn't know is that I already am. Sometimes it's all I can think about. Men, sex, bodies, lust, passion. I imagine what it must feel like being pressed against the wall, his body covering mine, his lips on my neck, my breasts, and everywhere else.

I like to imagine the weight of a man on top of me and the sensation of having him *inside* me. The version my imagination cooks up is usually rough in nature and wild in passion.

The very few kisses I've shared with random boys at school were nothing more than sloppy and overly aggressive expressions of lust. There were no real feelings involved. Nothing to write home about. I let one of them, a college kid who assumed I'd be as loose as my sister, put his hands up my shirt, and it was nice—just nice. But when he tried to unbutton my jeans, I pushed him away. He called me an ugly tease and left.

Later that night I drew a naked sketch of him with a tiny penis and gave it to Cadence. When I told her what he did, she was livid and posted it on Instagram and Snapchat —she even tagged him.

Then, she came into my room and lay with me on the bed. Then, she told me to wait as long as I could before having sex. According to her, she lost her virginity too young and regrets not taking the time to find the right person or finding what felt good instead of letting desperate horny teens paw all over her for as long as she did. She made me promise I would wait.

And I did.

I was fifteen at the time.

A shriek comes from the front of the house, jolting us both from our laughter. Cadence tenses next to me.

"Caaaaaadence," our mother howls.

"I better go see what she wants."

"Tell her we're out of tequila," I mumble without looking back as my sister climbs off the bed. "Get her high instead. It chills her out."

When I turn, my mother is standing at the door. Thankfully, she's too far gone for any of my words to register. Her eyeliner is running down her face, and she looks sad. For a moment, I feel bad for her. I almost miss the woman beneath the shell, but then she looks at me, and I know there isn't a filter in place to stop her from what she's about to say to me.

"You were so rude to Mr. Caldwell today," she slurs. "Couldn't even get up and talk to him. I raised you to have manners."

"He was talking to Cadence. I didn't want to steal the attention from her." I say this because I assume it's what she wants me to say, to acknowledge that my sister is a piece of meat we're trying to take to the market for the highest price.

My mother lets out a loud cackle. Cadence tries to lead her out of the room because she knows this interaction can only go downhill. My presence alone triggers her.

"You were being an ungrateful little bitch, Sunny. And you know as well as I do that you weren't stealing any attention from your sister."

When I glance up, I see her eyes pointed at me as she sways in her spot. There is hate and resentment in her eyes.

Cadence has noticed it too. She says our mother's disdain for me is from jealousy. It's because Mom's beauty is plain, mass-produced, sugared, and canned, like peaches. Whereas mine is natural and unique, like an exotic fruit right off the tree. Not perfect, but authentic.

She might be right, but I think my mother hates me because I'm not like her. I don't feel the need to smile all the time, just because a man shows me attention. I'm not hung up on things and money like her. I'd rather be single forever than stuck in a loveless marriage like she was for twenty years.

I don't care about men like Alexander Caldwell like she thinks I should.

If I say nothing, I'm being rude. If I say what's on my mind, things get physical. We do this dance every night, where she stands there with her hatred and I stare back, silent and fighting tears.

But I do not cry. Ever.

"Come on, Mama. Sunny's sorry. She'll be nicer next time. Let's go get a drink." Cadence pulls her out of the room, glancing back at me as I shake my head at her.

My sister is the bubble wrap of this family, keeping everyone at a safe distance and avoiding the shattered mess that would inevitably result if she was not there.

I know the day will come when Cadence will leave, and I certainly won't be around to see what happens when she does.

Chapter 2
Alexander

"Have the movers delivered everything?"

"Yeah," I answer, staring at the unopened boxes in my living room—all full of junk I can't even remember now and don't give a shit about. My sister's voice carries through the house from the smart speaker set up in the kitchen.

"I'll drive out next weekend and help you unpack," she says, sounding a little too eager.

"Don't bother. I can do this on my own."

"I know you can. I just don't think you will."

I don't answer her, and the room grows quiet except for the white noise hum coming from her side of the call. She must be in the car. She always calls me on her long commutes.

"This is a good move, Alexander. Put down some roots. Try to just be alone for a while. Maybe think about getting back into business."

I'm listening to her, but my mind tends to wander when my sister starts lecturing. That margarita wore off too fast, and my buzz is fading. One of these boxes has the booze, but I'm not about to start rifling through them. I need to go into town and stock up.

Still, I don't answer her. This is the part where she says all the things she thinks she needs to say—like I don't already know. Like I care. Like it'll make any fucking difference at all.

"Fine, don't answer me, but I know you hear me. No more parties, Alex. No more trouble."

I'm a fucking adult, and excuse me if I don't want to listen to my big sister threaten me if I want to party my ass off until I'm dead. Who cares if I'm throwing my money and career away? What fucking business is it of hers? None.

She doesn't know everything about what went down with Tyson, my business partner—why he kicked me out, his marriage ended, and we don't talk anymore. But I'm pretty sure she figured it out. I think everyone did.

"Yes, Mom," I groan, my forehead resting against the quartz countertop.

"Don't be a dick." Her voice is clipped, and I expect her to hang up. That's usually what she does when I call her *Mom*. It's cruel because our mother was a fucking saint, and she's also dead. Comparing Charlotte to her only reminds my sister how different the two of them were. My sister chose to skip the marriage and kids gig, breaking our mother's heart before she passed.

"Sorry," I chuckle, though I'm really not.

"Meet any neighbors yet?"

"Yeah, there's a nice family behind me. Had me over for drinks today."

"That's nice. I can just see you out there around the grill with other guys in cargo shorts and Crocs." Her husky laugh fills the phone line for a moment while I let a smile creep onto my face.

"No guys at this house," I add.

She groans. "Oh great. Well, stay away from that house then."

What my sister is implying is that I have a problem with women. I'm impulsive, indulgent, and reckless. Of course, it's all fucking true, but I won't satisfy her with that admission.

Just then, I peer out the glass patio door toward the yard. The trees just barely hide the view of the deck where I recently shared a margarita with a middle-aged woman hornier than a cat in heat.

It's dusk out now, and the air is getting cooler, but there's still someone out in the pool. At first, I figure it's the one I met. The busty brunette.

Then, I catch a glimpse of her long, slender legs as she dives in, disappearing into the water until she pops up on the other side, ducks back under, and glides across again.

Her head breaches the water, and this time, I can make out the softer features of her face. It's not the girl I met. It's the younger one. The one in the chair with the eyes that stopped me in my tracks.

She had a cold, harsh, no-fucks-given stare. The look in her eyes was like a line from a Dylan Thomas poem: dark, mysterious...sexy.

Granted, it was probably just a moody teenage sulking expression, and I'm looking too much into it, but still—she haunts me.

She steps out of the water and stops. Without a towel, she's standing on the deck, shivering in nothing more than a thin bathing suit. *What is she doing?*

Then, her head turns and her eyes trail up to my house where I'm sure she can see me watching her from my brightly lit window.

She doesn't wave. And neither do I.

We just...acknowledge each other.

Shaking without the sun to dry her, she finally turns away from me and rushes toward the house, hidden by the leaves of the tree.

"Are you still there?" Charlotte calls for the second time before I shake my head and answer her.

"Yeah, I am. Sorry, just tired."

"Get some rest. Call me tomorrow." We say our good-byes, and she hangs up.

The house is quiet, dark, and too goddamn big. There are four rooms in this house, three of which I guarantee I won't even touch, but this is what I wanted—a home.

Something quiet, calm, and a good place to focus.

This is what I wanted, and if I keep reminding myself, I might start to believe it.

Chapter 3
Sunny

Voices carry from downstairs. It's mostly laughter, high-pitched and obnoxious. They spill into my house, just like they do every Saturday night. Mom got the friends in the divorce apparently, because they never stopped invading my life, even after Dad left.

"Come have a swim with us," Cadence calls from the doorway.

"No, thanks."

She should know by now; these are my painting nights. If I go downstairs, everyone will want to tell me how much I've grown. The men will talk to me like I'm a child while simultaneously trying to get me to hug them or sit on their lap, and it's just not worth the hassle. So, when I was about fifteen, I decided my parents' party nights were my painting nights.

Putting the paint on the canvas is a lot of work. It involves mixing the colors, getting the supplies out, making a mess, and cleaning it up. Plus, I hate stopping once I start, and since their parties go all night, it's the perfect amount of time. I keep my music loud and pull an all-nighter.

"Shut the door, please," I say over my shoulder with a smile while my sister stands in the doorway with a spiked seltzer in her hands. Her hair is down, curled and hanging over her shoulders. With her tanned skin, that white bikini looks stunning on her, and it makes me so jealous I want to hate her.

But I don't.

Liam appears behind her, wrapping a hand around her waist and pulling her away from my doorway.

"Shut the door," I yell as their laughter fades away.

My sister broke my noise-canceling headphones when she fell into the pool with them on, so I'm stuck blaring my music to try and drown out the sounds coming from downstairs. It works out fine, except for the few times Mom inevitably complains.

A couple of hours go by when I finally sit back to see the progress I've made. Billie Eilish croons from my Bluetooth speaker on the dresser, and I'm pretty pleased with how my portrait is turning out. I decided to paint a sketch I've had in my journal for months. It was a woman I saw in a sunglasses ad once. It popped up on my Insta feed, and something in her eyes spoke to me, so I screenshot it. Then I added a few things, having a little fun with her expression. I changed the slope of her nose so that the bridge started up a little higher than the real model's. Her mouth is wider, her lips thinner. There are freckles scattered around her face, dark ones too, not the light spatter most people are used to seeing.

Cadence called it exotic beauty. Undefinable. Unattainable.

The sketch on the canvas is done with the beginnings of some color, but I'll be up until at least three if I want to get the shading in tonight, which I do. I'm afraid if I leave it, I'll never come back to it.

I need to clean my palette and mix some new colors. Climbing off the floor, I sense someone standing in the doorway and almost scream when my eyes meet his.

"Sorry to scare you," he says without smiling.

Goosebumps erupt along my arms and neck. Alexander Caldwell is standing in my bedroom, closer than ever. He steps forward, and I struggle to breathe.

Being this near him, I notice things I couldn't see from across the yard. Things that don't translate to his online photos and cell phone videos. His brown eyes are so dark they almost match the black irises in the middle. His nose is long, and like mine, the bridge rises up to his eyebrows. On him, it makes him look like a bronze statue, a face they might have etched into stone. The sharp lines of his lips steal my attention.

I've never been so affected by a man in person before. So…attracted.

He steps in again. Still, I don't move. At this point, I realize I'm in a pair of lounge silk pants that are too long and gather at the bottom. They're covered in paint. My shirt is a light cotton tank with two peaks where my braless breasts hold it up.

I suddenly feel so exposed. Why is he here? In my house. In my room.

"I was looking for the bathroom, and I heard your music." He steps farther in. He's walking right into my room like he owns the place, and I *should* tell him to leave, but I don't want him to.

"What are you working on?" he asks.

His eyes travel across the room to the easel on the floor. *Oh, God.* Please don't laugh at it, this supermodel portrait that is basically the artistic rendering of a Snapchat filter that looks like me if I was far prettier and sexier than I am in real life.

"Did you do that?" He walks toward the painting, looking closer, then comparing her to the sketch on the floor. "I like the painting better."

My heart is hammering so loud, it pulses in my ears.

He stands up and looks at me, locking eyes for a long moment. "Say something."

"What do you want me to say?" I mumble, my voice coming out with a shake.

"I don't know," he laughs. "Are you always this quiet?"

"Maybe," I answer.

He smiles. Then he lands on my bed, sitting on the edge, kicking his feet out and crossing them at the ankles. "Why aren't you downstairs? Your sister got all the social genes, huh?"

I can't help the smile that cracks on my lips. "That's an understatement." Before I drop the heavy trays on the floor, I take them to the attached bathroom and put them in the sink. With my back to him, I quickly rinse the trays before they stain the porcelain and my mother loses her mind.

"You're good," he says, and I peer over my shoulder to see him taking a sip of whatever is in the glass he's holding.

"Well, I had an expensive education."

He lets out a clipped laugh behind me, and I peer up into the mirror to see him in the reflection. Alexander Caldwell is sitting on my bed like it's not the craziest thing that's ever happened to me.

He catches me watching him.

"You don't mind me hanging out in here, do you?"

I shake my head. "Nope."

"Thanks. Sometimes I just need a break. Can I admit something to you?"

After I dry off the trays, I turn back to him, giving him a quick nod.

"I snoop at every party I go to."

"Everyone does that," I answer with a laugh.

"Yeah, but I like to go find quiet rooms and just hang out in them like they're my own."

As I step closer to him, I can make out the weathered skin around his eyes, where the tiniest crow's feet have started to form. Other than that, he barely shows his age. His shirt fits him snugly around the arms, strands of muscles peeking out of the light-colored fabric.

He glances up at me, and I nearly lose my breath again. How can someone else's face make it so hard to breathe? I want to sketch him, the darkness of his eyes. The slope of his nose.

Instead, I turn away and kneel next to the easel again.

Zayn starts playing, and I feel Alexander's silent presence behind me while I work. He just watches me while I mix the paint and stretch my arms before I get back to it.

Is he just going to sit there and watch me the whole time? It should make me uncomfortable...but it doesn't. I normally hate when people watch me paint.

The ice in his glass clinks when the song changes, and I focus on the lines around the portrait's eyes.

"Did they teach you to do that?" he asks. His voice has a little slur to it.

"Do what?"

"To paint that look in her eye."

I smile back at him. "What look?"

His eyes level with mine. "The look that says she wants you."

It gets quiet while he glances between me and the painting. I swallow.

"I don't know," I mumble, looking back at the canvas.

He should be out there with my sister. He's forty. I'm nineteen. He should be mingling with my mom's friends and not hanging out with me, but for once, I actually like one of the weekend partiers.

"How old are you, Sunny?" His voice is husky, and his words dance through the space between us the same way ink swirls through water, slowly changing the color of everything. A moment ago, it felt like he could be my friend. But now…

I'm nothing more than a blip on his radar. An itch to scratch. A notch on his bedpost. A weekend indulgence.

"Nineteen," I mutter, leaning over to finish the charcoal around her left eye.

I'm waiting for him to invite me over to sit next to him. Maybe he'll be one of those guys who asks me to sit on his lap. Have a drink with him. Give him a little kiss on the cheek.

The goosebumps on my skin turn cold.

I hear him stand up from my bed, and my breath gets caught in my chest.

"Stay in your room, Sunny. When your mom has these parties…you just stay up here, okay?"

My head snaps toward where he's standing in my doorway, his gaze down on me, kneeling on the floor.

"Okay?" he presses, sounding impatient and assertive.

I nod.

"Bring me that painting when it's done," he orders, jerking his head toward the canvas.

Looking back at the girl, I let my brows furrow in confusion. "You want it?"

"Yeah, I'll buy it. Can you finish it by next weekend?"

I nod again.

"Good. Bring it on Saturday."

Then, he just turns and leaves me speechless on the floor of my room.

* * *

I finish the girl on Thursday, but I barely sleep that night, overthinking and worrying about the curve of her lips. Is it too much like a smile or not enough? Should I redo it?

I've never sold a piece before. Not really. So, this has me on edge. Is the color right? Does she still have the *look* Alexander wanted?

The interaction in my room kept replaying in my head the entire time I painted it. I can't read him. At first, I figured he just wanted to hang out, be a friend, as I was the safe option. The person he didn't have to try so hard around. With my sister, he had to put in effort. But with me, I thought we could just relax...but there was something more. When he asked my age, it changed. Like he was checking to see how illegal it would be to touch me. Then he told me to stay in my room like he was my dad.

Did he want to protect me or preserve me?

Super gross thought, Sunny.

Finally, by 9:00 a.m. Friday, I can't take it anymore. While Mom and Cadence are still sleeping, I wrap the canvas in paper to protect the texture of the paint and walk it through the backyard, between the hedges and up to Alexander's house. It occurs to me as I reach his back porch that I should really be going through the front door, but I'm already here. I could just leave the package by the door, but what if the wind knocks it over or he doesn't notice it?

This was a terrible idea.

When I reach the sliding glass door that leads to his kitchen, I find myself about to knock.

"For a girl named Sunny, you move a little more like a black rain cloud."

I jump, letting out a howling scream. He steps out of the pool house on the other side of the porch, and I spin toward him nearly tossing the painting in the pool as a way to defend myself.

He laughs. "I scared you again, but you are on my back porch, so you can't blame me this time."

"I'm sorry," I stammer. "I just finished early, so I wanted to bring this to you."

"Bring it in, let's see it."

He turns toward the pool house and beckons me to follow. The expansive room is mostly windows, large shades keeping the sun from roasting the inside. All of them are up at the moment, so I can see that he seems to be renovating it. There are boards across the floor and a table saw in the corner. Is he working on it by himself?

He catches me looking at the scattered mess.

"My little project," he says, and when I look up, I realize for the first time that he's shirtless. In only his shorts, sweat beads across his tan body, down his sculpted pecs and over his abs.

I've seen men shirtless before. Hell, I've seen them naked, but I've never felt like a speechless idiot in front of them before.

"What are you doing?" I breathe.

He looks confused as he stares back, catching my eyes on his chest.

"I mean with the wood. On the floor. What are you building?"

"Oh," he laughs. "I'm redoing the moldings and building a bench seat across that window. I don't know if it'll be enough. This room is so boring."

Looking around, I can see what he means. It has plain

windowed walls, a small kitchenette, bathroom, cabinets. But it is just a pool house, and our house doesn't have one, so I'm impressed anyway.

"Okay, let's see it," he says, motioning to the painting again. Taking it to the large worktable, I pull off the paper and bite my lip. If he says it's nice, then he hates it. Anything less than speechless means he hates it.

His eyes don't change as he looks at the painting, and I can't stop staring at the curve of her lips.

Meanwhile he lets his gaze drift over every inch, absorbing each brush stroke like I bled into each one. I wait.

Finally, they settle on her eyes, and his lips turn up into a smile.

"Fuck, Sunny. This is good."

"Really?"

He looks at me like I just called him ugly. "Really? Come on. You have to see how good this is."

I shrug. "I don't know. I can't see what you see. Everyone sees something different, right?"

"If anyone sees anything less than fan-fucking-tastic, they're insane."

A laugh escapes my lips.

He looks at me again, clearly surprised to hear my laughter. Then, his gaze drifts to something behind me, and I turn to see it's nothing more than a blank wall along the back of the room.

"I want it there," he says decisively.

"You want to hang it there?"

"No. I don't want to hang it there. Sunny, I want you to paint it there." He steps away from me, standing in front of the blank wall and staring at it like he's picturing it. "Paint this girl on my wall."

What? He wants me to repaint the whole portrait on his wall? Is he insane?

"Are you serious?"

"Do you know how to do a mural?" he asks. I let out a heavy breath.

I nod.

"Good. Will you paint her on this wall? As a mural?"

I've wanted to do a mural for as long as I can remember. I used to try to paint my bedroom walls when I was little, thinking that if I just painted one square at a time, I could cover the whole thing without anyone really noticing. My mother nearly broke my backside when she found it.

"I don't know," I mumble.

Of course, I want to paint a fucking mural in the most famous guy in Pineridge's pool house, but this wasn't a good idea. What would my mother say? Would she think I was getting in Cadence's way?

Then, I realize something—he would pay me. How much I don't know, but probably enough to finally get out. Quickly, in my head, I do the math. I think most artists work for $40 to $50 per square foot. This is probably a twelve-by-fifteen-foot wall. I can't add it up fast enough, but it definitely feels like enough to start up in my own place.

Then, there's the exposure. If he shared it with his friends, I could do murals all over town.

"What do you mean you don't know? You have something better to do?"

"I've never done one before."

"So just paint this...bigger." He motions toward the wall. "I'll give you the keys to the pool house. I won't bug you. You can come and go as you please. Get it done in your own time."

Questions swirl around in my mind. Mostly it's doubt. I

can't do this. What if I royally fuck it up? Am I even good enough to paint a mural that big?

I'm biting my lip furiously, staring at the painting and the wall like they'll give me answers. Permission to say no.

Then a hand lands on my shoulder. "Hey there, little rain cloud."

When I look up at him, he has a crooked smile, but his eyes bore into me with a fierceness. "Breathe," he says quietly, so quiet his voice doesn't travel anywhere but straight into my ears. Straight into my heart.

So, I do. I take a deep breath and look at the wall again.

Reasons I should take the job: I deserve this. I need the money. He wants me to.

Reasons I should not take the job: none.

"Okay," I say finally. "I'll do it."

He steps back, crossing his arms over his chest. "Now wait a minute. Never accept a job without asking questions first, understand?"

"What questions?"

He walks over to the fridge in the corner of the room and pulls out two sodas. "Anything, but least of all, you should always ask how much you'll be getting paid."

"But I don't care how much," I lie. I actually care very much but I don't feel brave enough to admit that.

"How does ten sound?"

"Ten." My mouth repeats his words without registering in my mind. Ten...thousand?

Suddenly, my heart is picking up speed, but I try to maintain my composure like it means nothing to me. He hands me one of the sodas, and I stare at him, biting my lip again.

What does he want me to say? Does he want me to accept it?

"Fifteen," I blurt before I can stop myself.

Finally, his poker face melts into a smile. "That a girl."

Squaring my shoulders, I pull my lip from between my teeth and keep my eyes on his face, which is desperately hard when the sweat beads on his shoulders, I'm suddenly so desperate to touch it. To rub my body against it. To absorb every drop.

"Twelve, final offer," he says, and I nearly gasp. Instead, I lock a deep breath in my chest and take a drink of my soda. It's ice cold which helps with the fire that seems to be seeping from my pores at this moment.

Finally, I reach out a hand. "Deal."

He takes his before time shaking my hand. Slowly, he sets down his drink, every one of his movements so deliberate and driving me wild. He reaches forward and grasps my hand in his, squeezing just right.

"Deal."

As I walk back to my house, my thoughts are so clouded I can't react properly. Twelve. Thousand. Dollars. The keys to Alexander Caldwell's pool house. A real mural.

Fucking pinch me.

When I reach the back porch, it's not even eleven in the morning, and I can already hear the slur in my mother's voice. As I walk through the patio door, she's standing there watching me. Cadence is sitting at the table, leaning over a cup of coffee.

"Good morning," I say with a smile before my mother aims her angry eyes on me.

"Where were you?"

"I had to take something to Alexander's house."

Mom turns her face and stares at my sister with her mouth hanging open. "What is she talking about?"

Cadence shrugs.

"He bought my painting," I mumble, trying to walk past her and out of the kitchen, away from this mess.

A loud laugh echoes through the kitchen. "Gosh, I wonder why he would do that?" My mother is vicious with her words when she's drunk.

For some reason, I'm in the mood to fight. I want to defend him and prove something to them. So, I open my big fat mouth. "He's hiring me to paint a mural in his pool house."

Silence fills the room.

Cadence speaks with the cup up to her lips. "You can't be serious."

My face flips up to see hers and betrayal clouds my vision. She's acting like Mom. Is she drunk, too?

"Sunny," she says, trying to explain herself. "You know what he's doing, don't you?"

I squint my eyes at my sister. She knows I'm not sleeping with him. She knows I'm not like that...like her. But I won't stoop to this level. I won't join this circus of misery and act like them.

So, I refuse to answer her. "He hired me to paint a mural in his pool house because he liked my painting, not because he's trying to sleep with me. I'll have keys, and he's paying me."

"How much?" my mother asks, and I cringe. I shouldn't have said that. She won't touch my money. Not a fucking dime.

"I don't know. I didn't ask. Maybe a couple hundred."

"Cadence, you should go with her. Spend some time over there with him. I swear if you're lying, Sunny..."

"I'm not lying." My voice is cold and angry.

30

Cadence won't look at me. "Yeah, sure. Someone has to keep an eye on Sunny."

My sister...the ultimate traitor. This isn't about protecting me. If anything, she's jealous. Jealous that I can hold a conversation with a man that doesn't end in sex, and I want to tell her that, but I'm not cruel. Not to her.

Before anyone can say another word, I rush out of the kitchen and up to my room. As soon as I get that mural done, I'm out of this house. Forever.

Chapter 4

Alexander

She moans against my ear as I slam into her again and again. I like the way Lea purrs, but I wish she'd move a little. Grab my ass. Run her nails down my back. Through my hair. But she doesn't. She just lays there and mews.

I said I wasn't going to do this anymore, but after working in the pool house all morning, I needed to indulge in something. Lea is one of my go-to calls, and man does she answer. It's never a bad time for her. She was at my house in fifteen minutes; on her knees in less than twenty.

But now, I'm over it. Sinking into her on my bed in my brand-new bedroom, still cluttered with boxes, I look out the big window that overlooks the backyard, and I wish I would have just jacked off instead.

"You feel so good, Alex," she whispers as she wraps her legs around me. Grabbing one of her ankles, I try a new angle, hoping it will light the spark I need. She digs her fingers into her own hair and starts gasping like I'm pounding her lungs or something.

Fuck, this is not what I wanted.

Movement across the yard steals my attention for a moment. Sunny is walking out to the pool in one of her little bikinis. Chills run up my spine. She lets her hair out of a ponytail and shakes it free. Through the trees, I can just make out her long legs before she dives under the water. Dropping Lea's ankle, I crash against her body and try not to watch the nineteen-year-old cross the pool in slow strokes while I fuck a thirty-year-old cocktail waitress.

But my eyes find Sunny anyway.

And I think about the way she bit her lip this morning, standing in my pool house.

I think about her leaning over the easel in those silk pajama pants.

Fuck.

My skin tingles with electricity as I slide into Lea. I'm a fucking monster, but I can't help myself. Looking up, I find her again, climbing out of the pool, water cascading down her back, over her hips, and the perfectly round shape of her ass.

I lose myself, eyes squeezed closed as I come, imagining it's someone else kissing my lips. I picture someone else moaning and getting off instead of faking her orgasm because she thinks it's what I want.

When I open my eyes, Lea is looking out the window, too, and I tense, afraid she'll see what I see and know my secret. I just thought about that teenager while I was fucking her.

She lets out a deep breath and plants a kiss on my cheek before she climbs away. "Thanks, babe. That was fun."

"Yeah," I say collapsing on the bed, pulling off the condom and wrapping it in a tissue. "I needed that."

She leans down and ruffles my hair then fishes her underwear out of my bed.

"What you need is to unpack your boxes."

"Yeah, I know."

"You wanna go grab a drink?" she asks without really meaning it.

"Nah. I have work to do. Thanks, though."

"You got it." She slips on her dress and fixes her hair in the mirror. I catch her watching me cautiously as I lay back in my bed. "I feel a little bad leaving you here. You sure you're okay?"

I climb out of my bed because that's clearly what she wants to see. That I'm okay. That I didn't have a nervous breakdown and leave my old life behind for this suburban fantasy. Everyone seems to have the same worry these days.

Kissing her on the side of the head, I smack her ass and lie. "I'm fine."

* * *

After she's gone, I open up a bottle of bourbon and pour a glass. I should probably order dinner, but I don't have the energy to even look up anything. Instead, I walk out onto my patio and plant my ass in one of my lounge chairs. Sunny isn't swimming anymore, but I watch her yard like I'm waiting for her to come back. Counting the windows to her house, I try to guess what each one is, based on my drunk night at the party stumbling through the rooms and finding Sunny sitting on her floor like a child. There's a large window overlooking the yard on the right and a couple smaller ones on the left. I'm pretty sure the one on the right is hers.

God, I hope it's hers.

Fuck. What is wrong with me?

I'm not the barely legal kind of guy. Horny teens were

never my thing, and I certainly don't get off on the idea of being anyone's first anymore. That ship has sailed.

So, what the fuck was that shit in the bedroom? It wasn't about Sunny's age. But man, I'd like to fuck someone who actually feels things. Who makes me feel things. I can't remember the last time I met someone who oozed passion the way Sunny does. Not just in her art, but in the intensity of her eyes.

I'm tired of these emotionless lays, like mutual getting off and moving on. I'm over it. I'm not making any more booty calls. It feels like a weak resolution, but I repeat it to myself over and over. I'm not calling any more girls over here for a quick romp just so I can feel like shit about it afterward.

I mean, I'm not giving up sex entirely. But the next person I fuck, I want to feel something. Someone with life in her eyes.

Sunny's eyes pop up in my mind again.

Fuck.

Looking over at the empty wall in the pool house, I realize this is probably a very stupid idea. If I have her over here every day, sweating in that hot little room, in those silk pants, I'm screwed.

I should probably cancel the offer.

But I'd be lying if I said it was about the mural. I want those eyes of hers—even for just a few minutes every day. I want to see her in my space, looking at me, quiet and nervous with the whole fucking world behind her stare. I want it.

And it's not sexual. I'm not trying to get in a teenager's panties. I just can't handle empty stares anymore. No more fake tits. Fake eyelashes. Fake orgasms.

Sunny is real, and right now, I'm craving something real.

Chapter 5
Sunny

B y the next morning, I'm standing in Alexander's backyard with my paintbrushes and other supplies loaded into my backpack. Just like yesterday, he's there waiting.

"Good thing there's space to get through the hedges in the yard."

I smile at him as he lets me in. He's shirtless and sweaty again, and I wonder if he realizes what a distraction that is.

The interaction with my mother yesterday had my head spinning all day. Could they be right that this is all a ploy to get me into bed? I didn't talk to Cadence at all yesterday, and I never go that long without talking to my sister. She's my ally. Without her, I have no one. But the way she looked at me yesterday, with spite and bitterness, and...jealousy, had me feeling betrayed.

Alexander is forty—a *man*. And while his face is the sculpted kind of beauty that makes my heart pitter-patter right out of my chest, I don't see myself with someone like him. To him, I'm a scrawny, quiet kid. Next to my sister, that's what I feel like.

When I came out to the pool yesterday afternoon, I swear I saw someone else in Alex's window—a woman. I tried not to stare, but with the way the sun sets behind his house, it was so easy to see in his window from the pool. I wonder if he can see in my bedroom that easily. I wonder if he wants to.

He unlocks the door and guides me into my workspace. It's hot in here, hotter than I think it was yesterday.

My breath catches as I take in the scene. There's a two-level scaffolding in place next to the wall. On the first level, there are new brushes, a new apron, drop cloths, paper, mixing cans, and palettes. My jaw hangs open. He bought me all new supplies.

"I went out this morning. I hope this stuff works."

"Yeah," I breathe as I look through it all.

"I know you don't have the paint yet, but let me know what you need, and I'll order it."

Looking at him, my mind is reeling. He bought everything for me.

Today, my plan was to set everything up, take stock of what I need, and make a few sketches, but now that he's done everything, what will I do?

I look over at him, the sweat glistening, yet again, on his shoulders. He tenses as his gaze stays on my face. I break the spell by looking back at the supplies.

"This is awesome. Thanks."

"I know it's hot in here, but I can kick on the fans and close the shutters so you're not roasting. I hope you don't mind the noise because I'll be working in here too."

"That's fine," I say as I drop my bag.

"And if you want anything to drink, the fridge is stocked. Help yourself."

He's busying himself, trying not to look at me. As he talks, I can't help but think about the woman yesterday.

Was he having sex with her in his room before I saw her? Is she his girlfriend? Does he love her?

Like always, my mind takes it a step too far, and I start imagining his feelings for her. Overcome with lust. Does the thought of her touch on his skin keep him up at night, like he can't live without her? Is he obsessed with the shape of her cheekbones and the way she steals his breath when she's near?

"Does that sound good?" he says, and I realize I haven't been paying attention. I was too busy picturing him burying himself in that pretty blonde and thinking about how rough their sex was.

I clench my thighs together picturing the expression on his face when he comes.

"Um...what?"

He lets out a clipped laugh. "Little rain cloud." Then he walks past me and opens the door to the small room at the back. "I was just telling you the bathroom is back here. Now, you tell me what you were daydreaming about."

My cheeks flush with heat. "Nothing."

"Head up, rain cloud."

Turning away, I pull out my sketchbook and pencils to start on the grid for the mural. I desperately need to get my head out of the clouds and focus or I'm never going to get this thing done.

He stops watching me work as he goes over to the kitchen area. There are crystal blue glass tiles piled along the floor in stacks, and I watch him measure the area around the sink, realizing he must be putting up a back-splash. His back muscles stretch as he leans over, and it steals my attention.

Cadence's friends do not look that good without a shirt on, and I see them all the time. Fischer is bulky with muscles, but I've never been rendered speechless by the cords of his biceps or that deep V along his stomach that leads to somewhere I'm almost afraid and yet hungry to see.

He catches me looking again, so I turn my head back down to the sketchbook.

"Mind if I put on some music?" he asks.

"Not at all."

A moment later, his phone is hooked up to the speakers almost hidden along the ceiling and something soothing and sexy comes on. I find myself nodding along to the beat. This time I catch him staring.

"You like it?"

I nod.

"It's Sam Cooke."

He smiles when he realizes I have no idea who that is.

"Girl, you need an education."

A laugh escapes my lips.

"And you're going to get one while you're here."

My body freezes, and I stare up at him, but he's already back to his measuring and cutting. Did he hear how that sounded? Or am I making something out of nothing?

A couple hours go by, and I finally get comfortable working on the sketch. With the grid laid out on the paper, I can transfer the design and start laying out the lines on the wall. Alexander has a couch in the pool house, but it's covered by thin plastic. So, I sit on it while I draw, my legs sticking to the plastic and rustling every time I move. He continues playing his music, and he almost has the backsplash done when he walks over and lands on the couch next to me.

"Almost done?" he asks.

I realize now that I could probably do this part at my house, but being in this space helps me to get an idea of what I want.

"Almost."

"You want a drink?"

"No, thanks," I mutter without looking up.

"I mean a drink-drink. You like those spiked seltzers your sister drinks?"

My hand freezes. Is he trying to get me drunk? A chill runs down my spine. Maybe my sister and mother were right about him. As much as I find myself pining for him, I don't like the idea of him trying to get me drunk to get into my pants.

"I'm nineteen."

"Oh shit. I forgot about that. I'm used to having older people around. Well, you want me to make you something light? It's not like you're driving anywhere, right?"

Leveling my stare at him, I smile and shake my head. Holding back my suspicion that he's laying the moves—whether or not I want him to—I finally throw up my hands.

"Sure, what the hell."

He gets up and goes to the bar, pulling out a heavy bottle and two-liter of seltzer water.

When he comes back, he has two bubbly clear glasses with lime wedges in them.

"Don't worry, I made yours very light, and you're only getting one."

"Thanks," I mumble as I take a drink. It's not sweet, which is what I expected. In fact, it's refreshing, cold, and not as disgusting as the drinks Cadence has given me in the past. It's not disgusting at all. It could go down way too fast if I let it.

"You like it?" He's sitting back on the couch next to me with his feet planted on the wicker coffee table. Fuck, even his feet are perfect, tanned, and not covered in callouses. I catch myself staring at everything from his shorts down.

"It's not disgusting."

"Good." He gets comfortable and watches me. "You're nothing like your sister and mother, are you?"

"I hope not," I mumble.

A breathy laugh comes out of his mouth. "What does that mean?"

I let out a heavy sigh. "Nothing." I shouldn't have said anything.

"I'm glad you're not like them. I mean I like your mom and sister. They're great, but you're just...young. You should stay that way."

It's silent for a moment while I try to hold back a smile. Finally, he adds in quietly. "Did you listen to me last weekend? Did you stay in your room?"

I nod, pulling my gaze up to his face.

"Good girl."

Why does he care?

Burning under his stare, I finish my drink, and the room gets quiet with tension. Setting the glass down on the table, I look at his hands not too far from me. I wonder what it would be like to feel them on my back. My eyes shut just imagining the pleasure of it.

I wish I could read his expressions. He's not staring like he's hungry for me, like he'll devour me, but there is something going on behind his eyes. He's thinking. Wracking his brain. And I wish I knew what was going on in there.

Finally, he looks away and I go back to my sketch. He gets off the couch and walks back to the kitchen, but he doesn't get to work. He just stands there and takes deep breaths like he's thinking or deliberating something.

I only wish I knew what.

* * *

41

After about an hour, I have the sketch done. When I show it to him, he reacts the same way he did when I gave him the portrait. His lips don't reveal much as he stares at it. He takes a long look before he smiles and admits he loves it.

With that, I pack up my stuff and write down the colors I need for the paints. "I'll grid it out tomorrow," I say as I get ready to leave.

"Perfect."

With his back to me, I stand in the doorway and allow my eyes to swallow up his form. With his T-shirt stuffed into his back pocket, the cords of muscle along his back stretch and tighten as he hefts a box off the countertop and drops it on the floor by the wall.

He looks up and catches me watching, probably wondering why I'm still there. It's only the early afternoon, and I don't want to go back to my house—if I'm being perfectly honest. I can't stand the idea of what my mother has gotten into her head now. She knows I'm painting the mural, but her mind will go to other places.

Like mine does.

He smirks at me. "Well, if you're not leaving, you might as well get over here and make yourself useful." Nodding his head toward an open tub of what looks like white dust, he hands me a trowel, or at least that's what I think it is.

"This is like painting," he says with a smile.

The music has changed to something faster but still as sexy as before. I find my shoulders twisting with the music, and he laughs at me. Holding a large pitcher of water, he starts pouring it into the mixture.

"Grab that drill with the mixer and start blending this up. Until it's like pancake batter."

He keeps pouring while I work. The drill almost gets away from me for a moment, and I have to bite down a laugh. I don't want him to think I'm an immature kid who can't handle a simple task.

"Hold onto it," he bellows as he pours more water. Bits of gray sludge fly up and cover his hands, and I manage to get the mixer under control. It starts to blend up nicely, and I feel his eyes on my face again.

"Good job," he mumbles.

Being under his stare is like sitting under a heat lamp. I could burn here for hours, but to ease some of the tension, I shimmy my hips with the beat of the mixer and the music. The corners of his mouth lift in a smile.

"You like the Rolling Stones?"

I nod. Just then the sludge in the bucket gets away from me and the whole thing starts to wobble under the momentum.

"Jesus, Sunny," he barks as his arms reach around mine to grab the shaking can. He quickly pours more water, thinning the mixture. He stands hip-to-hip next to me and holds the drill in place with his hands over mine.

"Control it with your body, not just your arms." His hands press down on mine, sending tingles through me from the tips of my fingers. The scent of cologne and sweat drifts up to meet my nose creating a scorch deep in my belly. I should not be feeling like this for him. He's twice my age, and Cadence likes him.

But his breath is in my ear, and I can feel the muscles of his upper arms against my shoulder.

I lose focus on the mixer, beating against the side of the tub in a rhythm that makes my thighs clench. Biting my lips between my teeth, I wonder what would happen if I kissed him. I could turn my face and meet his mouth with mine. Would he kiss me back? Would he touch me like he touched that blonde woman yesterday?

My grip loosens on the drill, and his hands tighten to pick up my slack.

Quickly, I recover, squeezing the drill as the mixture in the bucket swirls. "Good girl," he whispers, and my breath hitches. Does he know what he's doing to me?

I don't even realize I'm staring at him until he turns his head and his eyes land on mine. For a moment, it feels like I'm drowning him in the intensity of my gaze.

Suddenly, he jumps back, clearing his throat and breaking the spell.

"Alright," he mumbles, grabbing the trowel from the counter. "That's enough."

The room grows silent and awkward as he reaches into the bucket and scoops up the grout and drives it against the seams of the tiles on the wall.

He sounds out of breath, and I know it's from his heart slamming in his chest like mine is.

I open my mouth, ready to say something, but nothing comes out. Instead, a chirping laugh spills from my mouth. His head snaps over to see me, and he looks pissed. His eyebrows are creased, and his jaw is clenched. It only takes a moment for his expression to melt into an easy smile.

We laugh for a minute, cleansing away the tension that existed there a moment ago.

Picking up my own tool, I help him with the wall, but the space isn't huge so we're working in close proximity. Every few moments, his bare shoulder brushes mine, and sparks ignite in my belly.

"This looks nice," I say quietly after sponging off the excess grout.

Alexander's head tilts slowly in my direction. "Holy shit, she speaks."

I smile. We got so comfortable in the silence, but I love the way he looks at me, so I try to keep it up.

"Did you design it?" I ask.

"Sort of. The lady at the hardware store helped me."

Alexander Caldwell in a hardware store. Now that's a sight.

"Why didn't you hire someone to do it?" I know he can afford it, so this isn't about saving a buck.

"I like the work. Back in the day, whenever my business partner and I would open a new gym or restaurant, we did most of the work ourselves. It felt good to get our hands dirty," he says as he heaves another dollop of grout on the wall. "Plus, I get bored, and if I'm busy doing this, then I can't get into too much trouble."

His eyes graze the features of my face and down to my neck. I swallow down the urge to be the trouble he doesn't want to get into.

"What are you going to do next?"

Glancing around the room, a droplet of sweat falls from his brow, and he lifts his forearm to wipe it. "I don't know yet. Maybe the floor."

"It's hot. Mind if I jump in the pool?" I ask. I'm suddenly desperate to cool myself off. His eyes fall on my face, and after a moment of hesitation, he nods.

"That's a great idea."

Abandoning our tools on the counter, we both walk out of the pool house to the pool's edge. During the summer, I don't even bother with bras and underwear. There is always a bathing suit under my clothes since I get in and out multiple times a day. It's not even officially summer yet, and it's already been scorching hot.

Goosebumps erupt along my skin as I pull my sundress up. I can feel him watching me as it glides over my legs and exposes the skin of my stomach. Then my bikini-covered breasts.

Suddenly, there's a splash and he's under the water,

gliding to the other side. My shoulders sink, a little deflated that he didn't watch me.

I've lost my damn head. I'm trying to seduce this forty-year-old man who probably sees me as nothing more than a scrawny kid. Tossing my dress aside, I jump in headfirst, gliding through the water until I come up on the other side near him. He splashes my face as soon as I break the surface.

Letting out a laugh, I splash him back.

"Not such a rain cloud now," he says.

Watching him glide to the other side, I notice him looking toward my house. He's probably looking for Cadence, hoping she'll come out, too. Maybe even come swimming with us. If she sees me out here with him, she'll definitely come out, and maybe she and I can put the tension behind us.

Or maybe he's looking to check if anyone can see us. To him, this might feel inappropriate, to be swimming alone with a teenage girl.

"So, what's your story, rain cloud? You in college?" He leans against the wall of the pool and watches me. I hate that he asked that. It makes me feel like such a kid.

I also don't know how I feel about the nickname. I mean, on one hand, it feels special. But on the other hand, I want him to know that I'm not the moody teenager he sees me as. Sometimes I'm just quiet because I'd rather be silent than fill the conversation with small talk.

"Not right now."

"Why not?"

I shrug. I can't tell him the truth. I can't go to college because I tried it, and I hated it. Six months in, I felt like a fish out of water and dreaded every day. Then, my parents split, and it was all too much to handle. I finished the fall semester and never went back. "I don't know what I want to do with my life."

"Be an artist," he adds.

"And make money how?" I ask with a smile.

"Do murals. I don't know. You're too talented to let that go to waste doing something mindless just to make money."

The blue water reflects the light between us, and I try to memorize the way the water drips off his brow. I want to sketch it—right on my inner thigh, the way his thick, dark brow looks when it's wet. Then I want his fingers to trace the image.

I clench my thighs again.

Taking this job was a stupid idea. I keep reminding myself it was about the money. Getting out of my mother's house. Not being a kid anymore and finally doing something for myself...something I can be proud of. But then I realize I'm too fucked up, and I'll probably spend the rest of this year picturing him naked and putting off the actual painting.

I never should have taken this job.

Chapter 6
Alexander

This was a bad idea. This was a very bad fucking idea.

What I needed was to get out of the city and out of trouble. I have somehow landed in the suburbs with a teenage girl in my pool, and I can't seem to keep my eyes where they belong.

Something about Sunny steals my focus like she's tuned into a frequency that only I can hear. I'm picking up every goddamn word. Everything she says is all too familiar.

She doesn't know what she wants to do with her life.

I know that feeling. She's scared. Her parents fucking suck, and no one is giving this girl any guidance.

She wants a job that makes money.

She wants freedom. Man, do I know about that? When I was young, I wanted to be a part of it all. I started with some business investments, and I was desperate to be a part of something successful. And for a long time, I was. But I was still too stubborn to learn anything new, and I know I wasn't the easiest person to work with. My trust fund afforded me a lifestyle with absolutely no guidance, lots of money, and just enough fame to get me laid on a pretty solid basis. In other words, a recipe for disaster.

And now at forty, I'm facing a fork in the road. If I continue this way, I can kiss any chance of a barely normal life goodbye. Live hard and die young. Or I can pump the brakes and try to find something that actually fucking matters in this life.

I just want to find peace, freedom—fuck—even love if that's what calms my ass down.

But as I sent Sunny home and went back to work on my backsplash, my fingers itched to make a call. I had just spent the entire day staring at the one piece of ass I did not want to want, and I needed to get this shit out of my system.

I rush through the grout job, and it turns out messy, but I don't give a fuck. The sun is setting, turning the sky a hazy grayish blue as it disappears behind the trees. A light in the house behind mine flickers on, and I watch as someone moves around the room, but I can't make out the figure just yet. The window is wide open, giving me a gold-fish bowl view of the bedroom inside.

Familiar light tan walls are framed by thick white mold-ing, and I can spot a closet, a few pictures on the wall, and a mirror to a vanity in the corner. I remember the room from the night of the party.

Just then, Sunny appears in the window. In her simple blue dress, still wet against her body from the pool, she gazes out the window without letting her eyes drift toward where I stand in my pool house.

Reaching up, she pulls the band from her hair and shakes out the wet curls, letting the dark locks hang around her shoulders. I should look away, but I don't.

Suddenly, I feel her eyes on me, and the pool house becomes torturously silent. With nothing except for my breath, I stare at her while she stares right back. I almost lift my hand to wave, to somehow acknowledge that we can see each other, but then she reaches down and pulls her dress over her head, leaving her in nothing but her simple bikini.

My lips part as I watch her. She looks so fucking lonely in that window, as if she is desperate to be watched. So hungry for attention that she would latch onto the only eyes she can find. Some crazy part of my brain wants to go to her, talk to her, hold her, *kiss* her to keep her from being so goddamn alone. Or maybe to make myself feel it.

But then she reaches behind her back, her eyes still on me in my lit pool house.

"No," I whisper as if she could hear me—but it doesn't stop what I know will happen. Her barely-there bathing suit drops to the floor, and I can't move. There she is, like a painting etched onto the wall of her house, in nothing but a tiny pair of bikini bottoms. Her tits are bare, small mounds on her petite chest, and even from this distance, I can see that her nipples are puckered, hard, and cold from the exposure to the air.

"What the fuck is she doing?" I say to absolutely no one, but I don't look away. I beg her to move from the window. Put on some clothes. Stop letting me look at her when I could easily just stop looking at her myself. I want to scream at her.

I look because I want to look. I want to memorize it. Not just the bare tits. I could see tits any day, but this vision of her. The sad look on her face, the innocent sexuality of her display, of what I can only assume is her own way of flirting with me. She wants me to look. And maybe she wants me to do more than look.

What kind of man would I be?

She stands in the window for less than ten seconds, but

every moment that I stare at her naked breasts feels like a hundred seconds. It is blissfully excruciating, but finally, she steps away from the window and walks towards her en-suite bathroom, leaving me standing breathless and reeling, alone in my pool house.

I try to go back to what I was doing, finishing the back-splash, cleaning up my mess, and calling someone to come over and take away the raging hard-on in my pants, but I can't function now.

Instead, I rush into my house and reach for the expensive brand of bourbon in my cabinet. Pouring myself two fingers full, I gulp it down and try to think about anything other than the curve of her hips and the tan line that ran like a V across her chest. The pale skin of her tits and the pink circles around her nipples. I try not to think about running my tongue along the peak, and down to her belly.

Before I know it, I'm squeezing my cock in my hands, gripping it tight, and stroking it to my imagination and the image she left me with. I feel like a fucking monster as I come in my own hand just thinking about her legs around my hips.

Fucking the teenager I paid to paint my pool house.

"What the fuck," I mutter into my glass.

I've lost my goddamn mind.

Chapter 7
Sunny

*W*hat the fuck was I thinking?

That's the first thought that pops into my head the next morning. And honestly, I don't know. I was feeling sexy, exposed, ready for him to see me. So, I stood in my window topless, knowing the whole time that he could see me. I had no shame.

And the feeling was...hot. I wanted to touch myself in that window, knowing he was watching. I was dying for him to see me as something more than a teenager. I wanted him to see the woman there, aching to be seen and touched.

The next morning, I gathered my stuff and headed over before I even ate breakfast. The house was quiet when I left, and I figured my mom and sister were already gone. Their rooms were empty, and on occasion they would meet friends at the country club for brunch or go shopping at the outlets without me because in their eyes I was still a kid. The kid old enough to stay home alone but not old enough to drink in public so might as well leave her at home.

When I reach Alexander's pool house, it's quiet. He's still asleep. I pull out my key that he gave me and unlock the door. He's nowhere in sight while I start on the grid. This is the part I was most nervous about. If I screw this up, I screw the whole thing up. So, I take my time as I measure out the lines and draw them with care. I manage to connect my phone to his Bluetooth speaker and keep the music blaring while I work.

I love this work. It's mindless, relaxing. Thoughts about my mother, my dad, my ever-growing need to get the fuck out of my house clear my head, leaving room to fantasize about my new neighbor. Thinking about Alexander has become my new obsession. But not just him. This awakening he's caused in me has stirred feelings about any man. About how I would feel when the time was right. About how badly I want the time to be right now.

The craving to lose myself in another person and explore these new urges is overwhelming. It's what I thought about as I fell asleep, when I woke up, and sometimes in the middle of the night when all I could do to get back to sleep was rub myself raw until my body clenched in ecstasy, and I could relax.

Suddenly, a hand gripped my upper arm, tearing me away from the wall.

"What is wrong with you?" he asks as I fly against his body and stare up at his face contorted in anger. I didn't hear Alexander come in, but now he has me so close to his sweaty body that I couldn't think a rational thought if I tried.

"Wh-what?" I stutter.

"Standing in the window naked, Sunny. Anyone could have seen you," he says through his gritted teeth. I can feel his breath on my face and notice the pause in his anger when his eyes meet my lips.

"I'm sorry," I mumble.

Letting go of my arm, he lets out a frustrated sigh. "I'm not mad at you, Sunny. You just...have to be careful. You can't let guys see you like that." He paces away a moment before turning back toward me, his eyes wild and desperate.

He must have just gone for a run or something because he's shirtless and red in the face. I stand motionless while his wild eyes roam over my face, clearly deliberating on what he should say next.

Silently, he steps closer, closing the distance. "I just want to keep you safe, Sunny. Do you understand?"

My breath comes out ragged. "Why? You barely know me."

Pain settles behind his eyes, causing his shoulders to sag. "Who keeps you safe?"

I don't answer, but something stings in my throat.

"A beautiful girl like you. People...men...would take advantage of you. Hurt you, Sunny. People are monsters, and I...like you. I don't want to see you get hurt."

Something in his resolve wavers.

"Are you okay? I didn't mean to scare you."

I nod, unable to peel my eyes away from his lips.

"Is that okay? If I...take care of you?"

My heart hammers behind my ribcage, causing my stomach to rattle and my breathing to falter. I want to memorize the sound of those words coming out of his mouth. The way he says *you* and means me. The way he looks in my eyes while he says it. The way I matter to him. If this feeling was a color, I would want to paint it all over my skin, and let it seep into my pores, making it a permanent part of me.

"Yes," I breathe, my voice coming out higher than I intended.

"Good." He steps away and looks at the wall, but I can tell he's unsettled. "Sunny," he whispers.

"Yeah?"

"Cadence's friends. They haven't...tried anything with you, have they?" His lips flatten into a thin line.

"Last summer, one of them did, but I didn't let him. I haven't let anyone…"

I watch his features relax. He's relieved. "Good. If you ever need to get out of there, you come here, okay?"

"Okay," I whisper.

It's a long, tense moment before he steps closer and slings an arm over my shoulder. I breathe in this feeling of being secure, safe, and comforted.

"How long will the mural take?" he asks, looking up at the grid in place on the wall.

"I don't know."

With both of us looking up at the wall, he lets out a laugh, letting his back shake as he squeezes my body closer.

Something catches my eye across the yard. Someone is in *my* yard...a man.

My heart skids to a stop. With his sable black hair combed back and his crisp white button-up shirt, I spot my dad walking across the patio, tearing through the outdoor fridge behind the bar.

I don't say a word to Alexander as I bolt across the room and out the door. I cross the yard in just a few steps as I holler for my dad.

"Dad!"

He glances up, confused as I run through the hedges and onto the patio.

"Where's your mother?" he asks by way of greeting.

"I don't know."

"I need the keys to the boat, and I know she fucking lost them somewhere." He rifles through the bar, dumping out buckets filled with bottle caps and wine corks. "She used to put her keys in the freezer when she was drunk."

"How long are you staying?" I ask, trying to steal a moment of his attention.

"I'm not, Sunny. I have to find those keys and get out before she comes back. I don't want to deal with your mother right now."

"I can help," I chirp as I walk inside and start pouring through drawers and baskets with random items.

"Who the fuck is that?" my dad asks, following me inside.

"Who?"

"The guy in the yard. You were just over there."

I glance out the window to see Alexander standing by his pool with his hands in his pockets, watching us from his yard. Now that we are inside, he can't quite see me, but it doesn't stop his vigilant observation.

"That's Alexander Caldwell."

My father seems to ignore me as he keeps looking for the keys.

"He's paying me to paint a mural in his pool house. Isn't that awesome?"

Still, no answer, as I watch him tear through the house like he still lives here. I have to swallow down the pain of feeling so ignored like I am still waiting for him to call me back even though he is standing right here.

"Can I come with you?" I ask, not entirely sold on the idea, but I'm eager to see his reaction. Leaving home is what I want more than anything, and I thought I wanted to go with him, but I can still see Alexander watching from the yard, and I already hate the idea of leaving him.

He wants to take care of me.

"Come with me? What do you mean?"

"Can I come stay with you? I don't want to be here with Mom anymore."

He freezes, his eyes softening as he looks at me like he just noticed my presence. "Sunny…"

"It's fine," I mumble, turning back to the drawer I was looking through.

"I'm in a small apartment with Ilsa. It's just not a good time." He steps forward, but I keep my eyes down. I can't bear to see the pity in his expression. His fake fucking sympathy and regret. I am a footnote on my father's itinerary: *if possible, show kindness to the daughter you just abandoned with her abusive mother.*

"Besides, Sun. You're nineteen years old. Get a job and move out if that's what you want to do."

"I said it's fine," I bite back.

He turns away with a huff and runs upstairs to continue searching. As if being nineteen was all I needed to move out. Who is going to give me a lease? There are no jobs out there that would pay me enough. I hate him for saying that.

I hear the jingle of keys from the drawer just before I closed it. I pull it farther back and find the three keys attached to a plastic keychain from our trip to the Keyes, which my mother thought was hilarious and ironic.

My father's footsteps retreat down the stairs, and I hold the keys in my hand, ready to show him I found what he wanted. I was ready for his approval. Instead, I think about the countless messages I left that went unanswered, and I let that anger stew as I walk the keys to the garage and drop them in the garbage can.

Dad leaves in an angry huff about fifteen minutes later. He is too annoyed to give me a hug, and I watch him drive away from the living room window.

Turning back toward the kitchen, I try to swallow

down the sting piercing the back of my throat. I won't cry for him. He never once cried for me. But I let myself imagine him pulling back into the driveway, walking through the door, engulfing me in his arms, and whispering his apology in my ear. I let myself feel it in my mind, and then I make myself drown in the absence of it. A cruel trick I do to myself when I feel self-pity rise to the top.

Alexander isn't standing in the yard anymore, but I notice movement inside his house through the large windows next to his dining room. He's in his kitchen, and I know I can walk over there and suffocate this pain with the warmth of his eyes on me.

Instead, I walk upstairs and climb into bed with my misery. Instead of sleeping, I pull a green pen from my bag and draw the boat keys on my inner arm so that I will remember to think about how miserable my dad was at the exact moment when he realized he couldn't take his new girlfriend on the water.

Chapter 8
Alexander

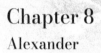unny didn't come back to the pool house, and after I made lunch, I heard commotion coming from her backyard. No surprise, Cadence was out there with her little tool bag boyfriends getting drunk and acting like dickheads.

Fuck, I could write a manifesto on the importance of parental boundaries based on this family alone, but it wouldn't change a thing.

From my little interaction with them, I can tell the girls were raised by an emotionally absent father and an alcoholic mom in denial of her own age. And now look at them. Cadence strikes me as the kind of girl who prefers to learn shit the hard way. Reckless and carefree, that girl has built up so much momentum partying, getting drunk, and having sex that she couldn't stop now.

I watch from the window of my kitchen as she starts making out with the blonde kid, even though I know I saw her with the other during the party.

Sunny hasn't shown her face outside since her dad left, and I can't focus on the one box I was supposed to be unpacking because all I keep seeing is that poor kid's face when her dad couldn't even greet her with a fucking hug.

My family wasn't perfect by any means, but at least my dad had the good decency to give me attention, and there was no doubt in my head that the guy loved me. Cadence is too busy filling the void of Daddy's love by filling other things, and Sunny is...well, I don't know. The girl barely speaks. She never leaves her house but seems pretty fucking eager to move out. So how the hell is she going to do that if she's too busy waiting for him to come home?

I step outside, knowing that the moment I do, Cadence will see me and invite me over. Which is exactly what I want.

Her eyes light up when she watches me step onto the patio. Well, they light up as much as they can seeing as how she's tanked.

"Come swimming, Alexander Caldwell," she croons, hanging her tits forward as she climbs out of the pool. Her tiny white bikini is about six shades lighter than her tan burnt-red skin, but she stumbles as she tries to walk down to the grass. One of the guys catches her by the arm and pushes her back into the pool.

I glance up to the window as I walk slowly toward their yard. Sunny's face appears behind the glass, those round blue eyes reflected by the setting sun, and I stop just outside the patio, staring up at her.

Calling her down without speaking a word.

She disappears from the window, and when she reappears through the sliding glass door, the red skin around her eyes tells me she's been crying.

I was a dick to her this morning about the window thing. Now, after seeing her practically beg her dad for attention, I feel like an asshole about it.

Cadence slides over toward me, and I steady her with a

hand under her elbow. The blond kid, Fischer, creeps toward Sunny.

For a second, he looks genuine as he gives her a warm hug and leans in to ask her a question. She nods and returns a warm smile to him. Normally, that kid is a little dick, so it makes me feel a little better to see him being real with her.

This is exactly what she needs, friends and support and people who care about her. I should leave and let her be with kids her own age. Fuck, I shouldn't even be over here, but Cadence wraps her arms around my waist and whispers in my ear.

"Wanna go inside and get high?"

I don't answer her. My eyes are still glued on Sunny. Now, Fischer isn't just hugging her for comfort. He's touching the exposed flesh on her stomach. She swats at him, but he teases her anyway. Walking towards the pool, I see the look in his eye. His gaze is laser-focused on her, like she's his next meal. It's predatory, and it makes me feel very fucking uneasy.

"Alexander…" Cadence drawls in my ear. I step away, looking directly at Sunny.

"You left all your stuff in the pool house, Sunny," I bark, my voice low and authoritative. Her eyes are round like saucers, and she stares at me confused. "Please go clean it up."

Sunny doesn't move, but I notice the way her chest heaves a little faster. She's searching my features, and I hope she can see that I'm just trying to get her out of there. Whether she sees it or not, I don't want her sticking around this crowd when they're already so far gone.

Cadence sways as she watches me, too drunk to look genuinely confused, but silent enough to tell me I threw her off.

After another long awkward moment, Sunny stomps away from Fischer and past me. I wish she would have put up a fight. I would like to see the girl stick up for herself, but she just grits her teeth and runs across the yard.

Following her to the pool house, I listen to the murmurs between the partiers in the pool, but they all die away when I shut the door, closing in Sunny and me. I hear her sniffles as she starts packing up her supplies.

I should explain myself. Apologize for acting like a jerk in front of her friends. But I see her standing there, and it grates on my nerves that she puts up with it. It makes me want to poke her more and see how far I can push before she pushes back.

"Don't go back there. Stay here and finish what you're working on. You can eat dinner here tonight."

"You don't own me," she mutters while throwing her pencils in her bag.

"Well, you made a commitment to do this, so I think you should do it."

"You're being an asshole." I hear it under her breath, and it makes me pause. I have to bite back my smile.

"Why don't you say that to my face?"

I stalk toward her, stopping just a foot behind her while she packs up her things.

She turns around, and I see the quiver in her lip. "You were an asshole this morning, and you're being an asshole now."

"Does that make you mad?" I ask, leaning in. She straightens her shoulders.

"Yeah. I thought we were friends."

"We are."

"Then, what's your problem?" she snaps back, leveling her angry stare on my face.

"You let people push you around too much," I say, ignoring the buzz under my skin having her this close.

"Who? Like you?"

"No, Sunny. Not like me."

Her jaw clenches even tighter as she realizes that I'm talking about her dad. And the boys she lets put their hands all over her.

Her shoulders soften as she backs away, her legs hitting the scaffolding. I have her cornered, pressed up against the cold metal.

Quickly, I step back, giving her space. I didn't mean to back her into a corner like that, but as soon as there is space between our bodies, I miss the proximity.

Her thin little throat bobs as she swallows, turning back toward her things. I have to turn away, so she doesn't notice my dick getting hard behind my shorts.

"I'm making pasta puttanesca for dinner. Have you ever had it?" I ask, stepping toward the kitchen.

She shakes her head, her chest heaving even faster than before.

"Text your mom and tell her you're working late. I don't want you going back there until the boys are gone and your mom's asleep. Understand?"

"Okay," she whispers as I leave the pool house.

She eats silently across the table from me. Her face is still swollen around the eyes, and I notice a fresh doodle in black ink on the inside of her left arm. In my empty dining room, she's dwarfed by the high-back chair I inherited from my mother, although I never really wanted the set. Formal dining arrangements aren't my style. I eat most of my meals alone around the kitchen counter or in restaurants where I am usually *not* alone. I feel about as out of place as she looks. Her dark hair is twisted into a round bun on the top of her head, and without a touch of makeup on her face, she looks sun kissed. It's like a thin layer of warmth over her already bronze skin from days spent in the sun. Ironic for a girl who never seemed to leave her house.

I can see the strings of her bikini under her tank top, and I wonder if she ever wears regular clothes. It looks like I picked up a stray dog from the side of the road and dropped it in the middle of a foreign planet.

She doesn't look up while she picks at her pasta. I wouldn't claim myself as a master chef by any means, but I do love to cook, especially for other people. On the very rare occasion I had a woman over to cook for, it was usually because I liked her a little more than the others. It was because I was trying. Trying for what...I don't know because it never worked. I could keep her devotion for a few weeks, maybe a month before I'd be sticking my dick elsewhere and undoing every goddamn good thing I worked toward.

"Do you like it?" I ask, but she only glares up at me, her leg bouncing under the table.

I'm about to drop my fork and give her hell for her ungrateful attitude, but she sits up a little straighter and speaks before I can. "It's good."

"Does your mom cook?" I already know the answer.

She stares at me through her lashes, and it's enough of an answer.

"Eat your dinners here. I'll cook for you."

Her eyes dance around the empty room with the boxes piled up, and I watch a question form on her lips like she's building the words up with her tongue one by one. It just isn't the question I expected.

"Are you trying to be my dad or something?"

"Look at me. I can barely take care of myself. You think I should be taking on wayward teenagers?"

She smirks. "You take care of me. I'll take care of you."

I try my damned hardest to swallow without letting her see the bob in my throat. My next question will be loaded no matter what I say. I mean, the kid walked me right into it. I know what she wants me to think, but fuck, she is making it very hard to not be a fucking creep right now.

"And how will you take care of me?" I ask, leveling her with my stare.

Leaning forward, she grabs the plate from in front of me. She stands from her chair, plates in hand, and sinks her hip into the table. "I can do the dishes."

She slinks away, and I let my chest relax, blowing out the heavy breath that has been lodged in my lungs. This girl is going to fucking kill me.

After the dishes are done, I pour us both a drink—hers a lot milder than mine. It might be wrong of me to give an underage girl alcohol, but I want Sunny to know I see her as an adult, although I'm not sure why. It's probably because everyone else in her life treats her like a kid—even when she's clearly the most mature one.

Drinks in hand, I follow her back out to the pool house. My phone is blowing up on the kitchen counter, but I flip it on its face and ignore all the invitations and bullshit calls.

For this reason, Sunny is a good distraction. I realize that I could leave her alone to work in the pool house and go get hammered at some random bar in town, but if I keep my eyes on the back of her head as she starts outlining her sketch onto the wall, it will keep me grounded.

Chapter 9

Sunny

Even though Alex gave me the scaffolding, I'm starting the painting at the bottom. It's unconventional, but I want to work my way up. The outline is done, so now I'm adding color. The girl in the painting is surrounded by tropical elements that will need layer after layer, and what might take an actual professional a few days or weeks will take me months.

The pool house is hot today. It's hot every day with that sun blazing through those big windows, but today seems unbearable. Every hour or so, I walk out back and jump in the pool to cool off, but I dry off too fast and it leaves my skin feeling dry, which makes me irritable.

"You're not getting paint in my pool, I hope," he says as he walks out with a towel to wrap around me as I pad toward the door, soaking wet.

Alexander has been keeping himself guarded since I started coming over to work. He still watches me paint, sometimes working on the window seat or other small projects, and he always makes me eat at his place. I'm here every night, and I can see in his eyes that he's fighting the urge to leave. Sometimes I wish he would. Go live his life. But then I hate the idea of this space without him. Him out in a club with a girl he barely knows doing God knows what.

I haven't seen the blonde woman since the last time either.

For the last five days, it's only been Alex and me. Cadence barely talks to me, and my mom hardly notices when I'm gone.

The towel he wraps around me is so big it reaches my knees, and it's the softest towel I've ever been wrapped in. The sun is starting to set, and I know this part of the day he'll ask me what I want for dinner.

With the towel around my hips, I climb onto the scaffolding on the lowest setting and open the paint tray, so I can finish the piece I'm working on. The stinging scent of chemicals in the paint brings that comfort I love. It smells like home. And I don't mean my house. Home like that feeling of comfort. Home like freedom.

The scaffolding shakes as he squeezes in, having to duck his head to keep from hitting the top rung. I can smell the sweet bourbon on his breath. He stretches one long leg behind me and folds the other in front of him so that he's facing me. He's sitting so close. Alex loses sense of boundaries when he's drinking. I'd be lying if I said I didn't love it. He's always trying to get me to drink with him, and part of me thinks it's because he wants both of us to forget our place—it's tempting.

My feelings for Alex are constantly changing, and it's only been recently that I can admit that I'm intrigued by the idea of something more than attraction. I've never been drawn to older men, and Alexander is miles out of my league, but the friendly connection between us has me wishing for more.

His piercing stare is on my face while I paint, something instrumental playing softly in the speakers.

"How long is this going to take?" he asks, glancing at the mural.

"Ready to get rid of me already?" Without taking my eyes off the wall, I keep up the blending before it can dry too much. The muscles in my right arm are already starting to tense and burn, but I have to get it done or it won't be perfect.

"I'll find another wall for you to paint," he says nudging me with the leg stretched behind me. Sometimes I think this is a game to him, to push me and tease me so that the ball is in my court. He's waiting for me to make the move, and I want to—so fucking bad I want to. But I don't have it in me.

Plus, it's only when he's drunk. He doesn't act so daring when he's sober. At least then he tries to hide his boners.

"Except when you go back to art school," he mumbles over his drink.

"I'm not going anywhere." A sad truth that burns when I think about it.

"Why not? Why aren't you going back, Sunny?"

"I just...don't want to." My hand tenses with the brush between my fingers. The feeling of inadequacy returns, making my breathing shallow and my heart race. It was all too much.

"You know...once you finish this, I can get my PR friend to get you set up on social media. You won't need art school. Celebrities will be hiring you left and right." He leans his head on the side of the scaffolding, watching my face as I keep my gaze away from his. Working for Alexander is different. There is a sense of freedom here, but with someone else...the pressure terrifies me.

"Say something, rain cloud," he says in a harsher tone.

I shrug, nudging his leg away. "You're going to make me mess up."

Again, he presses into my back with his foot, and I shove him away. "I'm here to work, not play with you," I growl at him, trying to look as stern as possible.

Next thing I know, the paintbrush in my hand is on the floor, leaving a streak in the mural, and I'm being hoisted up by my waist. "You little brat," he says, pinching my sides. My body jerks in reaction, and I let out a howling laugh.

"I will kick you, Alexander!"

"I'd like to see you try." He carries me over to the couch, dumping me on the cushions and attacking my legs, pinching them above the knee. I'm shrieking, laughing, thrashing—and growing more and more heated with every touch.

When he stops tickling me, his eyes are on my mouth, and when I finally take in a breath all I can smell is bourbon.

My lips part, and for the slightest moment, I think he's going to kiss me. I notice the crack in his armor, like he might actually do it. Instead, he stands up and shifts in his pants, turning his back to me and heading for the door.

"Where are you going?" I snap, sitting up.

"I'm leaving," he says, running his fingers through his hair.

"What?" My heart sinks. One minute, he's about to cross a line, and now he can't get away from me fast enough. He's all mixed signals, and I'm getting the feeling that he's holding back or even punishing himself for letting down his guard with me. It doesn't make any sense.

Moments go by when he doesn't return, leaving me to deflate on the couch; the heat he aroused in me still stirring under my flesh.

Getting up to my feet, I walk over to my stuff and throw the paintbrushes in the sink. Irritation boils beneath the surface, replacing the excitement I just felt. I turn the water on to rinse the brushes but decide to just leave them. He hates it when I do that, but I don't have the patience to clean them right now. Fuck that. All I care about is getting out of there as soon as possible.

Suddenly his arms are around me, his body hard against mine, and I let out a gasp that steals my breath. His body pins me against the counter so hard it almost hurts.

My heart hammers in my chest.

"Alex," I gasp.

"I would never hurt you, Sunny." His lips are against my ear, and I feel the tip of his tongue along the edge of my lobe.

I melt in his arms. He is the only thing holding me upright.

"Which is why I have to go," he mumbles against my back, and my heart sinks to the floor.

"Don't go," I beg.

"I have to. I'm so fucked up, Sunny."

His hands release my body, and I nearly fall to the floor. "You're drunk, but I can stay here with you. We'll watch a movie or something."

A laugh escapes his mouth, and it makes me feel about two inches tall. "You're so fucking sweet, rain cloud. I'm leaving because I need to fuck someone, and if I stay here with you…"

His drunk eyes find my face, and it sours my stomach to see him this way. This is not him. The light behind his eyes is gone.

"I'll go home," I say, struggling to get the words out.

Lifting his fingers, he grazes my cheek, pushing my hair back. "You don't think I'd crawl into that bed of yours?"

Suddenly, all his mixed signals make sense. Alex doesn't want to hurt me, and to him, that means keeping as much distance between our bodies as possible. Denying himself what he wants. Denying me.

A fire burns like an inferno between us as we stare at each other. His words replay over and over in my mind, the image of him sneaking into my room, crawling into my bed singes in my insides with arousal.

His hands pull away from my body, leaving me standing there cold and alone.

A chime on his phone alerts him that his driver is there, and he gives me one last apologetic glance before he jogs out the door.

* * *

Cadence is sitting on the couch watching TV when I run through the house. She turns to see me scampering up the stairs, and I'm not even on my bed before she's following me and closing the door behind her.

"What's going on?" she asks in a demanding tone.

"I'm fine," I lie, dropping my bag on the bed and grabbing my pajamas. I try to escape her attention by escaping to my en-suite bathroom, but she blocks the way.

"Did he do something to you?"

I laugh, a high-pitched cackle.

"Sunny…"

"He didn't do anything to me, I promise."

She lets me pass as I walk around her to the bathroom where I start the shower. Even when I untie my top, it doesn't stop her from standing there waiting for an explanation.

"Do you want him to?" she asks.

My laugh doesn't come out as sincere this time. Shedding my bottoms, I climb into the water, but it hasn't heated up yet, leaving me standing in frigid water, shivering and thinking about his hard body pressed against me.

Cadence sits on the toilet. "Sunny, Alexander is...complicated."

"I know," I blurt out against the water spray.

"I won't say he's too old for you because I do believe age is just a number, but Alexander comes with about forty years of fucked up baggage and bad behavior. I know girls who have been with him. One girl told me about how they fucked in a bathroom after they spoke two words to each other. He didn't even know her name."

My eyes squeeze shut, blocking out the pain. He is out doing that right now, isn't he? How many girls will he be with tonight alone?

Will he look at them like he looks at me?

"Alexander doesn't do relationships, Sunny. If you lose your virginity to him…"

"Cadence!" I shout from the shower.

"I'm being serious. I just want you to be careful."

"Everyone treats me like a child."

"I'm sorry, Sunny, but I've been worried about you over there. I mean, on the bright side, if he hasn't tried to sleep with you yet, you must be special to him."

I want to ask if he's tried to sleep with her yet, but I can't bring myself to do it. The answer terrifies me.

* * *

I can't sleep that night. I keep my eyes on his house, knowing he is out somewhere fucking someone else. Someone his age, who deserves him, but no one who wants him as much as I do.

Because I do. Somewhere in all the back and forth

today, I realized that I want him. I want to stay friends with him while also knowing the touch of his hands and the muscles of his body. I want to be the most special person to him, and that makes me feel like a fool.

He's gone for hours before I see the lights turn on in his house. After climbing out of bed, I watch him stumble through the house at 4:00 a.m. The bars closed two hours ago.

Go to bed, Alexander, I think to myself.

But he doesn't. Just through the window to the kitchen, I can make out his movements. He stumbles through the kitchen, knocking something onto the floor. He stops, and instead of picking it up, he presses his head against the cool stone countertop. I watch him from my bed.

Go to bed, Alexander.

He stands and walks toward the door.

Stay away from the pool.

I sit up in my bed, feeling my skin prick as he passes the edge of the water and walks into the pool house. From the doorway, he just looks at the painting, swaying where he stands.

My beautiful, broken Alexander stares at my art on the wall, and I feel it from all the way over here—the lava boiling in his soul.

I should quit the job and let someone else finish the mural. My presence is torturing him, and this desire is torturing me.

But I can't. I can't sleep, leaving him like that. He's never going to make it to his bed, and I couldn't sleep knowing he's too close to the pool in his condition. I could just see the headlines now. Billionaire trust fund prince dies in his own swimming pool.

In nothing but my tight cami and underwear, I tip-toe out of my house and through the backyard. The cool grass wets my feet as I run across. It feels like running toward danger, knowing this is a bad idea, but I can't stop myself.

He doesn't notice me as I step through the doorway, but I can smell the booze on him, like a strong cologne as I get closer. There are red footprints across the floor leading up to where he stands, staring at the wall.

When I touch his arm, he doesn't jump. I have enough experience with drunk people to know that when they're this gone, it's like they're not even there. There is no reaction, no life. You might as well be alone.

He turns toward me slowly, his reaction sedated. "Rain cloud," he slurs as he looks at me. His eyes won't focus on my face, so I don't look into his gaze.

"You need to get to bed," I whisper as I walk him toward the door.

I notice the way he walks is unbalanced.

"Alex, stop. Your foot is bleeding." He tries to lean against the wall but falls hard onto his ass.

Pulling his foot up to the light, I see the piece of glass sticking out the side of his foot and the deep cut there. Carefully, I slide the glass out and run toward the bathroom where I know there is a first-aid kit.

I grab a couple of bandages and head out to find him snoring on the tile floor.

Once I have his foot cleaned and covered, I reach down to pull his face off the floor. The sight of his cheekbones pressed against the cold tile makes me stop. Resting my hand against his cheek, I rub my finger across his bottom lip.

A thought crosses my mind.

He's so asleep he wouldn't even notice. And I need to get this out of my system so I can stop fantasizing about what it might be like. I just want to see, let myself feel it

74

once so I have the feel of his lips stored away in my memory.

I lean forward, straddling his sleeping body just to feel the hard frame of his body between my knees. Folding myself over his body, I pull his face closer so I can press my mouth against his. His lips are soft, perfect with that deep contrasted line against the skin of his face. For a moment, I imagine he's mine to kiss. And I let myself believe he's kissing me back. And I slip my tongue out to run it along the crease. He tastes like alcohol and perfume, a sour musk that assaults my taste buds, and I wish I could taste him instead. Tears prick my eyes when I realize he's been kissing other women tonight. I can still taste her lip gloss.

Sadness and regret bubble up inside me as I bury my face in his neck and wrap my hands around his waist. It's ironic that I'm holding him as he sleeps because that's how unrequited everything is with him.

Pulling away, I touch his face for another minute, letting this closeness seep into my pores. I want more, and I thought that kiss would get him out of my system.

"Come on, Alex. I need to get you to bed," I whisper. He doesn't move, and for a minute I consider leaving him on the floor. But I'm still afraid he'll get up in the middle of the night and stumble to his certain death.

"Alex," I moan, pulling him up by the shoulders.

He groans but doesn't move. I could try and carry him, but I probably wouldn't get far.

"Alex, come on!" I shout, shaking his shoulders.

He groans again as something grinds against my sex, sending bolts of lightning through my body. You've got to be kidding me. The man can walk through broken glass, crumble drunk to the floor and probably drown in his own pool but he wouldn't miss the opportunity to get his dick hard no matter how drunk he is.

"Sunny," he moans as he presses his hips up again.

Oh my god.

His eyes are still closed and for the most part, he's dead to the world—well everything except his dick, which is still pressing upward to meet me, and I should definitely crawl off him right now, but I can't bring myself to do it.

He tries to peel his eyes open as his hands reach for my hips.

"Wake up, Alex," I whisper as I climb off his body. The instant loss of that friction makes my body ache, but I can't be touching someone so intimately while they're too drunk to even walk. But oh God, do I want to grind myself all over him until I come...but I won't.

His hands fumble around my legs like he wants to fuck me, but his body is too damn drunk to manage it. He can't even get a firm grasp in his hands. Instead, he jerks his hips upward and reaches for my hands.

"Come here, baby," he stutters. Once he gets a hold of my hand, he pulls me down so that we're chest to chest and he tries to kiss me, but I pull away.

Not like this, I tell myself. My kiss on his lips was different. That moment belongs to me. But this? Kissing him so he can kiss me back while he's too drunk to remember it and still has some other bitch's taste on his mouth? No fucking way.

Not like this.

"Get up, Alex," I order him, my tone cold and level. The person who needs the most convincing at this moment is me.

"Bedroom?" he asks with one eye open.

"Yeah, let's go to the bedroom." Which is exactly what we're going to do but not to do what he wants.

Finally, he helps me get his drunk body off the floor. He winces when his foot hits the floor, but by some miracle, he stays on his feet. I've never actually been to Alexander's bedroom, and I can feel my hands shake as we make our way down the hallway. This could be a very, very bad idea.

What if we get to that bed, and I give in? Dear god, please don't let me lose my virginity like this.

Once we reach the end of the hallway, I wait for him to pull me in the right direction, and he stumbles toward the right. Of course. His room faces mine.

When we enter the dark space, I breathe in the smell of his room. It smells like him. Musk, cologne, something sweet. There in the middle of the room, looming like a warning sign is his bed. Sheets unmade, thrown about like he hasn't touched them since he rolled out this morning.

He seems to have sobered up enough to sit on the bed without collapsing, but not enough to stop him from pulling me with him.

"No, Alex," I say, keeping my voice calm. He yanks me onto his lap, but I pull away before I let my weight settle around his hips.

"Sunny," he mumbles, pulling me closer, and I start to panic that he's too strong for me to resist. "I wanna fuck you, Sunny." His voice is a low growl, and it warms me from the inside like a fire ignited behind my belly button. If only he knew how much I want him to, but I don't want my first time to be something he wouldn't even remember and likely pass out midway through. I would remember it for the rest of my life.

Plus, he's calling me Sunny, and that feels wrong now. If this ever happens between us, then I want him to call me what he always calls me. His little rain cloud.

I realize that pulling away doesn't seem to be working, but he's starting to drift off, too drunk and exhausted to keep his eyes open while in his bed. So, I let him hold me against his body, rubbing his groin against me a couple of times. He only gets in two thrusts before he stills, and his eyes roll closed.

I don't move though. Laying on him chest-to-chest feels intimate.

"I want to let you fuck me, Alexander," I whisper against his chest.

He doesn't react. He's out, which I knew before I said it. I won't admit the effect he has on me. Not to him.

Once I have his head on the pillow, I crawl over to his other pillow and lay down, looking at his sleeping face. I let myself imagine what it might be like to be the person on the other side of his bed every night.

It doesn't take me long to finally drift off, coasting off to dreamland with the scent of Alex filling my senses.

Chapter 10

Alexander

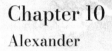y eyes pop open, and my chest is heaving like my body panics before my mind can. I slept with my guilt. I dreamt it and felt it in my subconscious.

Sunny.

I have a hazy memory of her body on mine, the feel of her tiny hips in my hands, grinding against her, the sound of her telling me to stop, the feel of her pushing me away.

Fuck. *Fuuuuck.*

After I got drunk and pinned her against the kitchen counter, which I remember better but don't feel any better about, I called a car and went to the first club my driver picked. Nobody I knew was out, but it wasn't hard to find some assholes to drink with me. People get excited to see me in public, and they like it even more when I buy them drinks.

Speaking of...I hope I paid my tab.

Fuck, I hope I came home with my wallet and phone.

Rolling over toward the wall, I freeze when I see the body in the bed next to me. She's facing the window, curled up on herself in nothing more than a tiny shirt and underwear.

Sunny.

My heart buzzes at the sight of her, something pinching behind my chest. I care about this girl, a whole hell of a lot. She deserves someone she can trust to not treat her like shit.

And I sure as fuck treated her like shit last night. Aside from touching her the way I did, crossing a line I should not have crossed, I know that in my drunken haze, I tried to fuck her. Hopefully not too aggressively. At least my barely lucid mind knows I didn't actually do it.

Turning toward her, I inch further toward my side of the bed, keeping my dick a safe distance. I'd jump out of this bed if it didn't feel like my head was about to explode.

She wakes as she feels my movement on the bed. She's probably afraid I'll try what I tried last night.

"I'm sorry," I mumble.

No answer.

But then again, I don't expect her to. Sunny doesn't talk unless she's the one calling the shots.

"You didn't hurt me," she breathes, not even able to look at me. "Did you have fun?"

I groan, holding my pounding head as I turn toward the ceiling. The light from the window feels like knives in my eyeballs. "Not really, but I was going nuts in my house, Sunny. I needed to get out."

She's out of my reach, crawling out of my bed, and I want her back. I want to bury her between my arms and keep her there, where she belongs.

No matter how much I want that, I can't.

"Whatever I did last night, I'm sorry."

"You fucked some chick at the club, then came home and tried to fuck me."

I wince. Damn, she's blunt when she wants to be. "Sunny, I shouldn't have done that. I'm sorry."

"Did you?" she says, swallowing. When I open my eyes, she's there in front of my large window in her underwear, and I want to cover her with something.

I fucked up last night. She was right. I went to the club, found some girl who remembered me from a couple years ago. Cute girl with brown hair and a big round ass, and she followed me to the spare apartment downtown I kept for extra space in the city, and I fucked her on the couch without fully taking my clothes off. Then she left. I vaguely remember her riding my cock and thinking about Sunny while she did it.

I remember the hunger for it, the desperate need for it...and the feeling it left when I got what I wanted. The decay it created.

I crossed a line last night. I touched Sunny in a way that was against the rules. Then I thought about her in a way that was definitely against the rules. I'm here in this house to settle down, stop throwing my life down the drain one pussy after another, and climbing between the sheets with a teenager is not how I'm going to do that.

"Did I what?" I ask with a frown.

"Did you screw someone at the club?"

My eyes find hers, and I see her hesitation. She's pissed, but she's also worried. I fucked up so royally last night, but now she's showing her cards. Sunny is jealous.

I can't look at her with the shame coursing through my body.

"Thank you for coming over to help me," I mumble without answering her. "Better get home before your mom worries." Her gaze doesn't move from my face. I can see the irritation in her eyes.

My sweet, beautiful rain cloud.

I am torn in two over all the things I want when she is around. Half of me wants to protect her, feed her, and keep her safe and comfortable. The other half wants to peel back that tiny shirt to see what she's hiding beneath. I want to know the face she makes when she comes. I want to watch her do it, her fingers buried knuckles deep...

Stop.

These are the things that make me the monster I am.

It doesn't take a genius to see what a guy in his forties who's fucked a different girl every week since he was sixteen would do with a nineteen-year-old virgin, and if I were any other guy, I would beat the ever-loving shit out of me for even thinking it.

"You cut your foot. Tracked blood into the pool house," she mumbles as she walks out of the room. I don't respond. I pull the black-out curtains closed, and I crawl back into bed, which is feeling a little colder now, and I sleep for as long as my body will let me.

Chapter 11
Sunny

Cadence comes with me the next time I go to work in the pool house. After our little talk yesterday, she seems a little more uptight about the idea of me spending so much time over here. Deep down, a part of me is nervous for her to see me and Alex together. Sure, we're not screwing each other or anything near it, but we have a familiarity now. And I'm afraid if she sees that, she'll get defensive again.

He comes out sometime in the late afternoon. It looks like he slept most of the day, which wouldn't be surprising. I can hardly look at him after the whole thing between us last night.

Every time I close my eyes, I feel him grinding himself all over me, begging me to fuck him, telling me he wanted to fuck me. I will never forget as long as I live the way it sounded to hear him say that to me. And how badly I wanted to let him.

"Hey," he says as he walks through the pool house to grab a water from the fridge. He's in a tight white T-shirt and gray sweatpants that are snug against his backside. I catch Cadence looking as he leans into the fridge. When he notices my sister sitting on the couch, he hesitates. I didn't tell him she was coming, and I hope he doesn't start thinking that I'm afraid to be alone with him now. When his eyes find me, searching for something, I see that question there.

Instead of trying to answer it now, I just get back to work.

"Rough night?" Cadence asks, her voice two octaves higher than normal.

"Yeah," he answers with an uncomfortable laugh. Inwardly, I stifle a groan. She thinks it's funny, and for her, it is, but for Alexander, it's a reminder that he failed. "About to take a swim to cool off. Care to join me?"

It's a harmless invitation. He would have said it to anyone. That's who Alexander is. The social being, party animal, never leaving anyone out, but he doesn't see how his actions are translated by others. My sister lights up like the Fourth of July.

"Sure," she squeals as she pulls off her see-through cover.

The hand holding the paintbrush freezes over the palette as I watch them talk on the pool deck. I have to make myself dip the brush into the paint, mix it until I find the right shade, and focus on what I'm doing and not on what they're talking about or how she's touching his arm.

I never outwardly admitted to my sister that I was growing feelings for Alexander, but I wonder if she would still flirt with him if she knew. She thinks it's a harmless crush, and maybe it is, but it still hurts to see her brush me aside, so she can get closer to him.

I stay in the pool house painting, letting the muscle memory in my fingers do all the work while I listen to them flirt in the pool, her laughing at every single thing he says.

When they come inside and he starts mixing drinks, I notice the way he doesn't hold her eye contact for long. Not like he holds mine. Not long enough to let her lose herself in those blue oceans.

"Sunny, take a break and come swim with us," she whines after her second margarita. Her hips are taking a softer shape as summer progresses, but the bikini bottoms still hang off her barely-there hip bones.

"I'm busy," I mutter, looking down at the chartreuse swirling with magenta, and I wish I could escape into the color.

My sister jumps into the water without another word, and it's a moment longer before a soft hand glides across the bare skin of my lower back, sending butterflies sailing through my stomach. I freeze under the contact.

"Take a break, rain cloud," he whispers, his mouth so close to my neck.

Every breath is heavy, like my lungs are filled with rocks. They come out slow and silent, but his hand doesn't leave my back. He's had two drinks already. He's slipping into the other version of Alex, the one who lets himself touch me.

Where I know my sister can see.

"Okay," I whisper back, and I turn toward him, our eyes meeting only inches apart.

And I let myself believe Alex is mine. He's mine and I'm his, and it's the safest and most fulfilling thing I could feel.

I hop off the scaffolding, and suddenly, his arms are around my waist and he's carrying me. I let out a shriek as he hoists me all the way to the water, my head hanging back on his shoulder as his laugh fills my ears. Then, I'm airborne. Flying through the air until I land, submerged by water, chilling me to the bone. My scream is cut off, and when I open my eyes underwater, I see him submerge just next to me, pushing off the bottom of the pool. He wraps his hands around my waist again and we glide to the surface as one.

When our heads come up, we're laughing. His smile reaches across his face, and his eyes look even brighter with the moisture pooling on his lashes.

Glancing over at my sister, I find her watching us with a hesitant expression.

After about an hour of swimming, Alex goes into the house for more drinks, and I head into the pool house to finish what I was working on before the paint dries. Which it already has. I get a little lost in the process, painting and mixing colors, the scrape of my trowel against the tray.

The sky is growing a little darker, and I realize that we haven't eaten. Those two have been drinking all day, and I bet they're both feeling it with how Alex mixes his drinks. It occurs to me that we should order pizza since I don't think he's able to cook at the moment.

Glancing back toward the pool, I look for my sister to make sure she didn't go and drown out there alone, but the water is still. Standing up from the scaffolding, I walk over to the door and see an empty pool.

She must have gone home. Or she followed Alex into the house.

As I turn around and face the kitchen, it becomes one of those moments that happens in slow motion because my brain already knows what it's going to see before I see it.

Without the sun hitting the patio window, I can see through the glass clearly, and it's the movement that catches my eye. She's standing with her back to me, her butt up against the kitchen counter, and he's standing close to her, most of his body hidden except for his hands which are firmly on the counter framing her in.

The blood drains from my face, and I imagine it pooling around my feet like I've been sliced open. I can feel it gushing from this wound, the pressure more intense than ever, slowly subsiding until I'm empty.

Her hands are on his face, tilted at an angle so I know their lips are locked. He pulls away from her face and looks up, his eyes meeting mine as soon as they open.

His eyes stay on me, and we're both frozen, stuck in a torturous moment while we both wait for his next move.

When she notices him stopping, she turns her head to see what he's looking at, and I wait for her to see me watching him, but he grabs her face and kisses her before she catches me.

My insides spoil, harden, break, and I'm lost in my jealousy as he kisses her against the counter.

I have to pull myself away, rushing toward the pool house. My breathing grows frantic, angry, desperate. My paints are still all out, and I realize in the back of my mind, I have to close them up before they warp and dry. The open can of magenta is sitting on the scaffolding next to the chartreuse, and I hate how bright they are. I hate how vibrant they look and how dull I feel in comparison. So, I grab the blue quart, considering for a moment that I could toss it against the wall, watch it splatter against the work I've done. I imagine the blue paint staining every surface around me.

Tears prick my eyes.

Instead of throwing it like I want to, I grab the lid and mallet, slamming it in place before I can do anything stupid. Bile rises in my chest as I turn and run. Dashing across the yard, I run up to my room. The house is silent as I crash into my bed.

When my face hits the pillow, I scream.

I hate Alexander Caldwell more than I've ever hated anyone in my entire life. I hate his beautiful eyes and the way he looks at me. He's made me feel like a stupid child who dreams of being his woman, and I hate him for letting me believe it for so long.

Chapter 12
Alexander

Sitting in the unpacked office, I scroll through old photos on my phone. They go back at least ten years when I helped my best friend, Tyson and his wife, Diana, open a new gym on the west side of town. Most of the pictures are of us working on the opening ceremony, the thrill of that day, the excitement of watching our hard work pay off and seeing those customers roll in. Tyson was the brains behind the business. I was the investor and his support. We ended up investing in and launching half a dozen more businesses—until last year, when I ruined everything between us, and he stopped talking to me.

When I hear Sunny's music in the pool house, I try to avoid going out there. I already know things are going to be awkward. I don't know why I kissed Cadence. I could blame it on her coming on strong or the five margaritas I consumed by that point, but those would be excuses. The truth is that I kissed her hoping I would feel something, as if my overwhelming attraction to Sunny was genetic, and I could feel something like that for her sister. I was wrong. Of course.

Or did I kiss her because doing so would drive away the one girl I want to keep safe?

Kissing Cadence felt like the kind of kissing that sad people do when they see another sad person. Cadence and I are too much alike for my own comfort, and I'm sure if we got together it would be messy, end badly, and wouldn't be all that much fun while we were in it.

None of this changes the fact that Sunny saw it.

I'm just one fuck up after another with this girl.

I'm just a fuck up in general.

When it's time to face the music, literally, I walk out there, lingering around the door while she works. She won't look at me. She thinks I won't notice, but even though I've been hanging around for at least fifteen minutes, she's been keeping her head down, working quietly without acknowledging me.

Technically, Sunny and I have no romantic ties to each other. To her, I'm her too-old neighbor and her friend. What she is to me feels much more complicated. But either way, kissing her sister *shouldn't* be any reason to give me the cold shoulder, and it only proves that I brought this on myself. I crossed a line, and feelings got entangled.

She turns her music up as she works. It's something moody and depressing. She loves that shit. I never should have let her connect her phone to my speakers.

I don't have anything to work on in the pool house, but I'm not leaving. I need to be around her. There's not a goddamn place in the house I could go that wouldn't feel like a hundred miles away from where I need to be. Plus, she's in a long skirt today, and she keeps it draped over her legs while she sits on the scaffolding, using one bent knee to steady her hand while she works.

"I can't listen to this anymore," I whine as I move toward one small box in the corner with plans to unpack it.

She doesn't respond. Playing silent treatment. Cute.

Snatching my phone out of my pocket, I immediately kick her device off the speaker's connection and replace it with my own. Her shoulders stiffen, but she doesn't do anything when I put on the Stones.

A couple songs play while she works, and I start growing irritated. I didn't realize how badly I needed her attention until she stopped giving it to me. It's like I'm suddenly the teenager, and she's the adult. I'd stomp and scream for her to look at me if it worked.

Satisfaction starts playing, and I watch her head tilt. She bites her lip.

"Dance with me, rain cloud."

"Don't call me that," she mutters.

"I'll call you what I want."

She shakes her head but keeps it down, her eyes glued to the paint on the tray.

"Dance with me," I say again, my tone more commanding this time.

When she doesn't move, I snake my hand around her waist and pull her off the scaffolding. I expect her to fight, but she doesn't. She lets me pull her to her feet and, once I have her in front of me, she stares at me with a blank expression. It's my favorite expression of hers.

"You're mad at me," I say, twisting her hips in my hand. Her body brushes against mine, and I realize how dangerous this is if I want to keep things the way they should be between us.

No response. Her hips move with my hands on them, but she's not moving on her own.

She's driving me crazy on purpose. Her big eyes

trained on the wall behind me and those pouty lips pursed in annoyance, my patience wears thin.

I can't go another fucking second denying this thing between us.

Digging my hands into her hair, I pull her close and whisper, my mouth only inches away from her ear, like a secret. "You're mad that I kissed her because you want me to kiss you."

She tries to pull away, but I hold her close, boring my stare into hers. I see her eyes widen, and I know she thinks I'm going to kiss her.

"Don't you understand?" I ask, letting my thumb graze the skin between her nose and lips, the soft ridges there, the warm breath from her nose.

"Understand what?" Her voice is just above a whisper.

"I care about you too much to kiss you. What I did the other night when I was drunk was uncalled for, and I'm toeing this line of insanity with you, Sunny. What I want and what I can have are two different things, and it'll drive me insane, but I won't give in because I am a stain, Sunny. You don't want what I would do to you. To me, you are perfect, pure, spotless."

"So, you kiss my sister? My *sister*, Alex." She has a look of disgust on her face.

"I'm sorry, Sunny. I'm all kinds of fucked up. I'm doing everything I can not to kiss you, and that was stupid. I know it. But not kissing you would be the noblest fucking thing I've ever done. And it will kill me."

When I finally let go of her face, she's breathless. The pure expression of understanding crosses her face, and I swear I might drown in her eyes if I don't pull away, but before I can move, she pulls me toward her, burying her face in my shirt. Hugging her to my chest, I kiss the top of her head.

It's like my fucking heart is being ripped out of my chest.

She finally backs away, and the song changes to *Beasts of Burden*. She smiles and twists her hips ever so slightly.

Fuck yeah.

Taking her hands in mine, I send her into a twist, and she comes back, pressing her body against me. Together we sway to the music, holding each other close but not too close. Her attention, her eyes, and her touch on me fuels the beating of my heart.

For the first time in my life, I feel completely fulfilled by another person. I may have unopened boxes in my house and feel like I'm floating on a life raft, lost at sea, but Sunny is my lighthouse, and as long as I have my eyes on her and she's shining those beautiful eyes at me, I'm not doing too bad.

I can't fuck this up. Coming here, buying this house was my last-ditch effort at growing up, getting a real grasp on my life, being able to look myself in the mirror without seething hatred at the reflection, and if Sunny is what keeps me moving in the right direction...I can't fuck that up.

It dawns on me when she laughs, the warmth in her voice sounding so familiar that my attraction to Sunny isn't just about her body, her age, her innocence but how she makes every goddamn cell in my body come to life. She defines me, accepts me, sees me, and I swear to Christ, it fucking feels like love.

And it scares the ever-loving piss out of me.

Chapter 13
Sunny

When I creep through the house that night, I get a bad feeling in my stomach. It's like a sixth sense, knowing when something bad is going to happen. The TV is too loud, but no one is sitting down to watch it. Cadence is in her room with the door shut, which is a sign that Mom is off the deep end. My sister has the good sense to ignore my mom when she's in one of her bad moods, but she has the liberty of being her favorite and not infuriating her by just existing.

Cadence is probably also avoiding me. We haven't spoken since the kissing at Alexander's yesterday.

I almost go back to his house then. I should, but hindsight is as they say twenty-twenty, and when I look down the hall and my mom is sobbing into her margarita, I know it's too late.

"What the fuck are you looking at?" she spits at me.

I don't answer, just turn and walk toward my room.

"You think you're so perfect. So smart."

Cadence steps out of her room. "Mom, stop," she says, either groggy with sleep or high...or both.

Mom ignores her. She stalks toward me, carrying her wide-rimmed margarita glass which is now almost empty. My mother is the kind of drunk who hides it well. She doesn't sway or slur, but her personality changes in a way that only those who are close to her have the honor of being able to see.

I swallow down my nerves in the doorway to my room, knowing that I'm cornered prey. If I disrespect her or shut the door in her face, I'm only fueling her rage. If I knew how to talk to her, I would defend myself, but I'm unable to form the words that would make my mother love me.

Cadence always tells me I was a mistake. That mom only wanted one, but I figured everyone heard stuff like that, in good lighthearted fun. More than half of the population was probably a mistake. It's not our fault. But my mother has been taking it out on me as if I was responsible for her not taking her pill or my dad not pulling out in time. If I could have stopped those cells from splitting, then I would have.

"Don't you fuck him, Sunny. Do you hear me?" she says, taking a drink.

"Mother," my sister whines, rubbing her head as if this is painful for her.

"I'm serious. Men like Alexander Caldwell would eat you alive, and you'd only be ruining your sister's chances. You keep your legs shut, Sunny. Men like him can't help themselves."

I want to vomit. My mother sees me as nothing more than bait. The virgin pussy walking around tempting poor unsuspecting men who don't know any better. She once yelled at me a couple summers ago for wearing a bikini in front of Cadence's friends, which to her wasn't fair, *if I*, and I quote, *wasn't going to do anything about it*. I didn't even know what that meant at the time.

Alex's name coming out of her mouth makes me want to punch her. I hate her for saying it, his first and last name, like that.

After what he told me tonight, as he held me in his hands, making me feel like I was actually worth something, worth keeping and loving, I hated the way she tainted that good feeling with her ugliness.

"Once men get the virgins, they never want to go back."

"Just shut up," I say before I can stop myself. It comes out through my gritted teeth, but I have to defend myself. I have to defend Alex.

But as my mother's fist comes crashing across my cheek, I regret it. The pain of being truly punched comes more from the shock and humiliation than the impact, and as I hold my face in horror, my jaw hanging open as the sting spreads through my face, I realize how badly I wish my life was different. I wish my family wasn't so broken and the love between these walls overpowered the pain. But it doesn't.

Lost in her rage, she swings again, making impact two more times: again on my face and once on my shoulder.

"Mom!" Cadence screams as she pulls her back. I'm already on the run, trying not to cry, as I take off in a sprint down the hall toward the back door.

I hear the scuffle between my mom and sister, and I sense the rage in my sister's tirade. Before I hit the landing at the bottom of the stairs, I hear Cadence shoving my drunk mother into her bedroom and shouting, "You're lucky I don't call the cops on you."

My head pounds and it feels like blood is pulsing out of my face as I cross the yard toward Alex's house. I pause in front of the pool house not sure where to go from here.

When I left just thirty minutes ago, he was already in bed, assumedly asleep.

He said he would take care of me. He'd want me to come in.

So, with shaking fingers, I open the patio door and step into his kitchen. The house is silent, and a sudden tempest of fear floods my body when I remember that I'm standing in someone else's house. I just *broke into* Alexander Caldwell's house, and he could think I'm insane for it and tell me to never come back.

I need water. The need to just do something other than stand there like an idiot is the only thing that keeps me moving, so I grab a glass from the cabinet and fill it, gulping down a whole glass full before the tears start.

What am I doing here?

I'm about to turn twenty years old, and my life still feels like it's in the hands of someone else. I always thought adulthood would be exciting, but all I feel is lost. I can still hear her voice, the loathing hatred in her tone when she spoke to me. Why am I still living with her? Why did I come back after one semester of art school?

A loud sob escapes my lips.

My mother's hatred for me has only intensified since Dad left, and it only makes me sob harder thinking about how invisible I am to him. She hates me, and he just doesn't care.

But I stay.

A sudden vision of me in ten years, still living with my mother's disappointment and begging for my dad's attention. Maybe I'll be like Cadence, searching for love between the sheets with the wrong guys.

The stabbing pain in my chest presses down with each gasping inhale.

"Alexander," I cry, hoping he can hear me in his room.

It's not even a second later before I hear a door open down the hallway. Immediately, I sense the panic in his features.

"Sunny?" His voice barely registers as I bawl into my hands in his dark kitchen.

He runs toward me, engulfing me in his arms without question. For a long time, he doesn't say a word, even when my cries get louder, and I feel my body shaking.

Finally, once I can manage a full inhale, he whispers. "What happened?"

He's in nothing but his tight boxer shorts, my wet face pressed up against the smooth skin of his chest.

I can't speak. For some reason, telling him what happened feels like reopening a wound I just stitched up. With care, he wets a washcloth and wipes the moisture from my face.

Since the tears started, they won't stop no matter how much I beg them to.

"What did she do?" he asks, looking into my eyes.

"She was drunk," I mumble.

"I don't care. Did she hit you?"

Biting my lip, I nod.

"Jesus."

He holds me against his chest again, and I try not to let the waterworks start running again and focus instead on the texture of his warm skin against my cheek, the sparse patch of chest hair beneath my fingers, and his hip bones pressed against my stomach. I am swallowed by him. I never want to come up for air.

Carefully, he refills my glass with water and hands it to me with two white pills.

"The good stuff," he says, and after I glare at him skeptically, he finishes. "Ibuprofen." With a small smirk lifting my lips, I toss them back.

His hands reach for my face, cupping my cheeks and pulling my gaze to his. "Are you okay?"

I try to nod, but he sees through it, giving me that knowing glance.

"You're not going back there," he whispers into my hair.

No words escape my lips because I want to believe him. For a moment, I'd like to pretend what he's saying is true. That this place is my home, and I never have to go back.

"You need some rest," he says, pulling my body away and cradling me in his arms. "I'll sleep on the couch."

Before I know it, he's resting me on his still-warm bed, and I cling to him like a child. It might be a cheap shot, but I want him near me more than I want anything else.

"Don't leave me," I gasp when he tries to pull away.

"I don't think that's a good idea."

I shift my body to the side, leaving him room to crawl in next to me.

"Sunny," he says as a warning.

"Just lay down next to me. We're just sleeping. We did it when you were drunk."

"Yeah, but that was different. I don't trust myself."

"I trust you," I whisper through the darkness as I curl my body into a ball, pulling my knees to my chest. Sleep is already threatening to pull me under, my eyelids getting heavy.

It takes him a moment before he releases a long sigh. Finally, his weight settles on the bed next to me. His soft touch along my hairline carries me under, and I drift off to the sound of his gentle breathing in bed next to me.

Chapter 14

Sunny

Alex is already out of bed the next morning when I peel myself up and walk to the bathroom. My cheek has a subtle bruise around the cheekbone, and my eyes are heavy with bags under the lids. My mother has hit me before—but not like that. For a moment, I feel a little humiliated that I sobbed the way I did. People have endured far worse than a closed fist across the face, but it was more than her hitting me. It was the weight of a long divorce, my family splitting in two, losing the love of my parents as they lost the love for each other, and desperately seeking that love in someone I shouldn't.

Alexander's words echo through my head as I touch the tender skin on my face. He told me I wasn't going home. Did he mean I could stay with him?

Would I?

Suddenly the idea of being in the same house as Alex, sharing this space and all of our time but maintaining our boundaries sounds like slow torture. Would it finally be enough to wear him down? Could I get him to cave and finally give in to what we both know we want?

The guilt of that scenario feels worse than the stinging on my face.

The nutty aroma of coffee sweeps in from the kitchen, and after a quick fix of my hair and a little toothpaste in my mouth to wash off the morning breath, I quietly walk out to the kitchen where Alexander Caldwell, my neighbor, major crush, and in-a-way best friend is making coffee in nothing but his gray sweatpants.

"Morning," I say, stepping up to the high countertop.

"Morning," he replies, glancing toward me. "How are you feeling?"

"I'm fine."

Staring up at him in the early morning light of the kitchen, I can't help but admire the strong angle of his jaw, the scruff from not shaving in at least a week, and the golden tint to his skin that almost shines in the light. Alexander doesn't look forty. He has the gray flecks in his beard and the soft crinkles around his eyes, but his expression is still youthful, and I don't feel like I have to look up to him when he talks to me. He treats me like an equal. Even when he takes care of me, protects me, like he sees my worth even when I don't.

"Coffee?" he asks, pouring himself a cup. I nod, taking a seat at the bar.

When he passes me my mug, I try to block out all of the thoughts in my head that I shouldn't have come here. Even before I take my first sip, he dives right into the heavy talk.

"I meant what I said, Sunny. You're staying here. I'll give you the pool house, or I'll sleep in the pool house, but I can't let you go back there." With his strong shoulders and narrowed expression, he seems almost fatherly, and I want to tell him that it suits him. That he should stop being such a bachelor and be serious once in a while. But I don't.

"Maybe for just a little bit," I mumble, warming my hands on the coffee cup. "Let things cool off."

His eyes linger on my face for a moment, and I can tell he wants to say something, but he doesn't.

"You hungry?" he asks, his eyes lingering on my face.

"No, coffee's fine for now," I answer, feeling antsy under his stare.

"Shower?"

His voice goes down an octave as he asks, and I can see the struggle in his eyes to remain nonchalant as he asks. My cheeks blush as I bite my lip. I know he means a shower by myself, but it doesn't stop the images in my head of his naked body under the water with me.

"That would be perfect."

He leads me down the hallway to the bathroom. Next to the door I assume is a linen closet is a box stuffed with folded towels and washcloths.

"Alex…" I say in a scolding tone.

Rubbing the back of his neck, he defends himself. "I haven't gotten around to that one yet."

"Or any of them," I tease as I wave my arms around to the boxes stacked in every corner.

"Yeah, yeah, yeah." He jabs me playfully in the ribs as I scurry into the bathroom with a towel under my arm.

Under the water of the shower, I can't stop the reeling in my mind. The events of the night are replaying in my head play-by-play. Alexander telling me that he wanted me, the reassurance I so desperately craved. He's so convinced that he would be terrible for me, but I only want to convince him that I'm not afraid of him. I don't worry about what he's done in the past.

The intensity in his eyes brings my excitement back down. Alex has done nothing but beat himself up since he moved in and my pushing him won't do him any favors. And now I've basically moved in...

This is a mistake. Isn't it?

By the time I come back out, holding a towel wrapped around my body, there's a folded pile of clothes waiting for me on the floor. Picking them up, I find a pair of basketball shorts and a T-shirt. The shorts hang off my hips, but I can roll them about four times to keep them up. It's enough to get me to my house to pack my things.

The thought of going back sends a cold chill down my spine. It's not that I don't want to face my mother. It's that I don't know if I can. If I had my phone, I'd text Cadence, but I literally came here with nothing last night. And I have to tell my sister where I'll be for a few days.

When I come out in Alex's clothes, he's waiting by the back door.

"I have to get some things..." I say quietly.

"I know. I'll go with you."

A smile fights against my lips as I try to bite it down. The proud look in his shoulders as he stands there, arms crossed, willing to protect me has me feeling all warm inside.

My hands won't stop shaking as I cross the lawn and spot movement inside. It's not a confrontation I'm worried about. I'm worried Alex will see that nothing will happen at all. That no one will apologize or ask about me or care at all.

When we walk through the back patio, my mom is sitting at the dining room table, her face in her hands, hovering over her cup of coffee. I feel myself hovering close to Alex's side. When my mom looks up, I see the swelling under her eyes, proof that she's been crying.

"Jesus, Sunny," she croaks as she stands up. "We were worried sick about you."

103

I keep my mouth shut as I walk past her and rush up the stairs to my room. There's no possible way they were worried about me. She knew exactly where I went and even if I did hitchhike across the country instead of running to Alex's house, why would she be worried after she clocked me in the middle of the hallway?

In a scurry, I collect up my phone, charger, and shove clothes into a bag. I can come back for more, plus I don't know how long I'll be staying anyway. My sister's door stays shut while I hurry, and just when I reach the bottom landing, I catch sight of Alex's body crowding my mother's in the corner of the kitchen. When he pulls away, she's crying even harder, rubbing her throat, and I freeze. My eyes trail to his face, but he avoids my stare as he approaches me and walks with me out the door. I don't spare my mother one glance as I leave.

When we get back to the house, I keep Alexander's clothes on as he makes lunch. Sitting on the bar stool, I look around at the boxes.

"You could have moved into a smaller house," I tease him.

He sends me a twisted smirk as he drops a grilled cheese on the counter in front of me. "I thought I wanted space. I had an apartment in the city, and I just envisioned something to grow into."

"Like a goldfish," I say through a bite of my sandwich.

"Excuse me?" he laughs.

"You haven't heard of the goldfish theory?"

He shakes his head slowly with a crooked brow. "Explain, rain cloud."

I stand and walk to the fridge for a bottle of water I know he stocks there. "There's a theory that a goldfish will grow as big as his fishbowl. So, a fish in a big bowl will be huge, but a fish in a small tank doesn't grow and dies."

Taking a long gulp of my water, I watch Alexander's expression fall. "Are you saying I'm going to get fat?"

A laugh bursts from my lips. "No. I just think...you have more room in your life now. For...people."

As his face grows more and more serious, flipping his grilled cheese and clearly contemplating what I said, I wait for him to say something. As he transfers his sandwich to his plate, he turns toward me and leans with his elbows on the surface. "Well, that would explain why I've already taken in one stray."

With a smile that lights up his eyes, he takes a bite of his sandwich, and I reach across the counter to swipe at him, but he dodges easily.

I tell myself this could work, and his smile makes me believe it.

Chapter 15

Alexander

Having her in my house feels right. She breathes life into these empty walls. After lunch, we take a dip in the pool and then a trip to Whole Foods for the essentials. She pushes the cart around the store, hopping on for short rides while I fill it with more than I normally do—which feels better than I expect it to.

I feel eyes on us while we shop, and I know what they are thinking.

Is she my daughter or new girlfriend?

And for the first time, I don't care. When we come around to the bakery, I buy a whole cake because I'm just in the mood to indulge. I catch her eyes on me more than once on the drive home, and I decide that I can do this. I can keep Sunny, take care of her, be the person she needs without crossing the boundary.

After dinner, the sinking feeling of bedtime looms closer. I hate to put her on the couch, but the guest bedroom is still in boxes. And if I'm being honest with myself, the idea of waking up to her again is tempting, but I don't trust myself to do that. So, I take a pillow and blanket out to the living room and toss it down as she comes out of the bathroom in her pajamas.

I watch her stand in the middle of the room, swallowing down her nerves.

"I'll sleep out here," I say before she can get anything out.

"I can't take your bed, Alex."

"It's fine, Sunny. I sleep like shit wherever I am, so it hardly matters."

A moment of silence passes before she speaks again, looking nervous as she picks at her fingernails. "It's a big bed," she breathes.

It feels like swallowing a baseball as I force down the thought. "I don't think that's such a good idea."

"It was fine last night."

I don't admit it, but I actually slept great last night. I didn't wake up ten times like I normally do, and our bodies never actually touched.

My shoulders sag as I think about it.

"I'll keep my hands to myself," she says with a smile, lightening the mood.

Something about her smile makes me give in. "Fine, but you stick to your side," I answer in a scolding tone. I watch the smile spread across her face.

As she crawls under the covers that night, I keep my eyes down on my phone. She curls her body into a ball around her pillow. It feels strange to go to bed with someone I didn't just fuck and feels a little like we're playing house or having a sleepover.

"Whatcha reading?" she asks quietly from her pillow.

"A boring email."

"Email," she giggles. "That's cute."

Dropping my phone to my lap, I turn my head toward her. "Are you calling me old, rain cloud?"

She muffles her laugh in her pillow, and it takes everything in me not to tickle the exposed flesh of her waist between her tank top and pajama pants.

Shutting my phone off, I don't reply to the email from my old work contact about a new investment opportunity that actually sounds pretty solid. The idea of getting back into business scares me. I should be glad he's even emailing me after the way I fucked things up last year. But I miss the days of having purpose. Having somewhere to go and something to work for.

* * *

The next day, Sunny spends the day in the pool house working while I unpack the box waiting by the linen closet.

As I work, I keep thinking about how it felt to have her in my bed. Our bodies never touched in the night, but I woke up a couple times just to admire her calm breathing next to me in the darkness.

Then, I start to think about how long she'll stay. How long do I want her to stay? How long until it becomes impossible to deny myself? Somewhere deep down I hope the desire goes away, and I just become used to her being around, but I'm not holding out hope for that.

The old Alexander Caldwell lived for weekends and late nights. Now, with her here, I want nothing more than pizza and movies on the couch like it's the equivalent to a new club opening and having VIP access.

Lost in thought, I stop when I hear her calling my name, sounding panicked.

Rushing outside, I find her standing near the back patio. "What's wrong?"

Behind her, I notice her mother crossing the yard and approaching the house.

"Do you want me to handle it?" I ask, touching her softly on the back of the arm.

She only shrugs. I understand that it's her mother, and her feelings are complicated. She doesn't want me to solve her problems for her; she just wants me there when she does.

Her mother walks straight up to the patio door and knocks. Her eyes have that same swollen shape like she'd been crying.

When I open the door, Sunny is standing next to me, holding her shoulders back and leaning toward me.

"What can I do for you?" I ask without inviting her in.

The woman bites her lip, glancing back and forth from me to her daughter.

"Thursday is Sunny's twentieth birthday. We want to have a party at the house. I just want—"

I turn my head and look at the girl standing next to me. I'll let her lead in the response.

"I'll think about it," she mumbles.

My harsh glare focuses back on her mother after Sunny answers, but she doesn't look at me.

"Are you okay?" she asks her.

Without any emotion on her face, Sunny answers. "I'm fine. Better."

"I'm so sorry, Sun. I just…"

"I don't care."

She grows quiet for a moment. "Since your dad left, you know—"

"I said I don't care. The party sounds fun. I'll be here until then."

With that she turns and disappears inside the house, leaving her mother without another word. As I close the patio door, I watch Sunny shield herself with a hard exterior, and I'm proud of her for it.

109

Chapter 16
Sunny

I wake up to the smell of pancakes on my birthday. Instead of getting up right away, I lay in bed for a moment and try to feel the difference. Being twenty doesn't feel any different than being nineteen, except for the fact that I'm one step farther into adulthood but feel no less like a clueless teenager.

When I do finally walk out, he's standing there with a smile, flipping pancakes in those practically illegal looking gray sweatpants.

"Birthday girl!" he chimes when I sit down at the counter. I love Alexander's warm moods.

I've narrowed down his behavior to warm, cool, and neutral, like the tones on a color wheel. Warm tones are when he's most alive. Passionate like amber. Lust-filled gold. Anger in crimson. I've only seen him truly hot once, and it was exhilarating, scary, and attractive. When he looks into my eyes, I find the warmth, the life, the real Alexander in an array of tones.

Warm is when he lets his guard down.

Alexander's cool moods are the ones that I notice

when he doesn't know I'm watching. When I see him relaxing by the pool, still and quiet for the smallest moment, and I see the ocean blue shade of his contentment. When we curl up next to each other on the couch, and he doesn't pick a fight, test the boundaries or relentlessly punish himself, he fades into something between blue and green.

The ones that frighten me the most, not because I'm scared of him but because I'm scared of how much I lose him are his neutral moods. That's when I'm afraid he's fading into the background of his life, hoping he won't mess anything up. The expression melts off his face and he's convinced that by doing nothing, he's doing the world a favor. I want to shake him when I catch these moods on his facade. I want my warm and cool Alexander back, the one with life in his eyes.

"I made you birthday pancakes," he says as he licks the batter off his fingers. Then, he piles four cakes on a plate and tops them with a mountain of whipped cream and syrup.

The attention warms my heart. This new Alexander, the one who wants to be domesticated and settled down makes pancakes, and he's doing it for me.

"Thank you," I whisper as I take a big bite. They're perfect.

"You are very welcome." He turns to wash the dishes in the sink, but I feel the silence in the room like a heavy weight. I know there are words on his lips. When he turns back around, he heaves a heavy sigh and speaks. "How are you feeling about the party tonight?"

"I feel fine," I answer, avoiding his eye contact as I keep my stare trained on my plate.

"Sunny," he says, and it sounds like a warning. Butterflies dance in my stomach when he says my name, and as much as I love his pet name for me, I do love hearing that one on his lips.

"I was thinking…" I confess after a bite when he passes me a cup of coffee.

"What?"

"You don't have to come."

He doesn't waste a second. "Do you want me to come?"

Yes.

No.

I want him with me, to walk in with him, sit by him, touch him and talk to him, claiming him as mine, but I don't want him there when Fischer makes an inappropriate comment about my virginity which no one will scold him for or when my mom drinks so much she makes an even more inappropriate comment about my virginity or my dad or how I was a mistake but chose to love me anyway.

I don't want Alexander around for that part.

I shrug. His face tightens as he clenches his jaw, and I know he wants me to say yes so that he can play this part of my protector, my guardian, but he doesn't want to over-step his bounds.

"Think about it, and I'll do whatever you want, rain cloud."

While I finish my breakfast and scroll through my phone, he comes out of his bedroom freshly showered and dressed, smelling like a million bucks and doing things to my insides that I don't exactly give him permission to.

"Get dressed. Before the party, I have a little surprise for you in town."

My head immediately snaps up to see him in a button-up shirt, rolled to his elbows over a snug-fitting pair of chinos. I wish Alexander knew that when he's dressed like that he drives me insane.

Without another question, I hop up and run into the shower. Not one thought barely registers as I get ready, putting on a thin layer of makeup and grabbing my favorite dress and wedges from my bag that I purposefully packed in case of a special occasion.

As I come out, he's sitting at the bar, one leg folded over the other and I wish I could snap a picture of him, but he moves too quickly. I don't know where we're going, but I crave being seen out in public with him. Not because he's famous but because he's radiant and, as far as everyone else is concerned, mine.

After a short car ride where he lets me pick my favorite songs—which are mostly ones he's opened my eyes to—we pull up to a parking lot by the river. It's mostly for joggers and walkers on the paved pathways, but as we get out, he doesn't walk down the paths. He heads up to the buildings along the main street.

"Where are we going?" I ask, running to catch up to him.

"It's a surprise," he answers with a laugh as he tosses an arm around my shoulders, pulling me close for a playful hug. He eventually lets go and drops his hand. I want him to touch me again so badly.

When we turn the corner behind the nearest building, my breath catches in my throat. Along the backside of the building, spanning the entire block is a mural of a woman and a tiger in front of a mountain landscape. I stop in my tracks, taking in the overall scope and size of the painting.

"I found this online, and I knew you had to see it. The artist just finished it a couple weeks ago." His fingers graze the small of my back as a couple moves around us, and I can't focus on his touch. I'm too overwhelmed with this. The gesture, the mural, the perfection that he brought me here on my birthday.

As his fingers glide off my back, I catch them in my hand. His eyes linger on my face as I pull him down the street, taking in every detail of this magnificent piece of art. I'm not familiar with the artist, but I find his or her signature near the bottom and touch it softly. I have Alex's hand clutched awkwardly in mine, but when he winds his fingers with mine, he smiles at me.

"Do you like it?"

"I'm obsessed," I answer, feeling breathless.

"I can show you the article they posted in the news. I just wanted to surprise you and let you see it in person first."

When the next cluster of people pass us, I notice how they each turn their heads, noticing Alexander, and I hope they take note of how close he's standing to me and how our hands are still locked together.

After we walk the length of the mural twice, he takes me to a little spot in the city with his favorite sushi. We share a couple rolls, laughing over stories he tells me of his first years on his own, and I revel in the way his eyes light up more than they have in a long time.

When we make the walk back to the car, our hands painfully separate, I tell him I want him there with me at the party. I haven't braced myself for what he might witness from my friends and family, but I can't stand the idea of him not being around me for the rest of the day.

* * *

Later that afternoon, we walk together to the party, which has seemingly already started. My mother had it catered and rented a bartender, so now my backyard looks like a circus. All of Cadence's friends are over, and since I don't actually have any friends, I didn't invite anyone.

"My birthday baby!" my mom shrieks as I pass the tall shrub into the backyard. Everyone starts clapping, and I feel myself lean into Alexander. He puts a hand on the small of my back again and it gives me the sense of confidence and comfort I need to keep walking.

I look up at him, hoping he can read the frightened, desperate expression on my face.

"I'll be right here all night," he says as we walk hip-to-hip up the slope to the rest of the party. My aunts are gathered around my mom, and they all kiss and hug me, but it's my mom's eyes I can feel on me as she pulls me in for a tight embrace. When she pulls away, her eyes are misty, and she runs her thumb across my cheek.

We don't say another word as I join my sister and her friends in the pool. Cadence is acting as flippant as ever, like nothing is ever wrong and everything is wonderful.

She swims toward me, throwing her arms around me and handing me her spiked seltzer. "Drink up, girl. Twenty is close enough to twenty-one. We're getting blitzed tonight!"

Seems she already is. I glance over at Alexander as he stands by the pool in his chinos and button-up shirt, one hand in his pocket as he gives me a subtle wink.

He's trying to tell me to have fun. Lighten up. That I'm safe with him.

So, I take the drink and throw it back. My sister cheers, followed by her friends in the pool.

The rest of the night goes by much the same. Cadence keeps handing me drinks, and I keep one eye on Alex all night.

"I know you have swim trunks at home. Come swim with me," I beg while hanging on his knees as he sits on the edge of the pool, feet dangling in the water.

"You want me to swim with you?"

"Yes," I say with a drunk smile.

"How many have you had, rain cloud?" he asks quietly.

"I don't know," I slur.

Brushing my wet hair out of my face, he smiles down at me. I can feel eyes on us as I lean on him, getting a little too comfortable, hanging on his legs, my hands not far from the off-limits zone.

I wonder how many people question our relationship, and the thought excites me. Do they think we're screwing over there in his mansion? Do they see me as his secret side piece? His girlfriend?

"Exactly. I'm not leaving you for one second," he says with a serious brow.

"Are you worried I'll drown in front of all of these people?"

"That's not what I'm worried about, Sunny."

I bite my lip. His cool mood is growing warm, and I feel him getting demanding.

Hopping up, perched on his legs and practically between them, I loop my arms around his neck. His eyes grow wide. He thinks I'm about to kiss him. Instead, I lean in and whisper. "Fine, then."

I plant my feet against the pool wall and launch myself backward, pulling a fully dressed Alexander into the water with me. Once we're both under the surface, his hands grab my sides tight, almost painfully, as he pulls me against him.

A second later we pop out of the water, and I wait for the anger that I illicitly coaxed out of him. "You're dead," he snaps as he throws me across the water by my waist like I weigh nothing.

I let out a yelp as I crash, hearing the laughter before I go under. Quickly, I swim back to him and latch myself onto his back, trying to dunk him, but obviously he doesn't budge. He laughs, that silky smooth low chuckle that tickles my insides.

When it's clear I won't be dunking him, I settle for hanging from his shoulders as he wades in the water. People are most definitely watching us now.

Let the mother fuckers look.

Chapter 17
Sunny

J ust after it starts to get dark, Alex and I huddle under one towel at the edge of the pool. I'm at least four drinks in, and my mother walks out of the house with a three-tiered cake with a large number 2-0 candle on top. Everyone starts singing, and I can't hide the embarrassed smile on my face. Next to me, Alexander sits in his wet clothes, watching me with a flat expression. He isn't smiling, but he isn't scowling either. It's a private look, and for just a moment as everyone sings, it feels like it's just the two of us, and my birthday isn't just a celebration for me but for both of us.

My mother gives me a couple presents to open, but I'm starting to see double from the drinks, so I open them and try to keep a normal smile on my face. It's a new pair of headphones since mine were broken. I don't want to tell her that I like listening to music with Alex, without headphones.

After presents, I sit at the patio table with Cadence and Alexander, and for the first time in a long time, I feel happy. Then, my mother swoops in, sitting too close to me, alcohol on her breath as she squeezes me tight.

"Stay home tonight," she says, sounding like a request and an order.

My heart sinks. All I could think about today was crawling into bed with Alexander, hoping maybe he would let down this wall between us.

The table grows awkwardly silent. I watch Alexander grind his molars as he stays silent. She doesn't bother to look at him. I don't want to see what drunk mom and sober Alex would be like together.

And I don't want to stir the pot, so I figure one night would make her happy, but after that, I'd be back at Alexander's. I'm already drunk anyway, and my mind isn't thinking clearly. Tonight would be a terrible night for things to happen between us. I want to be sober and clear-headed the first time he gives in to this thing between us.

"Just tonight," I mumble, keeping my eyes down on my fidgeting fingers.

"We'll see," she says, brushing my hair out of my face.

Finally, chancing a glance up at Alexander, I meet his gaze, his eyes fixed on me. Cool and emotionless.

A moment later, my mother leaves us alone, but we don't continue our conversation. No one is laughing or talking anymore, so Cadence stands up and has to catch herself as she sways toward where Fischer is talking to a group of guys.

"Do you want me to go back with you?" I ask, feeling breathless.

"You're a big girl, Sunny. You make your own decisions."

Dammit, Alexander. If you want me to stay with you, tell me so. But he won't. He wants me to make the calls.

"Just for tonight," I say, feeling his eyes on me.

He looks like he could shoot daggers out of his eyes with the way he has them targeted at the boys around Cadence. I can see his discomfort, that he's worried about me, not getting bruised up by my mom's drunken tirades but from getting into something with these guys that I might regret.

I want to tell him that I can hold my own with them. They don't scare me, and I trust most of them to at least be cool enough to not force me into something I don't want to do.

But the look on his face says he's jealous.

And I like it. I want him to feel what I felt when the blonde woman was in his window. I want him to feel what I feel every time I scroll through his Instagram and see him with a model on his shoulder. I hope once he feels the true claws of jealousy, he'll stop avoiding what we both know is happening between us.

"I'm heading back to the house. The door will be unlocked." His face is set in a cool, straight line, not giving away anything as he stands.

But I can't let him leave, not yet.

"Let me walk you back," I blurt out and stand up to follow him.

He gives me a curious expression as we walk toward the shrub line. Once we reach the opening between the bushes, I nearly lose my breath when he turns on me and holds me against his body, his hands on my hips. We're hidden from the party. My pulse is flying a million beats a minute.

"I didn't give you your birthday present," he says, holding me so close to his body that I can hardly breathe.

"What is it?"

Moving my hair out of my face, he leans down, his face a breath away from mine.

"Happy birthday, rain cloud." Then his lips are on mine. They are so soft and warm, and I nearly melt from this unexpected moment. I feel his hands travel up my back until he's digging his fingers into my hair and tilting my head. His tongue slips through my lips, and I have no idea how I'm still alive because I swear, I haven't taken a breath in minutes. As his tongue glides with mine, my legs start to tremble, but his hold on my hair keeps me upright.

Our heads tilt in the opposite direction and he takes one last swipe of my tongue before he pulls away. I'm left feeling more drunk than ever and not entirely sure I'll be able to walk back to the party on my own legs.

"Alexander…" I whisper, afraid to open my eyes. At this point, it feels like there is no way I will leave his side. I am crawling into his bed and letting him do whatever he wants to me.

"Go have fun with your family," he whispers, planting a kiss on my head. "But don't ever let anyone kiss you with anything less than that right there."

When I open my eyes, he smiles down at me, fixes my hair, and walks away.

* * *

It takes me a long time before I have the focus to walk back to the party. That kiss was like three shots of tequila, leaving me feeling dizzy and disoriented.

Why did he do that? Because he wanted to or because he wanted to set the bar too high for anyone else to meet it?

Cadence is looking at me with a mischievous expression on her face. Fischer and Liam are still horsing around in the pool. My loud aunt, the one who barely ever acknowledges me unless it's to tell me what I'm doing wrong, walks my mom up to her room. She was starting to get belligerent, but Cadence and I don't even seem fazed today. We're both three sheets ourselves.

"Let's take this party inside," she says when it starts to get a little chilly outside. It's late summer, and I know our days of sitting outside in the pool are numbered.

The idea of going inside instantly makes me nervous because I know the guys are included, and both of them are currently eyeing me like I'm a piece of meat. Or in their case, pizza. Cadence is carrying a bottle of champagne in one hand and a stack of glasses in another. We park ourselves in the upstairs den, a circle of chairs and a loveseat in front of the picture window. She turns on music on her phone and pours us all a drink.

I sip mine slowly, feeling like I should be somewhere else, and if I drink the thoughts away, I won't feel it anymore.

Liam sits next to me. Close.

"You still a virgin, Sunny?" Fischer asks, being obnoxious and loud. Cadence elbows him in the ribs.

"Don't talk about my baby sister like that."

"What?" he said, looking defensive. "I know Liam's curious."

Liam's mouth drops open as he chucks a pillow at his friend. "Not cool, man."

The group laughs, and I finish my drink, feeling hazy and not all present.

"Let's play a game," Cadence says, ignoring the new awkward tension in the room. Liam scoots closer to me.

I wish Alexander was here.

"Never have I ever," Fischer answers.

"Perfect," she answers, over the top of her cup.

"You go first then," Fischer says, looking like he's brewing up something awful in that mind of his.

"How do you play?" I whisper, holding my empty cup tight between my hands.

Cadence smiles at me, like I'm a kid sitting at the grownup table. "We take turns saying something we've never done. Everyone who has done it has to drink."

Oh great. It's just another way to show off my inexperience and make me feel like a loser.

"I've never been a paid, commissioned artist," Cadence says with a smug smile.

My eyes don't leave her face as she refills my cup. "I think that's just you, sis."

"You're a brat," I mumble before sipping down my champagne.

When it's Fischer's turn, he makes some obnoxious remark about blow jobs, which makes Cadence the only one to drink. I bite my lip as I feel Liam's eyes on me.

Nope, not even a blowjob, I think in my head. Get over it.

When it comes around to me, I try to think of something to say, but it's humiliating. Everything I could say makes me feel like an idiot, like I should be humiliated for the things I haven't dived into doing yet, especially when it was Cadence who so boldly convinced me to wait.

"I don't know," I mumble. "Never have I ever..."

"Fucked Liam," Fischer blurts out, and my sister's jaw drops.

"Fischer, man!" Liam groans, dropping his face in his hands. Meanwhile, my cheeks turn about ten shades darker and the tension between Liam and me grows.

I like Liam, I really do. He's the nicest and most mature of Cadence's friends, and there's a little part of me that keeps considering him. Like a constant reminder that we should probably be together. That if my choices were presented already, the obvious choice would be Liam. And it wouldn't be the worst-case scenario.

To be totally honest, I just always assumed I would lose my virginity to Liam.

But that's about it.

I don't think about him when he's not around. I don't search for his flaws, thinking that he has none, but knowing that if I did search, I would find plenty.

Across the room, my sister puts down her cup, but I see Liam's eyes glued on her face.

"This game is done," she murmurs.

Awkward silence fills the room, while Fischer fights the urge to say something else. The truth is obvious. My sister avoided drinking because she didn't want to admit that she and Liam have had sex.

Fischer doesn't want to accept it because he wants Cadence all to himself. But he walked right into this without even realizing it.

And if I could choose for my sister, I'd push her into Liam's arms all day long.

Instead, I feel his arms wrap around my shoulders, squeezing gently.

"You okay?" he asks. "It's just a joke."

His tone is genuine, and I probably do look a little shell-shocked. And I must be drunk because I'm actually leaning back into his touch.

The room sways a little when I look across the space and see Fischer leaning in toward my sister, trying to whisper something to her while she keeps her eyes down and away from him. A moment later he's kissing her, and she's not ignoring him anymore. She's kissing him back.

I can't tear my eyes away because I realize at that moment how much I don't understand my sister. Fischer treats her like shit, and just when I think she's fighting back, she leans right back into his advances. Like she was in control all along.

When I turn my head to see Liam, his face is already turned toward me.

Our lips are inches apart, and I start to pull away, but he's already kissing me. His lips are soft, and my mind starts to replay the kiss from Alexander as Liam presses his tongue into my mouth.

His hand skims my stomach over the thin material of my sundress. Winding his hands around my back, he pulls my body against his.

"You okay?" he whispers.

I nod.

But I don't understand why he asks that. Am I okay with what? Kissing him? He'd know it if I wasn't.

Suddenly his hands are exploring my body, cupping my breasts through my dress and swimsuit, squeezing and kneading them in a way that I'm sure he thinks feels good.

The kissing is nice, and I can't say I'm all that surprised he's a good kisser. I expected him to be. But when I open my eyes and see Liam's boyish face, I'm a little bit disappointed, so I close them again and imagine it's Alexander's lips touching mine.

"Let's go to your bedroom," he whispers as his hands glide down my body toward the hem of my dress, pulling it up with his soft touch.

When I turn toward Cadence and Fischer, I notice they're already gone.

"They went to Cadence's room," he mumbles against my neck. The kiss there sends chills down my spine, and I move without thinking. Standing up, I follow Liam down the hall toward my bedroom. Once we reach the doorway, I stop. The light is on and the window is wide open.

My breath is caught in my chest. What if Alexander is

watching? What if he can see Liam standing in my bedroom?

Before I can think about it another moment, Liam is kissing me again. He moans lightly against my lips as he pulls the hem of my dress up, rounding the curve of my ass with his fingers.

"Let me know when I should stop," he says, and I smile against his mouth. Part of me keeps screaming, do not stop. Never stop.

But this is Liam. Not Alexander. And if it wasn't for that kiss today, I would rule out any possibility of Alex and me, and I would let Liam take me to bed without another thought. I'm ready to let go of my virginity. The over-whelming fixation on my innocence is suffocating. It feels as if I'm standing on one side of this door, ready to walk through and live my life, explore what is out there waiting for me, but also knowing that once I walk through, I can never walk back.

Liam presses my hips against his with a groan, and I feel the thick hardness there, grinding against my stomach. I'm suddenly desperate to touch it, see it, feel it against my skin, but I don't move toward his zipper. Maybe it's the alcohol, but I feel so fucking inadequate at this moment.

Liam's fingers move toward my bikini bottoms, drag-ging his finger along the lining toward the center, and it sends chills to my belly.

I'm overwhelmed, and I want this to feel good, but I'm too lost in my head about what I should or shouldn't be doing that I can't focus on the way his hand feels cupping me over my bikini bottoms, grinding the palm of his hand over my most sensitive part.

This is for the best, I realize at that moment. I like Liam and I trust him, and Alexander wants nothing to do with an inexperienced virgin in bed who won't touch him or move because she has no fucking idea what to do. I would be mortified if this was how I felt with him.

"Can I take these off?" he whispers with his face in my neck and his fingers tugging on the fabric between him and my sex.

"No," a deep voice barks from the doorway.

Liam and I both flinch and turn toward the doorway. There in his gray sweats and white T-shirt, looking stern and angry as hell is Alexander-*fucking*-Caldwell. I feel my heart pick up speed as his eyes travel down our bodies toward Liam's obvious erection and the center of my body where I can still feel Liam's touch vibrating like my body is just now reacting to the contact.

"I think it's time for Liam to go home," Alex says without any emotion on his face.

Sweet, innocent Liam doesn't even consider putting up a fight. With a sheepish look on his face, he bolts out of the room without another word.

"What are you doing?" I say, watching Liam run from my room like he expected a beating if he stayed another second.

"Saving you from giving away your first time to a guy who doesn't know the first thing about making you feel good."

A rush of heat floods my cheeks as I stare at him. Alexander peeks down the hallway, seeing that it's dark and mostly quiet except for the subtle movement and low moans coming from Cadence's room. Then, he closes my bedroom door, shutting us in together. My heart begins to beat itself out of my chest. This can't be happening.

"You don't have any say in who I sleep with. You're not my..."

"Not your what?" he cuts me off, stepping up to me, his

body flush with mine. The back of my legs hit the bed, and if he inches any closer, I'll be forced onto it.

"Not your dad? Is that how you see me, Sunny?" His eyebrows are creased, and his face is contorted in anger, but his breathing is shallow. I know this look on him. He's at war with himself again, fighting his demons and losing.

I shake my head slowly, not sure how he wants me to answer. Does he want me to treat him like my dad? That kiss he gave me earlier certainly says no. A flutter of warmth pools in my belly just thinking that. It's too dirty, too obscure to admit...the idea of him filling both of those roles. The one who protects me, punishes me, pleasures me. My eyes nearly roll back in my head just thinking about it, and I have to bite my lip to keep from moaning.

"I'm not your boyfriend either, Sunny."

The coldness in his statement cools the heat in my body. He's not my boyfriend, and judging by his tone, he never will be.

His fingers touch my chin, lifting it up until his eyes meet mine. "I am a man, Sunny. And Liam is a nice guy, but I know what he's thinking about you. I know that if you let him, he would shove his dick into you, but he wouldn't know the first thing about giving you what you need."

A gasp escapes my lips at his words. Alexander has never spoken so vulgar, so dirty, and yet...I feel the moisture between my thighs.

He steps an inch closer, and I fall back, sitting on the bed before he nestles himself between my knees.

"Lie down," he commands, and I listen. My mouth feels dry, and the only sound I can hear now is the thrumming in my ears and the shaky intake of our breaths.

Alexander leans over my body, placing a hand next to

my head while the other travels up my thigh. "Has anyone touched you here, Sunny?" he asks, his voice shaking.

"No," I cry, pleading with him to touch me. "Please," I beg.

"Please what?" he asks, looking into my eyes.

"Please touch me," I gasp, feeling so vulnerable.

"I will," he says, teasing me, drawing circles between my legs. "Know why?"

"Why?" My voice is strained.

"Because I want you to know how it's supposed to feel when a man touches you."

Leaning down, he nestles his face into my neck, kissing a line from my collarbone to my ear. Meanwhile, his fingers are creeping up my thighs to the wet bikini bottoms between my legs. When they finally reach the moisture there, he lets out a low growl. He nips at my jaw, slipping the fabric to the side and running his thumb from the sensitive nub at the top all the way along my slit to the very back.

My back arches from the contact, and I let out a deep moan.

He lays his body against me, grinding his erection into my leg.

I'm about ready to beg again when his thumb finds that sensitive spot again and flicks it gently, sending bolts of pleasure through me. Another finger perches along my entrance before slowly sliding. He keeps the pressure swirling around my clit, and my gasps in his ear are frantic. Every touch feels like an explosion.

I cannot fucking believe this is happening.

"You're so wet, rain cloud," he groans, sliding his finger in and out. When he works in a second finger, I feel my body building toward something that threatens to shatter me. All I know is that I never want his touch to leave where it is right now.

My head is spinning. Suddenly, his weight is off me and his fingers are no longer buried inside me. I gasp, until I feel both of his hands running along my inner thighs. He kneels between my legs, and his lips travel the same trail from my knees to my center. Hooking his fingers around my bikini bottoms, he pulls them down, letting them fall to the floor. The motion stirs arousal in me.

For a moment, I feel so exposed, afraid to let him see that part of me, but then his fingers are back to my center, teasing and exploring in such a way that I know he knows exactly how to please me.

I cry out when his tongue runs from the bottom to the top. My legs wrap around him as the warmth of his tongue floods my senses. His mouth closes over the top of my mound, his tongue circling my clit, sending me flying. I never want it to stop, but I need this release so bad I would die for it.

"Sunny, you're so beautiful," he murmurs against my core. "I want to worship you, my little rain cloud."

I let out a moan in reply. The words 'I love you,' hang on my lips because at this moment, I do.

With his mouth on my clit, his fingers slide back inside, curling inward and hitting a spot that makes me see stars.

"Alex," I cry out, arching my back and digging my fingers into his hair.

Without letting up, he applies more pressure to my clit, driving his tongue in circles and sucking while his fingers do that magic, and from there it doesn't take much more before my toes are curling, my thighs are squeezing around his body and my breathing stops. I feel this orgasm from the tips of my toes to the top of my head, buzzing through me like electricity.

I would cry out if I could breathe.

It takes what feels like hours before my muscles release, and I relax heavily into the bed. Reaching for Alexander, he kisses the inside of my legs again, then pulls my dress down, covering my bare sex.

He won't meet my eyes as he stands. "Please don't leave," I breathe. I don't know where this puts us now. Have we crossed a line or will he go right back to treating me like a piece of forbidden fruit?

"Get under the covers," he says in that same commanding tone. When I move to pull my dress off, he barks again. "Keep your clothes on."

"Alex—" I start to protest, but he glares at me, jaw clenched, so I stop. How does this man go from giving me the best pleasure of my life to scolding me in one second?

"I'm going to stay here tonight because I don't trust your sister's horny friends. We sleep though, do you understand?"

I nod, biting my lip. I don't care if we do anything else, but his body within reach is all I really need.

Quickly, he flips off the lights and crawls on the bed next to me. It's not as big as his bed, so we're forced to sleep with our bodies together.

My heart can't catch up, and I try to slow my breathing, but I'm still reeling from what he just did to me. Alexander touched me. He *kissed me...down there.*

And now he's going to act like nothing happened.

"Alex," I whisper, reaching for his hand in the dark. He wraps my fingers with his.

"Go to sleep, Sunny."

"I can't," I cry.

I hear his low laugh hum against my fingers. "Don't say I didn't give you anything for your birthday."

A smile creeps across my face. "Aren't you going to let me give you something in return?"

"No. Go to sleep." He leans forward and presses his soft lips to my forehead. I breathe him in, desperate for him to put his mouth on mine, but he doesn't. He just leans back and stays still until I hear his breathing change.

It takes me at least an hour before I fall asleep.

Chapter 18

Alexander

I slipped out of her bed before she woke up this morning. It wasn't easy. I wanted to pull her into my arms and kiss her beautiful face while she slept. My morning wood wanted it even more than I did.

But I kept it under control.

What I did last night should have left me feeling like shit, but I was too busy reliving the way she panted and cried out my name while I was tongue-deep inside of her.

In my head, I separated what we did with sex. I meant what I said. Sunny deserved to know pleasure in bed, and Liam—bless his stupid fucking heart—wouldn't know the first thing about giving her an orgasm. I would have given her a hundred last night if that *one* didn't almost break me. I had to put her to bed just to keep myself from pulling down my pants and burying myself to the hilt.

I felt the way her legs nearly swallowed me whole when she came. That girl would be coming back for more. She'd be an idiot not to.

Now, in the light of day, I know things have to go back to the way they were. No more sleeping next to each other and toeing the line like we have been. I know what a stupid idea that was.

My struggle is about to get a whole lot harder. I came to this neighborhood to straighten up. Settle down and stop fucking everything that moved, including my too-young neighbor.

Although, Sunny has become more than that now...hasn't she? The girl I hired to paint my pool house isn't just a lust magnet for me. Sure, her perfect little lips keep my attention, but it's the way she looks at me, the way she talks to me that keeps me grounded. She listens to me. I mean, she came over in the middle of the night to make sure I didn't drown in my own goddamn pool for fuck's sake.

I can't go back to being the guy that lusts over her. We've made it so far with her staying with me, and I had an inkling that the full, satisfied feeling in my chest might be pride. For once in my life, I'm taking care of someone else with absolutely nothing in it for me.

Why can't she and I just have that relationship without all the goddamn lust involved? Why can't I just be a normal fucking guy who plays the guardian instead of thinking with his dick all the time?

* * *

After a quick shower, I decide to tackle the guest bedroom. My sister gave me a spare bed and a few extra pieces of furniture to make it a proper room for the kinds of guests that don't actually sleep in my bed.

The bed is already put together, and in the boxes Charlotte left me, I find the bedding, some decorations, and a few candles. By lunchtime, I have the space looking like an actual guest room. I even have a few extra pieces of artwork and a lamp my decorator bought before she quit on me—another casualty of my behavior.

I get the abstract hung above the bed when I notice movement in the pool house.

"Good morning, birthday girl," I say, standing in the doorway, watching her set up. She has her long, wet hair set in pigtail braids with denim overalls over a sports bra. The pants are baggy and rolled up to her knee. I find myself smiling at her even when I don't mean to be.

"Morning," she echoes with a smile, peeking at me over her shoulder.

I was afraid things between us would be awkward or what we did last night would change the dynamic between us, but Sunny seems unfazed, getting back to work on the upper half of her mural. The bottom is bright with color, reflected in the light, and I know it's going to be perfect when it's done.

"Can I show you something?" I ask.

She smiles hesitantly as she follows me toward the guest bedroom. At first, her face lights up when she sees the warm glow from the lamp and the cozy cotton aroma from the candle. Then, I see the smallest sign that she's disappointed.

"This is for me, isn't it?" she asks.

"You need your own space, Sunny. I want you to be comfortable, and I know that might sound ironic after what happened last night, but...it's for the best."

"It's perfect," she says with a smile. "Thank you."

Then, she walks away, back toward the pool house, seemingly more okay with this than I expected she'd be. I thought she'd put up a fight like she always does. "You're in a good mood today," I call after her just as she reaches the sliding glass doors.

She turns around with a mischievous smile. "I wish my birthday came around a lot more often."

My lips cracked a smile, watching her walk away. After finishing up a few more things in the guest room, I head out to the pool house. She's already deep into her work today. I figured Sunny might be working on a hangover, but she looks fine.

"Let me know if you need anything today," I say, walking to the fridge.

She giggles quietly at my statement, and I stop, realizing what I just said holds a certain connotation after last night. "I didn't mean it like that," I laugh back.

She giggles harder.

"I'm going to the store. Do you need anything?" I ask.

"No, thank you," she answers without looking back.

"All right." I'm standing only a couple of feet away, and I feel the need to touch her. I settle for tugging gently on one of her pigtails. She swats at me after I do.

As I walk out, she turns and calls toward me. "Oh, get me some of those chickpea snacks you had the other day. Please." She throws me a toothy grin, putting dimples in her cheeks. I'd buy her all the chickpea snacks in the world if she did that.

"You got it, rain cloud."

The solo trip does nothing to clear my head. All I can think about the whole way there and back is what I did last night, wondering if we could ever come back from that. No matter how much I keep trying to convince myself that my intentions were good, that I'm not a fucking creep who wanted to be the first tongue on that pussy, I still feel like one. Corrupting a sweet girl like Sunny because I didn't want a fucktard like Liam to be the one to do it.

And of course, the other thing I can't stop thinking about is that I want to be the first one to fuck her. Not because I have some fantasy about virgins but because I *should* be the first one.

Sunny feels like mine, and the thought of anyone else there, no matter how old or stupid he is, makes me want to drive this Audi straight into a wall. No, Sunny doesn't just feel like mine. Sunny *is* mine.

When I get back from the store, there's a car in my driveway. The hairs on the back of my neck stand up when I think about Sunny in there alone and one of my dick-head "friends" showing up unannounced to find a gorgeous young virgin who never wears enough clothes prancing around my pool house.

My nerves do not calm much when I notice a pair of long legs and a headful of blonde hair step out of the car. As I pull into my drive and pop the trunk, Lea slides up next to me with a smile on her face that used to light a spark in my dick...but doesn't anymore.

"Alexander Caldwell, did you just go grocery shopping?" she asks with a sugar sweet grin.

I smile back, faking the pleasantries as she comes in for a hug. "Even single guys have to eat."

When she pulls back to look at me, ruffling my hair and rubbing the three-day scruff on my face, I actually worry that she can see the guilt in my expression. Like what I did to Sunny last night left marks on my body, and she'll be able to spot it in seconds. "The suburbs look good on you," she lies. I know for a fact that I look like shit compared to how I used to look in the city.

"Thanks, Lea. To what do I owe the surprise?" I hoist the two paper bags under my arm and shut the trunk, hoping she'll leave without walking into the house.

"Oh, just checking in on you. I don't see you online much anymore, and I miss you. Thought we could do brunch."

She follows me into the house, and in my head, I'm making all kinds of excuses and lies for why I can't go out with her right now when the only reason I can't is that I just fucking don't want to. But for some stupid reason, I'm too afraid to just say that. I'm also internally panicking, knowing that she's about to be face-to-face with Sunny, and I can't quite put my finger on why that freaks me out.

She doesn't stop talking as we walk into the kitchen, going on and on about our friends and what they've been up to since I moved—which isn't anything new, so no surprise there. As I drop the bags on the counter, I peek around the window to see Sunny in the same spot working on the upper half of the wall. She has the music playing as she works, loud enough that we can hear it in the house. Lea doesn't seem to notice yet.

"So, what do you say?" she asks, looking at me expectantly.

"Um...now's not a great day, Lea. I have stuff to do around the house." I gesture toward the pool like a fucking idiot, at which she turns her head and sees Sunny's movement.

"You have workers in the pool house?" she asks, peeking around the corner.

"Just someone painting a mural on the wall," I answer casually, rubbing the back of my neck.

It clearly piques her interest. Without another word, she walks out the patio door toward the pool house. "Oh my gosh, it's gorgeous, Alexander," she drawls, looking at me as if I'm the one painting it.

"The credit is due to the artist." I point toward Sunny who turns around and nearly drops her paintbrush when she sees the blonde woman standing next to me. Her cautious eyes find me, and I try to apologize with my stare. Less than twenty-four hours after I had her writhing with

138

pleasure on her bed, I'm standing here with another woman.

"Aren't you adorable?" Lea squeaks toward her.

She walks over, sizing up the painting, and I watch my girl squirm, her music blaring from the speaker.

"This is Sunny Thorn," I say, introducing her, trying to act normal. "The most talented artist in Pineridge."

Sunny glances at me, her tight-lipped expression focused on my face. I want to pull her off of that scaffolding and show this woman that Sunny is so much more than my adorable decorator.

Lea looks back at me with something sneaky in her eyes. Turning her back on Sunny, she saunters toward me. "You've changed, Alexander Caldwell."

Then she leaves me standing in front of Sunny, feeling like the world's biggest piece of shit as Lea disappears into the house with a 'come fuck me' face on. And like the good little boy I am, I follow. Sunny doesn't say a word as I walk away.

The sound of a champagne bottle pop coming from my living room makes me pause. "This calls for a celebration," she says with a laugh, pouring the bubbly into a flute, glaring at me with a smile.

"What are we celebrating?" I ask.

"You're growing up, Alex. You have a house in the suburbs. You're decorating, spending your days doing housework, *grocery shopping!*"

I let out a laugh, amusing her for the time being. I could put aside the annoyance of feeling like the butt of the joke for a moment, and acknowledge that yes, I have grown up. But I'm forty-fucking-years old, so it's about damn time I grew up, and if the woman only five years younger than me who acts half as mature wants to have some fun with it, then I'm okay with that.

She raises her glass. "Here's to shocking the hell out of everyone."

I let my hand drop without a clink to her glass. My smile fades as I stare at her grin. Even my fucking friends expected me to fail.

"Oh, come on," she teases. "I'm proud of you."

"Yeah, you seem it. You're proud that I didn't fuck up like I always do, right?"

"Don't get salty about it, Alex." Her hand drops, and I have to step away to keep from saying something I'll regret.

"How do you know I haven't fucked up?" I ask, leaning against the counter and watching the girl that tempts me every day just sitting in her overalls like she's not a walking crisis for me.

Lea notices my unfocused gaze. "Have you?"

"All I do is fuck up, right? Just like everyone expects me to. My sister, my friends, my business partners. Why even try anymore if I just fulfill their expectations of me?" I don't know if I'm saying this to Lea or to myself.

She sets her glass down next to me and rubs her hands along my forearm. It's not a sexual movement. She's touching me as a friend, a seemingly concerned one. And why wouldn't she be? I don't even recognize myself anymore.

"Alex, this transformation is good for you. You're out of the city, getting time to reflect. Everyone is cheering for you."

I'm not buying it, but it's nice to hear.

"Besides," she says, pressing her body up against mine. "I know for a fact you haven't fucked that teenager in your pool house. So, that's progress." There's a little laugh in her voice.

But my face contorts into a disappointed expression as I move away from her, not even bothering to correct her.

Sunny is technically not a teenager, but I don't even know if that matters anymore. I'm putting space between us because that's what's right for her.

"Come on, Lea," I complain. "She's just a kid."

"Just a kid?" she echoes, eyebrows up. "Alex, *I'm* having a hard time keeping my hands off that girl."

"How do you know I'm *not* fucking her already?"

"Oh honey, I can tell."

Something about that statement doesn't sit right with me. How the fuck can she tell? "How so?"

She lets out a laugh as she gulps down her champagne. "If you were screwing her or have screwed her at least once, she wouldn't still be working for you."

"And why the hell not?"

This time her laugh is louder, and I'm not so convinced she hasn't already started drinking today. "Alex, come on! Girls that age don't do casual sex without commitment. Not with guys like you. The Alex I knew would have bedded that sweet thing weeks ago. She'd grow attached, you'd break her heart, and she'd probably have burned down your pool house by now. No, there's no way you fucked her."

"You should read fortunes," I tease back. "Because you're right. I haven't. I forgot to feel proud of that. Treating women with dignity."

A snicker escapes her lips as she steps closer. "It was never really your style."

My blood boils. Lea was always one of my closest friends and favorite fuck buddies, but she's putting a distorted mirror in front of my face, and I'm starting to feel like a real asshole for it.

"I think you should leave."

She freezes. "What? Why?"

"Because you want to celebrate how much I've changed, but you're not rooting for me."

"Alex," she whines, reaching for me, but I grab her bag from the table and push it toward her chest. From my periphery, I notice that we have an audience, standing by the open patio door.

"Next time you want to check on me, don't try to get me drunk so we can fuck, okay? Actually, just don't fucking check on me at all, how about that?

Standing in the doorway, she twists her face in anger at me, but I'm numb to it at this point. "You're a joke, Alex. Everyone knows you're just putting a big ol' Band-Aid over a gun wound, trying to pretend you can just buy a house and stop being such a loser. No one is rooting for you, Alex because no one fucking cares."

She storms out the door, slamming it as she goes. I'm standing there, jaw clenched and swallowing the anger in the back of my throat when I feel Sunny's soft hands on my arms.

"Alex."

"You shouldn't stay here, Sunny." My voice comes out harsher than I mean for it to, and I see her flinch, but she doesn't leave. Her hand doesn't even leave my back as she keeps rubbing circles between my shoulder blades.

"Breathe."

Lea's words just keep repeating in my head, and no matter how much I try to argue with what she said, I can't. She's right. How many girls did I fuck over the years, ignoring their emotions, leaving them high and dry, not giving half a shit for how they feel about it? How long until I do the same thing to Sunny?

"Fuck!" I bark, my voice echoing around the room as I walk away, fighting the urge to put my fist through the wall.

Sunny doesn't follow me, not at first. She only stands in her spot, watching me.

There's a tingling in my hands, and it's snaking its way up my arms, pooling in my chest, making my heart pound and my breathing become shallower. I plant my hands on the counter and try to control my breathing, but it's futile. All I can manage are short, shallow inhales.

"Alex, breathe." Her hands are rubbing circles on my back again. Her head is resting against my shoulder.

These things come around from time to time, and they just love to make an appearance whenever I give up drinking and convince myself I'm going to turn my life around. It's like nature's way of saying, *nice try, asshole. Not today*.

"I'm fine," I mumble.

Her hands keep up the rhythmic motion on my back. It helps.

Now the heat is in my cheeks, across my chest, making my skin crawl and my ears pound. It's like my heartbeat has traveled from my chest up to my throat and fills my head. I fucking hate it. Feeling helpless. Weak. Broken.

Once the panic subsides, I let my grip loosen on the countertop. Part of me wants to reach for the Klonipin or whiskey, which is what I usually use to make these things fuck off, but instead, I breathe in the reassurance and the girl standing next to me. Her fingers are in my hair, sending goosebumps down my spine and easing all of the tension in my back with the way she's moving her nails against my scalp.

"Talk to me," she whispers without pulling away or stopping her movements.

"She was right, Sunny. I haven't changed at all."

"Why do you need to change?" she asks, leaning her cheek on my shoulder so her voice is in my ear.

"Because I couldn't live like that forever."

"So, change what you do, not who you are."

"I have to. I have to change who I am," I growl, keeping my eyes closed tight.

"Why do you have to change?"

Pulling away, I look down into her wide eyes, those eyes with the world in them. The knowing, wise, welcoming eyes that make me feel like I'm being seen and not just looked at.

"Because I fucking hate myself, Sunny. And I can't live like that anymore. I don't do anything worthwhile. I don't make anyone happy or make anyone fucking smile. I don't even disappoint people anymore because no one has any faith in me at all.

"At night I want to know that there's someone in my bed that will be there the next night and the night after that. I'm tired of being lonely, Sunny."

Her hands are on my cheeks now, the soft pads of her fingers, with the scent of acrylic paint wafting to my nose stroking the unshaven scruff on my face to my neck.

"One day at a time, Alex," she whispers in the silence, and I want to kiss her so bad it hurts. It actually stings the back of my eyes to keep myself from gathering her into my arms to taste her lips, but I don't.

Instead, I settle on pulling her in for a hug. "You're the fucking greatest, you know that?"

Her smile against my neck eases away another layer of tension in my body.

When I finally pull away, she stands there awkwardly, and I hate myself for how tense I've made things between us. I had to go and do what I did last night, and now the girl doesn't know where we stand or what I'll do next. When we'll do what we did last night again. Fuck, she actually asked when she could return the favor, and it nearly killed me.

But what Sunny did for me today was more than that. These lines have been crossed, but I promised her I'd take care of her, and it's up to me to walk back over the lines to the side where we both belong.

"So…" she says, carefully, leaning against the counter, and I dread the next words out of her mouth, sure she's going to bring up last night.

"Sunny…"

"Did you get me those chickpea snacks?"

A laugh bursts through my lips as I take the bag out and toss them at her. "Knock yourself out, rain cloud."

"Thanks," she calls back to me, as she disappears through the door and back to her place in the pool house.

Chapter 19

Sunny

I'm having a hard time with this blue. It's either too green or too gray, but I need it to reflect the water from the pool, but no matter how I mix it, it just keeps turning out wrong, and it's distracting me. When Alex calls me in for dinner, I ignore him.

"What is all this?" he asks, seeing the different shades of teal, blue, cerulean scattered around me.

"I'm working on something," I mutter. The music has stopped playing, and he walks over to check on me, but I'm not in the mood. It's been almost two weeks since the incident on my birthday and the girl that came over to see him. Things between us have not changed, and we are at a standstill. It's making me restless.

We never talked about my birthday or the woman. Every night we crawl into different beds, and I have to admit the guest room is nice. I've brought over a few more things from my house, and I've managed to make it my own.

Alex and I still swim together, grocery shop together,

eat together—everything a couple would do—except for get naked and have sex.

And for that reason, tension is building.

I never really had the heart to tell him that it bugged me to see the woman at the house. I don't know if he called her over after our night together or if she just showed up out of the blue. Every night I go to sleep, tossing and turning, wondering if anything between us is real and if he called her over to be with a real person, instead of a kid.

"I'm not hungry," I mutter, going back to the first teal I had, hoping if I put in a dash of green it will even out.

"Sunny," he barks at me, giving me that tone I hadn't heard in so long. By instinct, I turn toward him. "Come eat," he says a little softer this time.

I listen, hopping off the scaffolding and stalking past him without a second glance. I'm irritated with him without really knowing why. At the table, I pick at my dinner while he watches me, and I know he's just as frustrated.

Finally, after a few moments, he throws down his napkin and stands up. "You have clean-up duty."

My eyes widen. "What?"

"You're cleaning up after dinner," he says again, reaching for the wine bottle. "You ate it, right?"

I've been working all day in the pool house, painting his goddamn wall, and now he wants to treat me like a kid who needs to do chores. My jaw hangs open. "I've been working all day, Alex."

"So what, Sunny? You can help out if you're going to be living here." My mouth goes dry. He doesn't want me staying here anymore. I knew things were getting tense between us, but I still held onto hope that if I stayed, things would eventually evolve, that he would at some point give in.

The thought that he's pushing me out, and that everything between us is over chills me to the bone.

"Then maybe I won't live here anymore," I threaten, feeling stubborn but also desperate to see his reaction.

"Then, don't." He's pushing back. He's not serious.

I stand up in a huff. "What the fuck is up with you right now?"

Stepping closer, he corners me. "You're not going to be like me, Sunny. You're not going to grow up without any responsibility or expectations. When you're here, you're going to pull your weight."

"Since when did you become my parent, Alex? I'm twenty years old!"

"Since I started giving a shit about you, Sunny. Can you say the same about those other two?"

"Fucking harsh, Alex."

"Get over it, Sun. Life sucks sometimes. Toughen up and stop expecting handouts. You know how much I wish my parents would have given enough of a shit about me to make me responsible for myself, but they didn't. No one did, babe, so you're welcome."

He steps away, leaving me reeling, leaning back against the table. The anger in my stomach is mixed with something else...lust.

But he's already gone, walking out to the pool to drink his glass of wine. Stomping over to the sink with my plate in my hand, I scrape off the food into the disposal and start on loading the dishwasher.

The whole time all I can think is that I don't need him treating me like a kid. It's the last thing I want for him to see me as. If he thinks I'm so fucked up already, then it means I am fucked up, and it's too late to fix me now. He just wants to take all of his self-deprecating angst out on me. I nearly break his plates tossing them around the sink.

Once the kitchen is cleaned and wiped down, I stomp out to the pool house, ignoring him sitting in his chair by the water. Sure, my parents aren't the most attentive, but at least they never make me feel like a spoiled brat like he does.

For a moment, I actually consider going home. I could pack my things up and show him that I don't care that much about him or what he thinks I need, but the thought of crawling back into my mother's house is a non-starter.

Climbing up on the scaffolding, I'm kneeling on the second rung, packing up my unused shades of blue when I feel something cool and wet along the back of my leg. Letting out a gasp, I turn to see Alexander standing behind me with an ashy shade of turquoise smeared across his finger.

Without another word, he picks up a dollop of the seafoam green with the same finger and spreads it across my arm.

"Alex!" I shriek, pushing him away.

"Stop being so angry at me," he whines.

"Well, stop treating me like a kid."

"Stop acting like one." This time, he plucks a blue finger on my forehead.

"You're one to talk. This stuff is toxic, Alex."

"No, it's not," he laughs.

When he reaches for another glob of paint, I swat his hand away, sending the tray flying, splattering blue paint all over his tile floor. Before he reacts, I slather my hand with sky blue and spread it across his chest, all over his shirt, mixing it with the strands of chest hair peeking out of his collar. He grabs my wrists tightly in his hands, stopping me. We're not playing anymore, but we're not quite fighting either. It's charged, and my heart is thudding harder than ever as rage boils up from my gut. I feel like a kid who can't have what she wants, bursting with emotion and desperate to let it out.

I let out a scream, yelling it in his face. Suddenly, his paint-covered hand is around my waist as he hoists me off the scaffolding. I let out a desperate shriek as he carries me out to the pool, hanging under his arm like a bag of flour.

"Put me down," I scream. But it barely gets out of my mouth before he's tossing me in the water, jumping in after me. The summer has recently faded into a warm autumn, leaving the evenings cooler, and the frigid water in the pool sends waves of electricity through my body.

When I pop up for air, I give him a snarl. I want to hit him, more than ever. "You're an idiot for what this will do to your pool water." The usually crystal-clear water is starting to look murky already from the paint all over his hands and my waist.

"Chill the fuck out, Sunny," he says, pulling me closer by the waist.

"No. you want to act like I'm not responsible, but you're the one who acts like an impulsive teenager." When my body slams up against his, his arms tight around my waist, I shut up.

Without a word, he brushes my wet hair out of my face. "Do you have any idea how hard it is for me to *not* act like an impulsive teenager around you?"

My breath slows, staring at his face and the soft wrinkles around his eyes. "Oh yeah?" Suddenly, I know exactly how I want to use this pent-up aggression. I want to push him, test the strength of his convictions.

The pool wall is against my back and he frames me in with his hands on the ledge on either side of me. I watch the movement of his chest as he breathes. The water clings to his wet T-shirt flattened against the cords of muscles that run down his arms. My fingers move to touch them.

"How would you act then, Alexander? If you were an impulsive teenager?" I clench my thighs together, feeling the arousal warming my center.

I expect him to swim away, stop himself from saying anything that he would deem too risky like he normally does. Instead, he leans in, as if speaking directly into my throat. My heart stops when I feel his cool breath against my wet skin.

"I would have fucked you in this pool at least a dozen times by now, Sunny."

His lips don't touch my skin, but he blows softly, sending goosebumps along every inch of my body.

It becomes harder to swallow when his fingers slide down the length of my shoulder, starting from my earlobe and traveling down to my elbow. My arms close around his neck as he presses me against the wall, grinding his erection into my lower belly.

"What else?" I breathe.

With his breath against my cheek this time, he continues. "I would have filled every single one of these precious holes, Sunny. I would own them all."

I can't help it, but a soft moan escapes my lips at his words. In response, his hands lift my legs until they're wrapped around his waist. My brain is lost in the sensation, but there's an acceptance there that he will never do these things he talks about. The things he wants to...*we both* want him to. This is what he needs to feel better about himself, to deny himself these indulgences until he knows he can trust himself to be a better person for me. I can accept that now.

But still, I want his lips on my mouth so bad, it hurts.

I don't beg. It wouldn't be fair.

But there are no rules against my lips on him.

Tilting my hips, I grind myself against his stiffness and let my lips absorb the moisture from his neck. Tiny droplets of saltwater on my tongue, I feel his pulse in my mouth.

"What else?" I want this game to last forever.

He grinds me roughly against the side of the pool. "I'd have you on your knees for me, Sunny. Hungry for my cock, every fucking day."

"Yeah," I moan into his ear.

"Jesus Christ," he groans, grinding into me again.

"What else?"

"Tell me not to touch you, Sunny." His hands are on my sides, digging his fingers into the flesh around my ribcage, and I understand what he's asking me to do. He's asking me to define the rules of this game. We can imagine it. We can pretend it could happen, but it can't actually happen. For his sake, this is what Alex needs. To know he showed restraint, that he is not the guy who takes without repent, that walks away from the version of himself he can stand.

His fingers are creeping toward my breasts, and for a moment I consider that my tits don't count. This doesn't cross the line. His hands fondling my nipples would be fucking heaven and if it's the only thing I can get, I'll take it. But I don't. Because it is crossing the line, and these are the boundaries he needs.

"Don't touch me, Alexander." It comes out in a croak, and his hips drive harder against me as I say it.

"Good girl."

"Tell me not to kiss you." He's holding my face in his hands now, staring into my eyes, and my gaze falls on his lips. How beautiful I already know they feel against mine.

"Don't fucking kiss me."

"I want to," he groans against my cheek.

I want him to, as well. So bad I'm about to throw all the stupid rules out the window. I could let Alexander have his way with me right now, and none of it would matter. I could nurse him back to understanding that he's not all bad. That what I see isn't what he sees. That he's not to blame for this. That he's not the monster he sees when he looks in the mirror.

This time when he grinds against me again, he grabs my hips in his hands, and it's too rough, but it doesn't hurt as much as his words. "Tell me not to make you come."

My chest deflates, and I want to ignore him. I know that if I don't say anything, he would grind his dick against me until I throbbed with pleasure. I can almost taste the orgasm.

"You can't make me come, Alex," I whisper, feeling defeated, hanging on his shoulders, wishing I could take it all back.

His movement stops. Our breathing slows. Hanging onto his shoulders, he lets go of my body. "Good girl, rain cloud." My eyes squeeze shut at his words.

I hate that the idea of being with me makes Alex feel like a monster. I wish that there weren't twenty years between us and that giving him every single part of me didn't warp his self-image, but it does. And it always will.

He pulls away, leaving my cold body in the pool as he walks toward the stairs.

When he reaches a hand down to help me out, he gives me one of his signature winks like nothing happened between us. "First rule of being a responsible adult is we don't always get what we want."

Chapter 20
Sunny

My phone buzzes behind my head, and I reach back and silence it without looking at the name on the screen. Alexander and I were up until almost two a.m. binge-watching something on Netflix, and I know it's probably at least eleven in the morning already. I smell the coffee from the kitchen.

He didn't touch me again after the encounter in the pool, which I had to admit grated my nerves. I wanted to keep playing that little resistance match, but that was the difference between us. For me, it was a game. For him, it was his life.

I don't know if Alex will ever get over our age difference and be ready to let me in. Somewhere in his head, he thinks he belongs with someone else, someone his age, better suited to his lifestyle instead of a teenager he won't even introduce to his friends. I have to live with the fact that if he did give in to what I tempted him with last night, it would just be sex. And that's it. And that would kill me.

My phone starts buzzing again. My dad's picture pops

up on the screen. Sitting up in a rush, I click the green button and hold it up to my ear.

"Hello?"

"Where the hell are you?" he bites across the phone line without a greeting.

"What?" I stutter.

"Your mother said you're sleeping over at the neighbor's house."

The blood drains from my face. In a rush, I jump out of bed and run to the kitchen. Alexander is sitting on his laptop with a coffee cup in his hands. I take a mental picture of how hot he looks in the early morning light.

"Well, did Mom tell you *why*?" I respond.

Alex tilts his head in question at my conversation. I just shake my head at him.

"I'm staying in his guest bedroom because I can't stand to be in that house anymore, Dad. I can't be around her anymore."

"What the fuck did she do?" my dad asks, sounding exasperated. I'm still waking up, but now I can make out the sound of his car in the background and realize that he's on the road somewhere. Whatever effort he put into calling me was just enough to put in a call on his way somewhere.

"Don't worry about it," I mumble. I'm not protecting my mom. I just don't need the added anxiety. If I tell him what she did, then he'll get involved. And it's prolonging something that I just want buried in my past.

"So, what? You're sleeping with Alexander Caldwell now?"

I flinch at the accusation in my dad's tone.

"We're just friends, Dad."

Alexander's eyes are on me, and I avoid his gaze as I

defend our relationship—our strange, undefinable relationship.

"Well, I don't know how I feel about you sleeping in a strange man's house. I know Caldwell, Sunny. He's not the kind of guy you leave your nineteen-year-old daughter with."

"I'm twenty, Dad." Staring out at the pool, I feel Alex's presence behind me, putting his hand on my shoulder.

"Well, whatever, Sunny. Same thing. I think you should go make up with your mom. Whatever she did, I'm sure you had a part in it, and you two need to figure it out."

"You've got to be kidding me," Alexander mutters from behind me, hearing my dad's voice blaring across the line. Before I know it, the phone is out of my hand.

"Listen here, asshole. Your daughter showed up in my house at midnight with a shiner on the side of her face that she got from her mother."

"Alex!" I shriek, trying to take my phone back. I hear my dad raging on the other line.

"Be a fucking man and take care of your family, you piece of shit." In a huff, he tosses my phone into the grass and stomps off, seething with anger. The tin sound of my dad's voice blaring from the phone calls for me, and I turn toward him to pick it up, but something stops me. I should stop chasing his love. I should walk inside with Alex and stick up for myself, but I'm frozen in place.

I hate that I pick the phone up, but I do.

"Dad, I'm sorry."

"Who does that fucking asshole think he is?" he barks at me, making my throat sting with oncoming tears. "He has no right talking to me like that. Sunny, you get your ass out of that house do you hear me? Go home and stay the fuck away from Alexander Caldwell. Has he tried anything with you yet? I swear if I find out he touched my little girl, I'll kill him."

"Dad, I'm just working for him. Painting a mural in his pool house. He hasn't tried anything. He's just helping me."

"You're what? Painting his pool house? What kind of idiot can't paint—"

"Dad, he hired me to paint one of my paintings on his wall. It's... never mind," I stammer. Trying to explain my art to my dad feels about as good as peeling my own skin off.

"Just go home, Sunny." I can hear the anger in his voice, but it doesn't penetrate anymore.

"Okay, Dad," I lie.

"I have a meeting, Sunny. I hate having to deal with this shit while I'm trying to work. Just keep your shit together, okay? And for fuck's sake, go home."

Before I can say goodbye, the line goes dead.

When I walk into the house, Alex has his running clothes on. A pair of shorts without a shirt, looking good enough to eat. The seasoned flecks of gray in his growing beard have my mind almost completely forgetting about the fight with my dad.

"Your dad really is an asshole," he mumbles as he grabs his earbuds off the entryway table.

"He's just...under a lot of stress," I lie. My dad is under the same amount of stress that he's always been under. This is his base standard of behavior, and I realize that I've been making these excuses for him my entire life. Alex catches my bullshit right away with a cocked brow.

"Can I come with you?" I blurt out, suddenly feeling motivated to be outside, with Alexander, working up a sweat in a way that doesn't have to end in a cold shower and frantic touching myself to relieve some of the pressure.

"You want to go for a run?" he asks, looking a little excited about it.

"Yeah, if that's okay?" We don't have to look like a couple while we're jogging next to each other. We can still look like friends.

"Of course. Suit up, rain cloud," he says with a smile, and I run back to my room to grab my shorts and sports bra. When I walk out, he immediately shuts down my outfit. "Nope!" he yells and points at the bedroom.

"You're not wearing a shirt!" I shout from the bedroom as I dig a tank top out of my bag that is now strewn all over the floor.

When I stomp past him, mumbling, "Happy now?" he answers with a quick swat on my butt that makes me laugh while sending a surge of excitement through my body.

We start off with a brisk walk until we get to the top of the hill where the neighborhood starts to level out.

"Why do you make excuses for him?" Alex asks as he starts to jog.

"I'm not. He's just…he's never been a great dad, but I still love him."

"That doesn't mean it's okay to let him talk to you like that, Sunny. Just because you love someone doesn't mean they have a free pass to treat you like shit."

"I don't know," I mumble.

I can tell Alexander is keeping his pace slower for me. I haven't jogged in almost a year, but I could remember loving long jogs in high school. I didn't play sports, but these runs around the neighborhood were one of the only ways I could escape my parents fighting.

"Keep up, rain cloud," he calls as he starts pulling ahead. It only makes me push harder, working to jog beside him.

"What about you?" I ask, losing the ability to speak and breathe at the same time.

"What about me?" he asks. The jerk doesn't sound winded at all.

"Why haven't you had kids? Gotten married?" My voice comes out in huffs.

"Never wanted to."

He answers like it's just that simple. He didn't want to get married, so he didn't. I realize that it must be nice to not be under so much pressure to find the right person, get married, and push out a ton of babies.

"Ha," I answer because it's about all my lungs can handle.

He laughs at me, that deep timber chuckle as he stops and lets me catch up. "Breathe, Sunny." His arm lands around my shoulder, and I lean into his body, wanting the contact but also the support. I guess I'm in worse shape than I expected.

"Are you laughing at me, rain cloud?"

"I just think it's funny that you can just live your whole life without any pressure."

"So, you think I don't get pressured? Please. My sister has been breathing down my neck to get married since I was twenty. It's probably why I haven't."

"Why does she pressure you so much?" I ask, finally regaining the ability to breathe and speak at the same time.

"My parents died when we were young. Left us with money and not much else. I had the whole world and zero responsibility. All I had to do was keep up the investments, stay in touch with the business managers, and spend more money than I could make a dent in in one lifetime. To my sister, I was throwing my life away. She thought that if I didn't settle down, find a wife, build a family that it would all be for nothing."

"And has it? Been all for nothing?" I ask, peeking up at him through the bright sun. There's a sheen of sweat along his forehead, but he's barely out of breath.

He smiles down at me, sending my stomach into a twirl. "How could I complain?"

I know he's making light of a lifetime of behavior that has sent him spiraling and left him unfulfilled, but I see that somewhere in the levity is a hint of truth.

When we come to the top of the next hill, we decide to take off in a jog again. This time, he keeps up a slow pace to stay next to me. I notice movement across the street, a flash of light, but I don't think anything of it. I just smile at him and jab him in the ribs like he always does to me.

As we get back to the house, I follow Alexander to the pool. He smiles at me as he tosses back a bottle of water. Then without another word, he peels off his jogging shorts and dives into the water. I barely get a look at his pale, bare backside before he's in the pool. Water spits out either side of my mouth as I hold my water bottle to my lips.

"Oh my god, Alex!" I spew. There's not much privacy in this neighborhood. I can see directly into his house from my room, so it's easy to assume other people can see him jumping naked as a jay bird into his pool.

He laughs, another hearty chuckle that lights my heart up.

"Better than a shower, rain cloud. Your choice." He splashes me from the edge of the pool. The weather has cooled, but not too cold to swim by any stretch. I bite my lip, looking around at the neighbor's yards. The trees still have most of their leaves, so I know my mother and sister can't see over, unless they're in my room and even then, it's sparse.

No one in their right mind would pass up skinny dipping with Alexander Caldwell. So, after downing the water bottle and dropping it on the table, I peel my tank top off, leaving me in just my sports bra. He turns around, as if he's going to cover his eyes as I let my jogging shorts drop to the ground. I feel so exposed, the bare skin of my ass on the pool deck as I dangle my feet in the water. Last, I pull up my sports bra as I sink into the water.

He's right. The cool pool water feels amazing on my blazing hot skin after that long jog.

When he turns around, I'm submerged to my shoulders, but I know he could see my tits through the water if he really looked.

Is he looking?

Swimming toward him with a smile, I circle him. He reaches out and takes one of my legs. I feel the bareness of his hip as he pulls me toward him.

Just when I think we're about to play the same game we played yesterday, the stakes a whole lot higher being naked, he plants a hand on my head and pushes me under the water. I laugh until I realize I'm under the water with the bare bottom half of Alexander's body. Once my face is submerged, I open my eyes and see him, the dark hair around his thick manhood, which looks a bit harder and longer than it should at a moment like this.

Did I do that to him? The vision of me naked aroused him. Did he push me under so I could see it?

When I pop back out, I laugh at him, but I keep my distance. Our exposed bodies, especially him with that growing erection, is a recipe for disaster if he wants the both of us to keep our hands to ourselves.

Instead, I perch my forearms on the pool deck and look at the mess I've made in the pool house. I imagine him saddling up behind me, pressing that thick erection against my back. Kissing my neck and dragging his lips down my spine.

The sound of him getting out of the pool and walking toward the table where his towel is waiting interrupts my daydream. I catch a glimpse of him before he covers himself. His solid body, the dark hair drawing a subtle line down his stomach from his belly button to that hidden place that suddenly disappears behind the towel.

"Where are you going?" I call after him. He stops before he disappears into the pool house.

Without fully looking at me, he tilts his head in my direction. "After last night, I thought it was clear that you and I shouldn't be in a pool together."

"What's that supposed to mean?" I don't know why his comment sours my stomach, but I was fucking proud of myself for doing exactly what he wanted last night. I played by his rules, pushing him away like he wanted, and now I'm being punished for it, and frankly, I'm really fucking sick of being punished for shit I didn't do.

Stirred by anger, I climb out of the pool and follow him into the pool house, standing before him naked and dripping water all over the tiles. When he spins toward me, his eyes nearly bug out of his head.

"What the fuck are you doing?" he blurts out, spinning away from me.

"I told my dad we were just friends. So, are we?" Stomping toward him, I yank his arm, turning him to face me.

"Jesus, Sunny. Cover yourself." He looks around at the windows afraid someone can see me, but at this point, I couldn't give a shit.

I don't even hear him. I'm too fueled by burning this angst between us. The limbo he's keeping me in is torture, and I'm done.

"Alex!" I shout. "Answer me."

Stuck with no other choice, he pushes me backward

until my back is pressed against the wall and I'm out of view of the neighbors. It leaves our bodies inches apart.

"Are we friends, Sunny?" he gasps. "I'm too old to be your fucking friend. I'm trying to do right by you, be what you need, but so help me God…" He leans his head back like I'm hurting him.

"I'm not a child, Alex. And you're not a monster." With my bare skin against the wall, I touch his face. His eyes meet mine, and I watch him swallow. He's about to kiss me; I can feel it.

He leans in, so slowly I wait for him to close the distance, and just when his face is close enough to feel his breath against my mouth, his forehead drops to my shoulder. The heavy breath moves through his chest like every inhale is full of pain.

Framing my face, his hands stay glued to the wall behind me, and I let my lips graze the skin of his arm. The pain I'm causing him will break me, and I'm certain at this very moment that neither of us will make it out of this unscathed. It occurs to me at that moment that if I cared about him at all, it's clear what I should do, and it absolutely kills me to admit.

I have to move out.

Chapter 21

Sunny

He doesn't say much for the rest of the day. After the tense encounter in the pool house, he made quick work of ignoring me and opening a bottle of bourbon. He's been in one of his moods ever since. It's not anger at me anymore. It's the neutral, non-caring version of Alex that shatters my heart into shreds.

It's well past midnight when I hear the sound of the ice clink in his glass as he walks into the pool house. I don't know if he's waiting for me to go to bed, but I can't sleep in this house tonight. I figured the best thing for me to do would be to wait until he goes to sleep and sneak back to mine.

Just thinking about it makes my chest want to cave in, but I have to. I know that now. As much as I want Alex, I know what it would cost him to let himself down after he's spent so long doing what he thinks is right.

I was supposed to be making this easy for him, and I know I'm not. I watched him grind his molars at dinner as I sauntered in with nothing but one of his T-shirts and a pair of underwear, but neither of us had done laundry for

164

days and it was the last thing I had. He's hardly one to talk with those gray sweatpants he walks around in. The house today feels like a ticking time bomb, and we're both about to let it destroy us.

And at this point, I'm ready for an all-out war. Once again, I'm left without a choice in this matter. Someone else is calling the shots, and my voice is silenced. Walking around in nothing but his T-shirt with my bare ass on the dining room chairs is just my way of protest.

With Dua Lipa playing in the pool house, I try to focus on the veins of these flowers in gold and blue when I hear him sit on the couch. He takes a drink but says nothing.

The music stops, and I know he's controlling it from his phone, leaving the room in awkward silence as I work, trying desperately hard to focus. There is a sense of expectancy in the air, like we both know everything between us is about to change.

"Did you see me under the water, rain cloud?" he mumbles, a cold edge to his voice.

My hand freezes. Why is he doing this? Bringing it up when he knows it will only make things worse. He's trying to start something, and I don't think I can handle him starting something he's not willing to finish.

"Did you?" he says again, his voice low and sexy.

"Of course, I did," I answer, trying to keep things casual. "Did you want me to?" The teasing tone in my voice doesn't come out genuine.

"I wanted you to see what you do to me."

Like this is all my fault. Like my presence alone is what drives the torment in him. On one hand, I hate him for blaming this on me. And on the other...the control turns me on.

I have to gulp down air just to swallow. My back is still to him, but I hear him moving, shifting on the leather sofa.

Setting the paintbrush down, I try to clean off the brush and catch a glimpse of what he's doing.

He's moving, writhing slowly against the couch, his hand on his crotch.

Then, there's the sound of a zipper.

My eyes close.

"Do you know what I'm doing, Sunny?"

His words punch the air out of my lungs as I turn my head enough to see the slow movement of his arm and the thick erection in his hand. I'm frozen in place. Is he drunk or does he finally want to tear down this wall between us? And do I play along or stop him for his own sake?

"Face the wall," he commands when he catches me looking. It's the tone that drives my toes to curl.

I do as I'm told and look back at the still-wet paint on the wall.

"Answer me. Do you know what I'm doing?"

"Yes," I croak, my mouth feeling dry.

His slow rhythmic movement has my thighs clenching, the muscles in my core pulsing at the thought of him watching me while he does that. Maybe this could be where we draw the line. We can keep our distance and acknowledge the fire between us without burning ourselves on it.

"Does it scare you?" he asks.

My answer is immediate. "No."

His next words come out in a rasp. "Do you want to touch yourself?"

I have to bite my lip from gasping, and I'm already practically grinding myself on the heel of my foot as I sit on my folded legs in front of him. "Yes," I breathe.

"Do it."

With my eyes closed, I snake my fingers across my thigh to the apex between, feeling immediate relief the moment I touch my sensitive, aching clit at the top. Letting my head hang back, I circle the spot, picturing Alexander palming his own erection. I imagine it's my hand around his dick, his fingers between my folds.

When he groans, I wait for his next instructions. Every inch of my body is waiting for him to touch me. I hope this is him changing his mind. After this, he couldn't possibly keep his distance. Once he sees how good he makes me feel and how bad I want him, he'll give in.

"Lie down." His voice is deep and hungry, and I can hear the strain. When I recline on the middle level of the scaffolding, I catch a glimpse of his movement, his hand pumping faster. I wish I could see it closer, desperate for the moment he lets me touch it. "I want to watch, rain cloud."

The skin of my cheeks grows hot as I pull up my shirt and slip my fingers into my underwear, writhing on the hardwood platform when they reach the right spot. The muscles of my thighs squeeze around my hand as I move closer to my climax.

His heavy breath as he strokes himself pushes me toward this cliff of pleasure. We're not even touching, and I've never felt closer to him.

"You feel that?" he whispers just loud enough for me to hear it. "That's me between your legs, Sunny. My fingers are there."

"Yes," I moan, my back arching at the thought.

"This is your hand around my cock. Your lips. Your pussy."

My legs clench, and I let out a loud yelp. When my orgasm takes over, my body seizes, riding the wave of blood rushing to my core.

"That's it baby. I'm with you," he groans as I hear his loud sigh of relief, and I know he's feeling what I am.

As my climax fades, and I regain feeling in my fingers and toes, I open my eyes, a smile stretching across my face. Turning my head, I search for his eyes, but I only see an empty couch. He's walking quickly out of the pool house and into the main house, leaving me in the throes of pleasure—alone.

A surge of anger propels me off the scaffolding and into the house.

I'm tired of being toyed with. I'm tired of feeling like a dirty little secret, when what we have feels like the realest thing I've ever felt.

"Alex," I shout at him as I shut the patio door. He's already in his bedroom, closing the door in my face.

I don't hesitate as I pull it open and find him washing his hands in the bathroom sink, knowing it's the product of our lust that he's rinsing down the drain.

"I'm sorry, Sunny," he mumbles, and I grab his arm, spinning him toward me.

"Stop apologizing to me. You didn't do anything wrong."

"That was most definitely wrong, rain cloud." His large hands grip my face and pull me closer, just out of reach of his lips. "You have me wanting these things, and I'm struggling to deny myself, Sunny. I want you so bad, it hurts."

"So, stop denying yourself," I cry, tears pricking behind my eyes. All of my chips are on the table, and I'm so desperate for his physical touch that I know I'll die from this. "I want you too, Alexander."

"I'm so fucked up, baby. You're perfect. Don't you see that? I can't do that to you. I can't." His face is contorted in anguish as he brings our faces so close, I can feel his breath.

"You're not fucked up to me," I sob, reaching for his lips.

"Do you know what happens to the girls that I fuck? I want them until I get them. Then, I hate them, and I forget about them. I can't take that chance with you."

"It'll be different with us, I promise. You won't ruin me. You won't forget about me. I trust you, Alex."

His lips brush mine, and I clutch his hair in my fist, trying to pull him close enough to feel his tongue on mine. He puts more distance between us. "You're the most precious thing in the world to me, my sweet girl. I haven't cared about anything in so long, and I care about you. If I lose that…"

"You won't lose me. You will never lose me, Alex."

His lips crash against mine, his tongue invading my mouth, and for a moment I'm lost in this sensation of Alexander. His smell, his taste, his breath.

Pressing my tongue through the space between his lips, he groans, nipping at my mouth. It becomes a battle of tasting each other, a sudden ability to feel the things we've been so desperate to feel for months.

I let out a shriek when his hands reach behind my thighs and pull me against his body, my legs wrapping around his waist. He walks me to the bed and drops me down, crawling over me, filling the space between my legs while I fumble with his pants. My heart is hammering in my chest as he lifts the hem of my shirt, exposing my breasts.

"I can't stop, rain cloud," he groans.

"Then don't."

When his mouth closes over the pink bud, I let out a soft moan. I had no idea it would feel so good. That his lips on my nipples would send such a jolt of pleasure to my core. But suddenly, I feel a frantic need to have him inside me.

It takes me a moment to get his pants unbuttoned, and

I have to use my toes to shimmy them off his body. When they finally drop to the floor, I see the hardness peeking out of the top of his boxer briefs for me, and I reach for it, anxious to hold it in my hands, this powerful thing that I do to him.

As my hand encircles the hard shaft, I have a moment of panic, suddenly not knowing what I should do. Slowly, I slide my hand along the length, watching him for a reaction. He jacks his hips forward to meet my hand, his mouth still devouring my left tit. He moves to the right, and I squeeze him harder.

"Am I doing this right?" I ask in a gasp.

In response, he nips at the skin of my breast and moans.

"Stop me, Sunny," he whispers.

"No," I answer honestly. I'm not doing what we did in the pool. I'm done pretending that we don't want each other, that his body isn't all I crave.

He answers with soft kisses up my chest to my neck, my earlobe, and then to my lips. "I'm afraid I'll hurt you."

"I want you to," I answer, and he thrusts forward again.

Moving the fabric of my underwear to the side, his fingers find my folds and dip inside, pressing his palm against my clit. A loud gasp escapes my lips. As he presses in a second finger, my back arches, and I pump my hand faster around his dick.

"Promise me you want this, Sunny." The strain in his voice both breaks my heart and turns me on. With his fingers still buried to the knuckles. I wrap my legs around him and pull him closer. I wait for his eyes to find mine before answering.

"I shouldn't want you as much as I do." Something in his features surrenders the fight when he hears me. With his lips against mine, I try to kiss him with every ounce of need in my body.

"I don't just want you, Alex. I need you." My voice comes out as a cry, desperate, and he's quick to answer the call.

He pulls his fingers out of me and shifts so far that I have to let go of him. For a moment I panic, that he's about to stop what we're doing. Instead, he pulls his boxers down and off as he walks over to the side table drawer for a condom.

My heart beats even faster. This is happening, and it almost seems too impossible to be real. In a rush, I pull my shirt off and shimmy out of my underwear, so that I'm lying completely naked in Alexander's bed.

Positioning himself between my legs, I watch as he puts the condom on, his eyes staying on my face the whole time. There's a new hunger in his stare that I could drown in.

As he rests his weight on my body, he kisses me softly. I feel the tip of his cock positioned at the entrance of my core, and I wrap my arms and legs around him, drawing him as close as I can.

"This feels like my first time, too," he whispers against my mouth, and I smile against his kiss as he presses himself inside. Keeping his lips on mine, he stops once he's in an inch. "Stay with me, rain cloud. This part will hurt."

I take a deep breath in and keep my eyes on his face, using his steady stare as the bullet between my teeth. In a quick motion, he thrusts, past the feeling of something popping, and I let out a small scream. It feels so tight the skin burns, but on the inside, it's like he's reached a new but different level of pleasure. I am consumed, knowing his touch everywhere on my body and never wanting to let it go.

"Are you okay?" he asks, dropping his forehead to mine

and keeping his hips still as he presses himself as far into my body as it will go.

I nod, tilting my hips up to accommodate him. Slowly, he backs out and thrusts in again.

"Oh my god," he groans.

When he does it again and again, these slow but powerful and deliberate thrusts, I am breathless and lost in this new lust.

His eyes squeeze shut with every pumping motion, and I never want his body to leave mine. I could explore this new feeling for hours. I want to feel him inside me and know this new sensation, but as he slams into me harder and harder, gripping my hair in his hands as he places a kiss on my forehead, I know neither of us will last long. I'm already lost in this new deep pleasure spreading through my body.

"Don't stop," I gasp, reaching up for his kiss again. My fingers claw at his back, feeling the sheen of sweat there as he picks up speed.

He calls my name as he buries his face into my neck, his fist still clutching my hair as the other engulfs me in a tight embrace. We are glued to each other, lost in a trail of ecstasy when he finally lets out a guttural roar, slamming into me so hard my body seizes again, the warmth exploding between my legs.

My thighs squeeze around him as I feel him pulling away. "Not yet," I beg.

Before he can move, I look down at the connection between us, the blood-streaked condom still buried halfway inside of my body.

"Are you okay?" he asks when he sees me looking.

All I have to do is look up at him and my face splits into a smile, moisture filling my eyes even though I don't think I've ever been happier in my life. A tear falls down the side of my face toward the bed. He kisses the trail it leaves, his lips eventually finding mine.

"Alex," I breathe, my voice coming out like a sob.

"Hm?"

"I want to do it again." Biting my lip, I run my hands down the length of his body. There is still so much of it I have left to explore. So many things I still want to experience and no one else in the world I want to experience them with.

He laughs, resting his head on my chest. "Give me a minute, rain cloud. I'm not as young as I once was."

After he gets up to clean himself up and throw away the condom, I curl up under the covers on his side and reach down to feel myself. There is a new sensitivity down there, and the idea of being sore tomorrow excites me.

As he walks back to bed, I find myself staring. His body is so perfect, sculpted and weathered, but still so ruggedly gorgeous, and I'm pinching myself. I just spent my first fucking time with Alexander Caldwell.

Chapter 22

Alexander

Standing in the bathroom, I try not to look in the mirror. I swore to myself three months ago that I wouldn't do what I just did. Funny thing is that I don't feel like I let anyone down.

Sunny doesn't see the same person that I see in my reflection. And I don't know which version to believe.

As I crawl back into bed with her, I plant a kiss on her lips, but she doesn't let me pull away. She fuses our mouths, sucking my lip between her teeth.

"You're not too sore?" I ask against her mouth.

"I want to be sore," she answers, skating her fingers down my chest to my stomach.

"Just take it easy, baby." I rest on my back, pulling her against my chest. "We have plenty of time."

Propping herself up on her elbow, I take in the way she looks with her sex hair, tousled and sticking up in different directions. I can't stop from kissing her lips again.

"I know that look on your face," she says, her eyes squinting as she stares at me.

I try to force a smile but nothing comes. "What look is that?"

"You're beating yourself up again."

Taking a deep breath, I run my hands through my hair. With Sunny, it's like I feel everything with more intensity. Nothing is easy or mild. "I'm not beating myself up, rain cloud. I'm just trying to be cautious. If we blaze through everything, we want to do…"

"You're afraid you'll get sick of me."

My chest deflates. "I could never get sick of you."

For the first time, it feels true, and I'm not proud of how many times I've promised a girl forever. This is the only time I actually mean it. Loving Sunny is real, natural, like I was supposed to be doing it years ago. Although I'm not quite ready to say it. This is new territory for me, and the paranoia is there. What if I give her everything I have and I run out of interest, passion, love?

Pulling her naked body against mine, I let my hands roam the landscape, trying to memorize every slope and valley, pinching the buds of her nipples and squeezing her round flesh in my hands. She starts to writhe under my touch, and I'm torn between wanting to rest and trying not to spend all of this new lust at once—but also feeling unable to keep my hands off of her.

Placing a kiss on her nose, I reach for the bedside lamp. "Let's get some sleep."

"I don't need sleep," she whispers across the darkness.

"Well, this old guy does, and I want to have the energy to do this all day long tomorrow. So, sleep."

"Fine," she answers with a yawn. Nestled against my side, she breathes softly against my neck as I drift off.

* * *

Somewhere in the middle of the night, I wake to her movement next to me. Against the silhouette of the window, I watch her stand from the bed and pull on my T-shirt. Without a word, she disappears from the bedroom, leaving me alone in the darkness. Pulling on a pair of boxers, I quietly follow behind her.

I don't disturb her as she climbs the scaffolding with a pencil in her hands. I've watched her do this so many times now, sketch out the plans onto the wall, filling the grids with detail and delicate lines.

Watching silently from the door, I drink in the sight of her sketching in the dim light of the work lamp that shines onto the white wall. Her bare ass peeks out from the bottom of my shirt, and my cock stiffens in my shorts as I stare at her.

I want to take her back to bed and get lost in her body again, but I can't disrupt what she's working on. There's nothing I'd rather do than watch her work, deep in her own visions.

When she takes a small break to stretch, I catch her touching herself again, and I know she's just checking the raw skin there. Does she feel different? The thought stirs something carnal in me.

There's a package of rubbers in the kitchen junk drawer, so I grab one, hiding it in my hand as I walk out to the pool house. She freezes when she hears me enter.

"I couldn't sleep," she mumbles, looking at me over her shoulder.

"I couldn't either once you left me." I walk directly up to the platform that puts her at just the right height to kiss her back, run my hands over her bare legs.

"I'm sorry," she pants as my fingers fill the space where hers were just buried. She's already wet for me. Spinning her body around to face me, I pull her ass to the edge of the platform and lick up the arousal pooling there.

Moaning, she drapes her legs over my shoulders, grabbing onto the bars of the scaffolding for support. Sucking and nibbling at the raw skin around her clit, she shifts her weight until she's practically levitating off the platform.

I bury my tongue inside of her, and all I can hear are her cries of pleasure.

"I need to be inside you," I growl, pulling her off the surface and carrying her toward the counter as she hangs limply off my shoulders.

"I need it too," she breathes.

When I set her down gently, she quickly takes my lips in hers, tasting her flavor there and moaning against my mouth. Quickly, I rip open the condom, desperate to fill her up.

This time, I ease in smoothly, gliding all the way in as she watches. Jesus, it turns me on how much she likes to look.

It nearly strangles my cock as I pump inside of her, so tight and wet. I could keep this perfect little pussy forever and never want for anything, but how long will Sunny want me? The novelty will eventually wear off for her, and by the time she's my age, I'll be sixty. Will she find me so sexy then? Will she still want me or will she move on to someone younger? Better?

Growling against her open mouth, I slam into her again. It hurts to think of anyone else here. Another man fucking my Sunny.

"Harder," she gasps, clutching onto my neck, and I oblige.

"Who do you belong to, baby?" I pull her off the counter, hanging her legs from my hands as I pound her gentle flesh, her moans growing louder and higher.

"You, Alex. I'm yours, all yours." Her voice is so strained I know she's close.

"That's my girl." I feel her coming, pulsing around my cock, and it practically milks the cum out of me.

Trailing my lips down her face to her mouth, I carry her back to bed, both of us still panting. This time, I don't have a hard time sleeping.

Chapter 23
Alexander

The music is blaring, so loud I can't even hear her voice when she talks to me, but she's trying to tell me something, a smile plastered on her face from ear to ear. She has on so much makeup that I almost don't recognize her. The strobe light overhead flashes, and with every glow, I see the face of a different girl I've screwed in this club. For a moment, it even changes to her mother, then her sister, before it's her again, writhing up against my body, looking so happy it chills me to the bone.

Suddenly, we're in the bathroom, and I'm banging her against the stall. Her face is pressed against the filthy white-tile wall as I pound into her from behind. Someone is calling my name, but I just want to come before I leave. When I pull her face up to kiss her, she turns away, keeping her lips from me, so that all I can make out is the streaks of filth from the wall and her eyeliner across her cheeks. I know that if she would just look at me or let me kiss her, I would come, and I'm starting to get frustrated.

No matter how fast or hard I pump, nothing happens.

Just when I feel the climax in my reach, my eyes fly open.

I'm flooded with that sense of relief when I realize it was just a dream. The guilt lingers, though.

Sunny's naked body is still molded to mine, silent and sleeping.

I hear a familiar voice calling again from somewhere outside the bedroom. When I hear the front door open and close, I bolt upright.

"Alexander," the call comes again as I hear them set down bags in the hallway.

Jesus, why can't she just knock?

Sunny stirs but doesn't wake. I climb out of bed hiding my throbbing erection as I grab my clothes and throw them on. The voice starts to fade, and I know she's going out to the patio and pool house.

Finally, my erection subsides, and I run out behind her, finding my sister standing in the middle of the room, staring not at the artwork on the wall but the underwear discarded on the floor and the open condom wrapper sitting next to it. Not far from there is a watered-down glass of bourbon from last night.

Fuck.

She turns to see me, the look of disappointment obvious on her face.

"Is she still here?" she asks, walking past me in a rush.

"That's none of your fucking business, Charlotte," I bark at her, following her into the house.

"Oh my god," she gasps as we both turn the corner to find Sunny walking out of the bedroom in only her underwear. I run toward her, covering her body with mine as she stares at the woman standing in my living room. Her jaw opens as she glares at me.

Quickly, I turn Sunny toward the bedroom and shut the door behind us.

"Don't panic," I mutter, grabbing her something to wear from the folded laundry on the dresser. "She's my sister."

"What is she doing here?" she asks, taking the clothes but not moving to put them on.

"She likes to control my life and walking into my house is just one of her ways of acting like my mother. It's complicated," I say, kissing her on the forehead.

"I'm going to shower," she mumbles, covering her face with her hands.

"Don't be embarrassed." Pulling her into a hug, I crush her mouth with mine, feeling her body soften. I'm tempted to push her against this counter and fill her up again. The poor girl has to be sore and needs a break.

After pulling away, I say, "Enjoy your shower. I'll have coffee and properly introduce you when you're done."

"Okay," she answers, biting her lip.

Leaving her is hard. Her perfect naked body is my new favorite thing to look at, and she's climbing into that big shower where I know there's plenty of room for two.

When I get to the living room, I don't look my sister in the eye.

"Jesus, Alexander," she mutters.

"Don't start." As I fill the coffee pot, I ignore my sister's presence behind me, looking around my house like it belongs to her. It doesn't matter that I'm forty. She will always try to control me, convince me I'm a fuck-up.

"Just answer this one question, and I'll drop it."

I don't answer.

"She's legal...right?"

"Fucking A, Charlotte!" Slamming the coffee pot on the counter, I'm surprised it doesn't shatter.

"You can't blame me for asking. She looks young enough to be your kid, Alex."

"So, what if she is?" I argue back.

"You moved here to settle down, remember? Not start banging teenagers."

"It's not like that, Charlotte. Sunny's a sweet girl."

"That's exactly what I'm worried about," she stutters before walking away.

Seething, I finish loading the coffee pot. My phone buzzes from the counter where it's been plugged all night. Reaching over I notice there are a bunch of notifications, mostly social media alerts.

"You and your new friend were spotted on a jog yesterday. You're lucky they didn't catch you doing whatever you were doing in that pool house. Maybe invest in some curtains before they do."

My heart stops, remembering Sunny prancing around my backyard fully naked. I don't answer her as I open my phone, seeing the pics of me tagged all over Instagram. Sunny hugging my side as I smile down at her. We look like a comfortable couple. The caption below our picture reads, "Caldwell and his barely-legal new suburban catch."

I want to throw up. I guess I should be glad there aren't any of her from the pool house.

The comments don't get any prettier.

He's fucked everything in the city. Recruiting them straight out of high school now.

He's old enough to be her dad. That's just disgusting.

Poor girl. Get out now!

Shutting the screen, I toss it onto the counter. I know how this part goes. They'll call me every name in the book, but in the end, they'll hail me as a lady's man, but Sunny will live with this label forever.

"Have you unpacked anything?" Charlotte calls from the dining room.

"Get off my back."

Just then, I hear the quiet steps coming out of the bedroom. Sunny is in her long cotton dress with her wet hair draped over her shoulder. My shoulders immediately soften when I see her, remembering how it felt to hold her body in my arms last night, fucking her against the counter when she told me she was mine.

I know I should feel like shit, giving into something I tried so hard to avoid, but I don't. I feel good, and I can't tell if it's false hope, but this time is different than any time before.

Sunny is different.

We're different.

She smiles at me, ready to walk into my arms until my sister enters the room.

"You must be Sunny," my sister says, holding out a hand and a fake smile. "Sorry about barging in on you earlier. My brother failed to mention that he had company."

"She's not company," I say, the words coming out without hesitance.

Sunny's eyes find mine.

"What's that?" Charlotte asks, looking like I just gut punched her.

"Sunny's been staying with me. For over a month now."

"Really?"

"Yep."

Finally, Sunny closes the distance and steps into my arms, kissing me with her warm soft lips. I'm about two seconds away from telling my sister to fuck off when she clears her throat.

183

"Coffee's ready," she says quietly, looking away.

Sunny smiles as she reaches for a coffee cup. I run my fingers through her wet hair, feeling my sister's eyes on me.

In my heart, I know she's just jealous. My sister took on the role of parent after ours died. She felt the need to be the responsible one while I filled the opposite role. It was a little exhausting.

Charlotte never married. Well, I guess you could say she married her job. It didn't matter that our parents left us loaded. My sister still managed a full-ride scholarship, law school, took the bar, and started her own firm, only adding to her exorbitant wealth. Why anyone would put so much time and energy into making that kind of money when you already had it was beyond me.

"How did you two meet?" she asks, sitting at the bar with her coffee.

"I live in the house behind this one," Sunny answers, and I shoot her a glare. Not because I don't want my sister knowing where Sunny lives but because I hate when she does that. Reduces herself to my neighbor, instead of the artist I hired. I heard her do the same thing with her dad, and judging by the way he treated her, I have a feeling she's used to being belittled.

Resting my hand on her back, I look toward my sister. "Sunny is a very talented artist. I hired her to paint a mural out back." Gesturing to the pool house, I watch the recognition dawn on my sister's face.

"You did that?" Her eyes are wide, and I feel a moment of pride.

"I'm planning a big press release when it's done. Have a couple influencer friends of mine come out and do a piece on her. She'll be the busiest artist in Pineridge by Christmas."

Sunny's head snaps to face me. "You didn't tell me

that," she deadpans. I see the panic settle itself behind her eyes, and I lean in to kiss her forehead, but she doesn't relax much.

"There's an excellent co-op commissioned by the university downtown," Charlotte says nonchalantly, stirring sugar into her cup. "It's a six-month program. City sponsored art is huge right now, and most of the artists who come out of it go on to do murals all over the world."

Beside me, I feel Sunny tense. Her eyes are fixed on my sister.

"Did you know about that?" I ask, looking down at her.

Quietly, she nods, and my heart sinks just a little lower in my chest. Why didn't she tell me? Sunny is more than qualified for that.

"You should definitely look into it, Sunny," Charlotte goes on. "It's all paid for by the university, and I don't think you'd have a problem getting in."

"Thanks," Sunny mumbles with her lips perched over her coffee cup.

I give her shoulder a squeeze again, and I can still feel the tension. Now I'm really anxious for my sister to get lost so I can pick Sunny's mind about this because she's definitely hiding something.

"So, what do you have planned in Pineridge today?" I ask my sister.

"There's a Cherry blossom festival at the park today. I figured I'd have to drag you out of the house..." She tries to hide a sneaky smile, but I catch her eyes on Sunny.

"I've always wanted to see that," Sunny says softly.

"Then, we're going," I answer too quickly. I shouldn't be surprised that her asshole parents never took her to anything like that, and even if we hadn't started what we started last night, I'd want to take her. I want to show Sunny everything. I want her to have everything.

185

"I'll go get dressed." Dropping a kiss on her cheek, I leave the girls to run toward the bathroom. About halfway across, I remember the pictures someone snapped and posted all over social media. Sunny doesn't know yet, but she will. And if we do this...there will be more.

"Rain cloud," I mutter from the door of the bedroom. She quickly excuses herself and runs over. The bright look in her eyes has me pulling her in for a kiss before I can get a word out. Hiding her inside the room, I let my hands roam the soft fabric of her dress and over her little round ass.

"Is this what you called me in for?" she whispers breathlessly.

"No," I answer into her neck. I fish my phone out of my pocket. While she watches, I open up the posts I was tagged in. I watch her eyes for panic, but there's nothing there. Instead, her lips curl at the ends, making her eyes crinkle with a smile.

"This won't stop. If it makes you uncomfortable, I'll keep my hands to myself," I say gently as she scrolls through the posts.

"And what if I don't want you to?" She's being cautious, checking the water. The old Alexander would have run scared at the slightest sign of commitment. She wants to know how serious I am about her.

"Then, I won't let go of you for one second. Let them take their pictures." My lips find the soft peak of her cheekbone as she smiles.

"And it doesn't bother you if they think we're together?" she asks softly.

"Think?"

Her eyes find mine, and she waits for me to speak. So often, I see Sunny's hesitancy to speak up, the fear that she's wrong, waiting for me to set the rules. My brave, headstrong, beautiful girl shouldn't hesitate for anyone. Kissing her nose, I look into her eyes. "I don't care who knows we're together, Sunny."

Winding my arms around her waist, I squeeze her closer, kissing her deeply and trying to feel the same confidence I just conveyed. Because it doesn't matter to me, but I know it will cost something different for her, to be labeled as one of Caldwell's flings. Even though I act like I don't care, in truth it terrifies me. I'm pulling Sunny into my world, and I don't know if she'll still love me when she finds what's hidden there.

Chapter 24

Sunny

Alexander's hand is warm in mine as we stroll through the park. We drove separately from his sister, but she still walks beside us, and after her initial reaction to my dating Alex, she seems to have warmed up. I can still tell she's keeping herself guarded, like she doesn't expect me to last long, so she won't get attached.

Which is fine. If Alex doesn't care about other people's reaction to our relationship, then neither do I. I notice people looking. They have the same initial reaction when they see him, then their eyes settle on me, and I'm not stupid. I know what they see. Young girl, excited to be seen with the most notable playboy in Pineridge. This month's headline, forgotten by tomorrow.

But it all feels like distractions. The only thing that matters is what Alex and I have, and it was born in that pool house, not out here in the public light of day. None of this will change us.

I trust us, and I know he does too.

He squeezes my hand and looks down at me with a

smile. His eyes are hidden behind his RayBans, but I can tell he's happy. I lean up and run my fingers through the gray-flecks in his short beard before pulling his face down for a kiss.

"This is beautiful," he whispers while his sister is distracted. "But I want to go home."

"Me too," I whisper with a smile, knowing what he's thinking. All day I've been letting the events of yesterday, from the skinny dip to touching ourselves in the pool house all the way to the moment he buried himself between my legs, run in a play-by-play loop in my head, soaking my underwear and sending flutters of excitement through my belly nonstop.

Being with Alexander was more than I expected. He's so passionate, and yet gentle. All the fears of him screwing me up by just being with me seem so trivial now. We're finally free, free to be together without these expectations. And even if he hasn't said it yet, I feel his love. In the way he looks at me to the way he touches me. I'm not just a quick lay for Alexander, and I knew I wouldn't be. He loves me.

"Thanks for inviting us, Charlotte," Alexander says as we reach the end of the park where the car is parked. He keeps my hand in his as he pulls his sister in for a hug.

"Yes, thank you," I say with a smile as she takes my hand in hers.

"Sunny, I really hope you'll look into that co-op. It's a great opportunity for talented young artists like you." She pulls me in for a hug, and I force the smile on my face. Any mention of that program sends a sudden pang of anxiety through my gut.

As we leave his sister, Alex and I practically run to the car, both eager to get home where we can be alone, but as we both climb into his Audi, it's clear neither of us want to wait. As soon as the doors shut, he pulls my face to his and kisses me so fiercely, I lose my breath. My heartbeat climbs up my throat and my need for him almost becomes painful.

"Let's go home," I pant. When he pulls away, I notice the way his chest moves, heavy and breathless.

Squeezing my fingers between his, he keeps our hands locked together as he starts the car. With a wink, he pulls out of the parking spot, and I have to bite my lip to keep from smiling like an idiot.

I don't want to jinx this, but things feel very good right now.

Tensions rise during the long drive home. It's only about fifteen minutes, but we're both shifting in our seats, like we're starving for each other. During the long red light, he pulls my face to his across the console and presses his tongue between my lips, and the sensation it creates down below takes my breath away. Neither of us talk much during the ride. The need is too much to make coherent conversation anyway.

He pulls into the driveway, and I'm already unbuckling. Just as he puts the car into park, his hands are around my legs. Before I know what's happening, I'm straddling his hips in the front seat of the car. He crashes his mouth against mine, and I let out a moan when the thickness in his pants rubs against my clit. My panties are so wet already, I'm sure I'm making a mess all over his lap.

"Sunny," he breathes against my lips, thrusting his hips up against me. "Get a rubber out of the glove compartment."

My heart beats even faster when I don't move for the box, and it almost makes me shake with anticipation when I whisper back. "I'm on the pill, Alexander." The second half of his name comes out in a whimper as he grinds against me again. He lets out a groan and bites my collar-bone gently. His fingers stretch my panties to the side, rubbing the pad of his thumb through the moisture pooling there. I'm so desperate for him to fill me, I could cry.

"I trust you," I say, my voice high pitched and pleading.

He stops his writhing as his eyes find mine. We're both panting as he presses his lips against mine. "You can always trust me," he growls.

Quickly, his hands move for his zipper and before I can take my next breath, his cock is out and perched at my still sore opening.

"I want to feel you so bad," he groans. "Go easy, baby."

I lower my hips, and he slides in easily. I hear the air leave his lungs as I move, lifting and dropping my hips to experience a completely new sensation to having him inside me.

His eyes bore into mine as I move, watching as the movement of my body paints an expression of pleasure on his face.

A few minutes later, we're both left panting, and I sit up to see the windows around us are foggy from our breath. When I look back down at him, his eyes are wide as he eats me up with his stare.

"You are amazing, rain cloud." His lips press softly to mine, and I want to stay in this moment forever. "But I'm afraid you might kill me."

I laugh against his mouth. We both wait for our breathing to level out and for the feeling to return to my limbs before we both climb carefully out of the car.

After cleaning myself up in the bathroom, marveling at what the aftermath of sex without a condom is like, I find him sitting on the back patio, sucking down a cold beer and offering me one.

"I want to order in for dinner. Sound good?"

I smile at him, nodding my head. We sound like a regular couple, and even though we've been doing the same dinner, lifestyle routine for weeks, this part is new. The feeling is so right together.

He pulls out his phone and orders Chinese delivery while I drape my legs over his. Rubbing my shins softly, we relax against our chairs and say nothing at all.

After what feels like an hour, he turns toward me. "Did you know about that program downtown that my sister was talking about?" He seems curious, but I can tell by his expression that this is something he's been thinking about.

"Yeah…" I answer, avoiding his eyes.

"Have you applied for it before?"

I shake my head, trying to show disinterest. Really, I just want him to drop the subject. The six-month program is intense and for serious artists only. I love what I do, but the idea of drowning myself in it sounds exhausting.

"Why not?" he asks.

I shrug my shoulders, looking out toward the sunset. "I don't know, Alex. It's intense. I mean…just because I can paint a picture on your wall…"

"What are you talking about? That program sounds perfect for you."

"I'm not *that* good," I say, touching his leg and finding his fingers with him.

He freezes, pulling my arm toward him. "Hey," he says in a sharp tone, and I glare at him, waiting for his next words. "Don't talk about my girlfriend like that." With a final wink, my cheeks explode into a smile. I have to bite my lip from looking like a real idiot.

"Promise me you'll look into it, okay?" He squeezes my

fingers again, touching them to his lips, and I have to nod my head because who can say no to that?

The doorbell rings, and he pops up to get our dinner. While I wait, I try to settle the worry bubbling in my chest. He comes back with a bag of food that makes my mouth water when I get a whiff of the spicy chicken and rice.

We eat right out of the cartons, and I struggle to keep the smile off my face. When I catch a glimpse of the mural behind him, I see the last quarter of the wall waiting to be finished. Then I remember what he told his sister about his plans for his PR and my painting.

"So, when were you going to tell me you were going to advertise my art with influencers?" I ask through a bite of Chow Mein.

"I figured you knew. What idiot would keep this a secret?" he asks, gesturing toward the pool house. "But you know, summer is winding down, Sunny. The sooner we get it out there, the better."

I swallow down my anxiety and a spoonful of rice. "I know."

"You're almost done, baby," he says, touching my leg. "Tomorrow, you can do nothing but work, okay? I won't bother you all day."

I can't do much to hide the slouching disappointment in my body language, which makes him laugh.

"You'll have breaks, of course." With a wink, he laughs, and I can't stop myself from leaning forward and pressing my lips against his. He pulls me onto his lap and drops his chopsticks, winding his arms around my waist and holding me tight against his body.

Chapter 25

Alexander

Keeping my promise, I lace up my running shoes and knock on the pool house window, letting her know I'm leaving. She's been on the top rung of the scaffolding since sunrise. To be honest, I'm looking forward to a moment alone, not because I don't fucking treasure every second around Sunny because I do, but I need to clear my head for a minute. It feels like everything has been going a mile a minute since that first moment two nights ago when she called me out on my bullshit.

It's a cool morning, a welcome cloudy sky for running. For the first mile, I don't think about anything. I let my mind quiet and go silent.

On the second mile, I replay every moment of the week. When I drank too much and pumped my own dick on the couch, watching her hands slip beneath her panties. When she ambushed me in the bedroom, pulling the distorted mirror away from my face so that I could see her more clearly than I have before. When she welcomed me between her legs, never making me feel ashamed or

194

wrong for wanting her so bad. And the way she wanted me back.

In my head, I was writing up excuses for letting myself have Sunny. I had pre-written speeches ready, detailing every reason I shouldn't feel bad for this, such as her being perfectly legal, an old spirit for her age, wise and mature beyond her years. I told myself that she was a good influence on me, keeping me grounded and happy. Although, I assumed I'd have to say these things to my sister, I knew the person I was really convincing was myself.

These runs were always great for opening up the real deep shit.

Of course, all of these things were true. Sunny wasn't like other twenty-year-old girls. She had more life behind her eyes than anyone twice her age.

But that is beside the point. The point is that I don't have to defend Sunny or our relationship to myself or anyone. Fuck, I've been happier in the last 48 hours than I've been since I was nineteen. I don't feel like I'm indulging or flying off the handle. I feel like I'm falling the fuck in love, and maybe that's what scares the shit out of me.

I've never truly been in love before. I wasn't even thirty before I just resolved myself to believe that I wasn't capable of it. Some are built for the long haul, but I was convinced that in all of my relationships if I hadn't found it by now, then I never would.

And it's not about Sunny's age anymore. It hasn't been in a long time. I don't know the exact moment that I stopped seeing a teenager when I looked at her, and I know no one would believe it, but who the fuck cares? My attraction to Sunny goes far beyond her years.

It's about her little mannerisms, the way she bites her lips while she paints, the adorable way she curls up in on herself no matter what she's sitting on, the little pen sketches all over her legs like she can't bear to not be creating something and will use her own body as a canvas if she needs to. I love the way her eyebrows crease when she's mad at me, how she's so quiet and yet when she's angry she erupts like a silent volcano. I love that she fell into my life so easily and although I hate how she was treated at home, I love that she doesn't let it harden her. She puts herself first.

When I turn the corner to the neighborhood off the main drag, I look down at my watch and realize I hit five miles. Fuck, I really did need this run.

And I'm glad I did. As tired as I am, I've never been more excited to get home to her. Call me crazy, but I want to spill everything I just realized about her. About us.

Before I make the turn on my street, I see someone familiar walking ahead of me. Her black ponytail and curvy waist grab my attention. At the same moment, she spins her head and spots me.

"Hey," Cadence calls, pulling out one of her AirPods.

I slow to walk next to her. "Hey Cadence." Our greeting is respectful, cordial, but as soon as we've gotten through the usual *how are yous* there's an awkward tension in our conversation.

She stares at me cautiously. We haven't spoken since Sunny's birthday, and I don't have the most respect for Cadence. She may be the only one in the family who really looks out for her sister, but she doesn't do so wisely.

"How's Sunny?" Cadence asks, walking slowly by my side.

"She's great," I say, rubbing my jaw. I feel her eyes on me, and I know she's keeping pace with me to have a moment to talk about her sister. "Almost done with the mural actually."

"Good," she says, pausing and staring blankly ahead. After a moment, she adds, "She's happy with you." It sounds more like a statement than a question, and I know it to be true. Sunny is happy, happier than she was when I met her.

It's silent and awkward for a moment, and I can feel her readying herself to say something. I want to tell her not to worry about Sunny, that I have it under control and will do what's best for her, but then Cadence stops our walk with a hand on my arm.

"Listen, Alexander..." she says, looking nervous "I don't want Sunny coming back home."

"That makes two of us," I answer with a laugh.

"But that doesn't mean I want her settling down with someone already. The thing about Sunny is that she's loyal...to a fault. She won't leave you, Alexander. No matter what it costs her."

Shielding my eyes from the sun now peeking through the clouds, I stare down at Cadence. I knew this about Sunny, didn't I? Cadence sees loyalty as a fault, but I know it's Sunny's passion, her integrity.

"What do you mean 'how much it costs her?'"

"She's only twenty, and she's the most talented person I know. Did she tell you she dropped out of art school because my parents split? Sunny could have stayed, but she took all the blame for their split."

"I'm trying to help her, Cadence. I'm not holding her back. I'm not your father. When the mural is finished, I'm doing a big PR campaign to get her name out there. I've even pushed her to take an internship with the university."

She nods with a small smile, but I can see the hesitation on her face. And I don't like how much I sound like I'm defending myself. I love Sunny. I'm not going to be blamed for something I haven't even done. I would never hold her back. Unlike the rest of her family, I'll be the one to push her.

"She won't take it." Cadence's words feel like a punch to my gut. Because I know she's right. Deep down, it rings true.

"I'm just looking out for her. She's better than us, Alex."

With that, she turns away, putting her earbuds in and starting up her jog. I try to ignore her words, shaking off the feeling she left me with.

As I walk up the front steps toward the house, I have to remind myself of everything I thought before I ran into her. I love Sunny. She makes me happy, and I'll do anything she needs me to do.

She's better than us.

Cadence's words echo in my ears as I walk in the house. I see Sunny in the pool house, still busy at work. Deciding to hit the shower first, I go to the bathroom, intent on washing off the weird feeling I have now.

Standing under the hot stream, I try to quiet the thoughts plaguing my mind. Sunny is better than me, but I can still take care of her. I can shower her with everything she never had. I'll give her the world.

Just then, the shower door opens, and a cool breeze hits my skin as Sunny steps through the steam.

"Mind if I join you?" she says with a smile. Feeling her bare tits against my chest as she wraps her arms around my shoulder and presses her lips to mine makes all the thoughts in my head disappear.

"Yes, please," I mumble against her mouth.

Letting my fingers drift down her back, wetting her hair in the water as she grinds against me, my cock stirs to life.

"How was your run?" she says with a gasp as I turn her around, her back against my chest.

"Not as good as this," I murmur with my lips on her shoulder. Cupping her soft tit in my hand, I drag my tongue along the back of her spine. She lets out a heavy sigh, arching her back and pressing back against me like she's begging me to enter her.

As I slide my dick easily into her folds, I wonder how I went so long without this. When I'm inside of her, it feels so fucking right. And not just because it's like heaven, but because Sunny and I fit. Every goddamn thing between us is meant to be together.

I start with my hands around her body, trying to kiss her while I move, wanting to taste her and be consumed by her at the same time, but she pulls away, planting her hands on the wall and rocketing her hips back against mine.

Fuck, this girl will kill me.

It takes the air out of my lungs to watch her move against me, hungry for her own pleasure, and I want to give it to her. I want her to have it all.

Grabbing her narrow hips, I meet her thrusts, deepening each one until she's so out of breath she can't even form a sound.

When I come in her, I gather her body up against mine again. I want to feel her orgasm, the tension in her muscles, the heavy beat of her heart, the strangled sound of her cries. I need to know it's enough for her, that I've done right by her, and I try to memorize it all. I have her orgasm in the palm of my hand, and still I'm left feeling like it's not enough.

* * *

When she crawls into bed with me that night after spending another four hours on the ladder, I welcome her warmth against my body.

"Guess what," she whispers, kissing my chest.

"What?" I smile.

"I'm done." Her smile is bright from ear to ear.

"What?" I ask, setting my phone aside to curl a lock of hair behind her ear.

"I'm fucking done!" She practically squeals with excitement, so I gather her up in my arms, kissing the top of her head.

"I'm so proud of you," I whisper. When she pulls away, her eyes fall on mine, and I do my very best to hide the lurking worry hiding in my mind. My smile is forced, and she senses it right away.

"What's wrong?" she asks, resting her chin on my chest.

"Nothing, rain cloud. I'm happy for you."

"Well, I still have to finish a few outlines and touch-ups here and there." She says it like it's supposed to make me feel better, as if her being done with the mural would be bad news for me. Does she think I'm worried she'll leave when she's done?

"Sounds good." My fingers trace her neck to her shoulders where a smudge of yellow paint has dried. Laying on my chest, she trails her fingers down my chest in the same way I trail them down her spine. It's quiet, comfortable, and I want to hold onto this moment, pushing the doubts in my head away.

I can talk her into the internship. And if she doesn't want to do that, she'll get plenty of jobs after we showcase her work here. Then, an idea pops into my head.

"We should have a party," I whisper. "Like a showcase for your mural."

"Who would come to that?" she asks, sounding skeptical.

"Lots of people. People with influence, followers, designers. It could be a huge breakthrough for you, Sunny. If that's what you want."

"Yeah…" she mumbles. "Or we could just stay in bed by ourselves." I know she's being playful, but her answer doesn't make me feel any better.

Just when I'm about to press her about it some more, she touches a tender spot on my side, just above my hip. "What's this?" she asks, fingering the raised scar about the size of her index finger.

"Oh, that's from a very careless trip to Mexico last year," I tell her, looking down at the warped skin that runs parallel to the elastic on my boxers.

"It looks like a mountain range," she says with a laugh. "Can I draw on it?"

I answer with a chuckle. "Have at it."

Jumping off my chest, she scurries to her bag on the floor and comes back with a felt-tip pen, crawling back on my body and facing the scar. The pen is cool on my skin and makes me jump a little as she stretches a long line along the ridge.

"So, tell me the story," she says, biting her lips while she concentrates.

"I wish I could say it was from bungee jumping or jet-skis, but the reality is that I drank too much in Cancun. Got myself in a little trouble with a friend, and he threw me against a table. A glass top table. Sliced through my side like a knife through butter."

"Ouch."

The sharp movements of her pen make me wince. I wish that story was better, and I don't have the heart to tell her the rest of that story. How I was so drunk, I didn't even know I'd been cut. Or how my best friend and business partner left me for dead because I fucked his wife in the hot tub the day before. How I spent two days alone in the hospital in Cancun and had to catch a flight home alone on my birthday, feeling like the world's biggest asshole.

"A little trouble, huh?" she asks, and I grab her arm with my hand, stopping her drawing.

She looks up at me with a question in her eyes. "What is it?"

"There are things in my past that I don't want you to know, Sunny. And it's not because I don't trust you to stay, but there's a lot of ugly back there. It doesn't belong anywhere near you."

Moisture fills her eyes, and I have to swallow the lump in my throat. Dropping the pen, she scoots her body up my chest until her face is inches from mine.

"I love your scars, Alex. I know that under your skin is a whole lot of shame that you think you need to protect me from, but I won't leave you for it. I won't let you try and scare me away."

Taking her face in my hands, maybe a little too hard between my fingers, I pull her lips just a breath away from mine. "I love you, Sunny."

She blinks, a tear spilling over her lashes. "I love you, too," she croaks.

I crush her lips to mine, like today is the first day of my life. There is nothing before now, and every moment from here until the end of my life will belong to her.

Chapter 26

Sunny

*C*adence: *Labor Day BBQ today at 1. You two should come.*

I'm busy finishing the outline on the girl's long brown locks when I hear the ping from my phone. Brush in hand, I glance down at my phone and see the text. Before I answer, I let the question stew in my mind.

It's been over a month since I've seen my mom. Not that I'm complaining, but I know things will only get worse if I don't make some effort to mend the bond. I realize it's not up to me, and that she's the one who screwed things up between us, but my sister is stuck mediating, and I hate to leave her like that.

Labor Day was always a major holiday for us. My dad loved throwing BBQs in the backyard, inviting his fancy friends over with their high maintenance wives and fresh out of rehab kids, none of whom I got along with, and everyone would have a pretty miserable time until they were properly drunk at which point I escaped to my room and pretended they were all gone, even when they weren't.

Since my dad left, the parties have changed. The guys rarely come to my mom's parties, but the wives do. The kids follow their mothers even though they're not kids anymore. Fischer and Liam will roll because Dad's gone and Mom can't handle it while she's drinking. Cadence will keep them company, and I will sit alone hoping the few guys who did come won't come over and talk to me because it always gets awkward when they do.

This year will be different though. I have Alexander. I can stay by his side. Hold his hand. Claim him as mine and pretend that none of them exist.

"My sister just invited us to a BBQ today," I call over to Alexander, who's lounging on the couch, stretched across the cushions while he replies to emails to his publicist.

"Okay. Do you want to go?"

He leaves it up to me, which I love, but it's not a choice I want to make. I miss my sister. I miss certain things about my mother. I don't want to meet them on their terms. I want to meet them on mine. I want the version of them that doesn't make me hate myself.

"I don't know," I mumble.

A few moments pass while I keep up my work on the scaffolding, outlining, fixing small spots, perfecting something that's already perfect. A gentle touch on my neck pulls me out of my trance.

"We can go for a drive, if you want." His eyes are soft, loving, and I feel connected to him. A drive would be nice. Get out of town for a while.

But as soon as I consider it, I know that I'm going to the BBQ. I only needed him to offer another option before I knew what my gut would settle on.

"I should at least make an appearance. I haven't been over there in two weeks."

He offers me a warm smile. "Okay then, rain cloud. We can go."

I touch his fingers with mine and lean down to kiss him. It's not supposed to be this easy.

His hands squeeze the flesh of my thighs as I deepen the kiss. I can't get into anything heavy at the moment, but I love the idea that we could just get into it at any moment.

When he pulls away and walks back to the couch, I set down the brush and text my sister back. *"We'll be there. What can we bring?"*

I smile at how much like a couple we sound.

"Just yourselves," she replies.

A heavy sigh escapes my lips, and I can't focus on the mural anymore. Placing my brushes in the cup to clean, I climb down and walk over to where Alex is lounging on the couch. It only takes one look before he's opening his arms to me.

"It'll be fine, rain cloud."

I crawl onto the couch, laying my body against his, and he wraps me in a tight hug. He doesn't have to say anything or make this right for me, but his support, his arms holding me down when I want to run settle the fear in my chest.

We walk to the BBQ hand-in-hand. He pauses before we cross the yard and looks at me with a question in his expression. He's asking me if I'm ready for this. For people to know we are doing this now. And I aim the question right back toward him. With a wink and a kiss on my forehead, he pulls me through the opening in the fence, and we enter the party.

It's bigger than I expected, and everyone's eyes are on us as we make our appearance. As a couple.

My mother is the first one to drop her jaw.

Cadence doesn't even look surprised at all.

Alexander hands her the drinks he carried under his arm, and she gives us both a hug, all the while we keep our fingers locked. When my mom comes down from the porch to greet us, I flinch at the fear of how she might react, but a gentle squeeze of my fingers makes me relax.

When she engulfs me in a hug, it's a strong one. I feel her chest quake as she holds me, but I don't feel anything. I'm not sorry or sad, but I'm also not angry, so at least I can be glad about that.

"I'm so glad you guys came," she says through her tears when she pulls away.

"Of course," Alexander says stiffly from beside me. He'll be cordial with my mom, but I know deep down, he's seething and won't bend that easily.

He and I settle by the side of the pool while Cadence fills us in on some courses she's signed up for with the community college. I'm glad to hear she's trying to do something for herself, but I can't help but notice the tension between her and Fischer and Liam. The guys haven't spoken to her since we arrived, instead standing soberly by the grill.

"Alexander, will you please go help out those idiots," Cadence says to him when a waft of smoke blows through the party.

I tense, smiling at my sister. I can already feel the onslaught of questions. She's about to interrogate me, and I brace myself for it.

"So," she says leaning back with her drink once he's out of earshot. "When did this happen?"

"Does it matter?"

"Are you happy?" she asks when I ignore her first question.

Considering her question for a moment, it's not a yes or no answer I'm preparing. The answer is emphatically yes. But there are other emotions there, too: fear, excitement, paranoia. I just don't know exactly how much I'm sharing with my sister.

"I am happy," I say truthfully. "He cares about me, Cadence. We care about each other. I know how it looks."

"Good," she says. "Because if you didn't know how it looked, I'd be worried."

When her eyes start to mist up, I bite my lip. When did things with my sister become so strained? So heavy.

"Why are you so worried?" I ask.

"I just want us to be close again, Sun. I wanted you to share this stuff with me."

By this *stuff*, I know she's referring to the sex. I lost my virginity, and I didn't go running to my best friend to tell her about it, like I always thought I would have.

"We will, Cadence. I just needed to be away from her for a while." My eyes glance over to where our mother is laughing with her friends.

"I know, and I'm glad you're happy. I just...want you to be careful, Sunny. It's easy to get attached to the first one…"

I have to clench my jaw to keep from looking too angry with my sister. I know she's looking out for me, but every cautious warning only taints the peace and happiness. Yesterday, Alexander told me he loved me. Nothing my sister says will ruin that.

When I don't answer, she continues. "I've heard stories about him, Sunny. About what he's like with women."

"Stop," I bark at my sister, and a few heads turn,

including Alex's. I send him a reassuring glance and a smile. I'm ready to go home, to be alone with him.

"I'm sorry," Cadence mutters, reaching for my hand. "I just...I don't want you getting hurt."

When I look at my sister, I see years of feeling like she was the only person who loved me because she gave me attention when my father didn't and stood between me and my mother when her tirades were the worst. I grew up knowing nothing but toxic cries for affection, and now I have someone who is actually trying *for me*, and I can't express this to Cadence because I know it will crush her.

So, I touch her hand. "Thank you."

Mom doesn't talk to me much for the rest of the day. She doesn't go anywhere near Alexander, but just when his eyes find mine from across the yard and we're both sending each other the *let's get the fuck out of here* vibes, she links her arm through mine, stumbling with me into the yard.

"I just want you to know that I'm okay with this." Her breath smells like vodka, but her eyes are still sober enough while she bores them into me.

"Okay with what?" I mumble.

"You dating a man twice your age, Sunny." She whispers it roughly against my ear, and it sends chills down my spine.

I pull away. "He's good to me."

"Yeah, middle aged men are good to young girls at first, Sunny."

I shouldn't be shocked. This was coming either way, but it still hurts to know her true feelings about me. This is how everyone will feel about us, and I knew this would happen, but it feels like a slap in the face regardless.

"I had a great time, Mom. Thanks for having us." With her mouth hanging open, I pull her into a hug, and walk away, meeting Alex in the middle of the yard so we can walk back home alone.

"You okay?" He squeezes my hand.

"Yep," I say, forcing a smile.

As we go through the motions back at the house, getting ready for bed—in his bed since we don't even mess with the guest room anymore, we talk about the party, and I think about the first time Alex walked over to my back-yard. What it was like seeing him in person for the first time. He was so out of reach, so mysterious, and I try to compare that first impression with the man I see now.

They are two different people.

The Alex I met then was confident, a beast I wished would devour me.

What I have now is a man who is struggling like me. No matter his twenty years on me, he still feels the same sense of loss, the same torn consciousness, the same daily fight with who he wants to be and who he sees in the mirror.

His age does not intimidate me or place us on different planes. We see each other through the same filter. Being alone with Alexander doesn't feel like being with my family. I'm no longer guarded, alone, or desperate for affection. For the hundredth time this week, I say a silent prayer that this thing between us sticks, because I need it to.

"What are you thinking?" he asks from across the room, pulling the sheets back from the bed. Wordlessly, I slip into my side and crawl over to him. When he sits down, I run my fingers through his dark hair, with the gray flecks at the temple, and I kiss his lips. I let my lips linger in that position for a moment, drinking in the sensation of his kiss.

When he draws me against his body, we fall into bed together, taking our time with each other tonight. Everything from peeling our clothes off to the gentle way he enters me is delicate, savoring each and every moment.

I push away my worries as he thrusts, deeper and deeper, force behind every powerful movement, so that when my body unwinds from the climax, I melt into him. We melt into each other, and I try to convince myself that I have absolutely nothing to worry about.

Chapter 27
Sunny

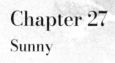ou're sure you're okay with this?" Alex asks, leaning over to brush his lips against my temple while I apply another coat of mascara.

"Of course," I say, feigning confidence.

He woke me up this morning with news that a friend of his, an art-lover from the city, wants to see the finished mural. It's nerve-wracking to imagine someone judging my work, and I keep thinking about the slope of the girl's nose, worried that I didn't put enough definition in her complexion and she looks too amateur.

Alexander keeps reminding me it's perfect.

The only thing scarier than someone seeing my artwork is meeting one of Alexander's friends. We've been good since the party at my mom's last weekend, but I don't know if he's ready to be official with his friends yet.

He answers my question when the doorbell rings, and Alex promptly grabs my hand. It comforts my worries, but doesn't make me feel any more adequate on his arm. He's grown his beard out, and his hair, which is gelled and coiffed on the top of his head, making him look too fucking good. He's in a white-button up shirt, sleeves rolled to the elbow and a pair of snug black chinos. Next to him, in my cut-off shorts and cheap tank top, I feel like a kid standing beside a grown-up.

It doesn't help that the couple standing behind the door is gorgeous and interesting. The woman is dark-skinned with a tasteful piercing through her septum and a hairdo cut short to her scalp. She's in a simple black dress that comes down to her mid-thigh.

The man has shoulder-length hair and is also dressed in black. He looks exactly like you'd expect an art-lover to look.

I immediately feel like a fraud.

"Gino, this is Sunny Thorn," Alexander says with a smile as his friend reaches for my hand.

"Such pleasure to meet you, Sunny. This is my friend Valerie."

The woman takes my hands in hers and pulls me in for a tight hug. The four of us fall into easy conversation as Gino and Alexander catch up and we give them a tour of the house, which is still littered with unopened boxes in every corner.

"I'm ready to see this mural," Valerie chirps, squeezing my hand with a bright smile.

Heat floods my cheeks as we walk out toward the pool house. When we reach the doorway, I tense up next to Alexander, but he meets my nerves with an arm around my shoulder and a comforting squeeze.

The couple gasps in unison, and I stand back and watch as they approach the ten by fifteen painting I slaved over for three months. From far away, I have to admire it myself.

It's bright, brighter than I expected it would turn out. The girl's blonde locks are highlighted with streaks of bright pink and gold. Her eyes are the same shade of blue as the pool behind us, and behind her is a collage of tropical colors. A turquoise bird, a yellow palm tree, the sun, the sand, the water.

"Does she have the look?" I ask Alexander, so quietly the other two can't hear.

"What look?"

"The one that says she wants you." When I glance up at him, he smirks at me before leaning down and dropping his lips against mine.

"This is phenomenal," Valerie says as she steps closer to us.

Hastily, Alexander pulls away from me and nods. "I agree."

"I have a wall in my apartment that needs something like this, Sunny. I hope you're ready to get to work on more."

We all laugh, and Alexander offers them something to drink. The four of us sit around the patio table while Gino tells us all about the art he's been buying, dealing, wants, and it's overwhelming for me. These were the people I went to art school with, the ones who scared me away, made me feel like I would never belong. Now, he's looking at me like he admires me.

"So, Valerie is one of the directors for the downtown art co-op," Gino says nonchalantly, and I freeze in my chair.

"Really?" Alex replies, and my eyes dash to his face. Did he know about this?

The sudden feeling of being ambushed makes my heart pick up pace.

"Have you heard about that program, Sunny? I think you would really belong in something like that."

Alexander's tapping foot freezes. "I've been telling Sunny about it. I thought she could apply," Alexander says, still holding my hand, tighter than ever.

"Oh, with work like this, I have no doubt you'd get in, Sunny."

The blood drains from my face. "No."

The table grows quiet instantly. "I mean...it's a lot to think about."

"For sure," Valerie says carefully, a tight smile aimed at Alexander.

Gino drones on about some artist who graduated from the program and went on to paint some award-winning art in Europe. I can't focus on his story. I let my mind consider this for a moment, what it might be like to spend so long away from Alexander. Him alone in this house for months on end. Would it be worth it?

He laughs along with his friends, and I start to feel more and more out of place. Every so often, they glance my way, asking me a question. I try to act as normal as possible answering, but I feel out of place no matter what.

They stick around for another hour, and it seems like they do more talking about me than to me, and I feel myself growing more and more irritated. Even Alexander mentions me like I'm not even there, and I desperately want them to leave so that he and I can return to normal and pretend none of this happened.

* * *

The room is silent and tense as Alex and I clean up the glasses around the patio. There are so many unspoken words between us, and I just keep waiting for one of us to break. But just when I expect him to say something, he comes up behind me and puts his arms around my waist instead. His lips touch the side of my neck, and I jerk away.

"I don't want to fight," he mumbles, and I believe him. In fact, I don't want to fight either, but there is too much fogging the air between us.

"You were treating me like I was a kid," I whisper, looking down at where his hands hold mine.

"You are a kid, Sunny."

"I'm not, Alex. I'm twenty. I know what I want, and I don't need you to try and push me into something."

I pull away from him and walk across the room. I don't trust myself to be touched by him, afraid I'll give in and let him pull me to bed so we can sweep all of these feelings under the rug where I know they'll fester and ruin us.

"Is it wrong for me to want the best for you?" he asks, crossing his arms and staring at me with a furrowed brow.

"I don't want to do that program. But you won't listen to me," I cry. "You think it's best for me because you want it for me. I'm telling you I don't want it."

He clenches his jaw and glances away. "You don't want it because you don't think you're good enough. You're too scared to do it on your own."

It feels like a punch to my chest. "I'm not scared of anything," I say through clenched teeth.

"You are. It's why you left art school. You blame it on the divorce and money, but I know it's because you were scared of being alone. It's why the farthest you made it from your mother's house is my house."

"Why are you being so mean to me?"

"I'm not being mean, Sunny. I'm trying to help you."

"No, you're not. You're trying to push me away because you think it's best for me. I see that, and I wish you'd stop." Tears prick the backs of my eyes as he walks across the room, his hands folded behind his head.

"Then, what is it?" he asks. "Why don't you want to do it? When it could launch your career farther than anything else. When I was your age, I blew off every single good opportunity that came my way. I threw my life away instead, and it took me twenty years to get here. Why don't you get it?"

"I don't know. I just don't want to. Do I really need a reason?"

"Yes. Sunny," he lets out a long sigh. "I didn't pursue anything I wanted to. I took the easy way and it got me nowhere. I want better for you."

"Stop treating me like a kid!" I cry. "What if I want nothing more than to paint and be with you? Why can't I do that? They said I could get jobs, so I'll do that. That program is six months, Alexander. Six months that I'll have to live there, work full time, almost never see you. What if what we have doesn't survive that? What if you..." my voice trails.

"What if I what?"

"What if you move on? What if you forget about me?" My throat aches as I force the words out. "What if you cheat on me?" I watch the expression drain from his face. He doesn't react in anger or sadness. A neutral tone takes over the features of his face and after a long breath, he walks away, onto the patio alone.

With my next blink, tears spill onto my cheeks.

Resting my elbows on the counter, my face in my hands, the moisture seeps through my fingers while he sits in silence on the patio. I wish I hadn't said those words to him because I know they hurt. The pain of knowing that I don't trust him. I *can't* trust him, and that's what will hold me back. It's the knife through his heart, one that I'd been holding onto since before we started this thing we have. I knew what I was getting into with him. I heard the stories, knew the man, heard the things he'd done, and I fell hopelessly in love with him anyway.

Now I had to face the cards in my hand. I can fold, or I can play.

After a few minutes, I step quietly out to see him. I drop into the chair opposite from him, and I watch him wrestle with these emotions.

"I'm sorry," I whisper.

"Don't be. You're right to be worried."

Another punch to the gut.

"That's not what I meant. Sunny, I want to tell you I'd never do that to you. I love you too much, but that's the kind of person I am, isn't it? Impulsive. Selfish. But that's not what has me worried."

My eyes lift to his face as he narrows his gaze on me. "What worries me is that you'd pass on this—the opportunity that would change your life—because of me. Because you love me and yet you know...I'm..."

There are tears in his eyes, and a sob wracks my chest. *Please don't say it.*

"I'm a monster."

"Don't say that," I whisper through my tears.

It's quiet for a moment as he stares out at the cool water rippling across the pool. The autumn air sends a chill in the breeze, and I bawl silently while he does nothing.

"If I say you can trust me, would you go?"

"I do trust you, Alex."

"Then, go."

"Let me think about it, okay?"

When his eyes meet mine again, the air between us is saturated with this new pain, the doubt, the guilt, the fear.

"Okay," he agrees finally, and I can't stop myself from crawling onto his lap. The need to touch him is unbearable. He pulls me into his arms and buries his face in my neck. I hold him tighter than ever, and I wish that I could take back every word I said today.

Chapter 28
Alexander

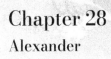e park the Audi in the garage under the gallery, and as soon as she gets out of the car, I take her hand in mine. I don't know why I do it—I did it when Gino came over, too, but it's my statement right out of the gate. I'm not afraid of people knowing we're together. I'm not hung up on this image of myself anymore.

Of course, her statement the other day about trusting me hasn't quite dissolved yet. It's still settled between us like pollution, clogging up the air we breathe.

I didn't want to be angry at her for that statement, but I was. I was angry she said those words to me, but I hated the situation she put me in. Again, and again, I'm backed into a corner with Sunny.

She's forcing my hand.

If she stays home for me, I will have to live with the fact that she gave up her future because I'm a piece of shit. At least in her eyes. I have been and always will be an untrustworthy scum of a boyfriend, and even if I can make up for the mistakes of my past, she will never have this opportunity again.

So how could I let her stay? How could I stop her from giving that up?

She has to go. Now more than ever, she has to go.

It's not up to me. The minute she uttered those words, the decision was made.

"Nervous?" I ask, kissing her on the temple.

She looks beautiful tonight. In a floor-length blue dress, she braided her hair and let it drape softly over her shoulder. The light fabric of the dress hangs over her curves, and I love the feel of the soft cotton under my fingers, inviting me to touch her all night long.

But I know I can't do that. This event is important for her. Gino's friend Valerie invited us to tonight's gallery showcase in hopes of introducing Sunny to the director of the program as well as a few of its alumni. Although it's really more than that. This is Sunny's induction.

This is her chance to meet people, be seen, heard, make her presence known.

Tonight, I will be the man on her arm.

As we enter the gallery, Sunny tenses next to me. "Don't let go, okay?" she whispers, glancing up at me.

"Promise."

My eyes linger on her face, and for a moment, I forget that she's only twenty. She's grown years since I first met her back in June. Sunny has always shown maturity in her eyes, but I was just waiting for her to express the confidence that I knew she should. Now, in that bold dress with so much prospect in her future, I wonder when she will outgrow me. When she will realize that I'm not worthy...just because I'm older, have money I didn't earn, friends who don't care about me, a lifetime of regret and mistakes.

"You made it!" Valerie shrieks as she runs over to hug us. Valerie is one of those women who is beautiful, but too intimidating to any man who might consider flirting with her. She's practically a goddess, and with her gold leaf headband tonight, she looks more like one than ever.

She takes Sunny's hand and pulls her away from me. "I have so many people to introduce you to."

As she pulls her away, Sunny's eyes go wide and she stares down at where our fingers are linked. "Wait," she whispers, but I pull her hand to my lips and place a kiss on the back of her knuckles.

"Go ahead. I won't be far." With a wink, I send her off with Valerie while I scope the crowd for Gino, who I find mingling toward the back by the drinks, naturally.

When he sees me, he greets me with a freshly mixed mule. The party usually starts at these gallery shows, but I've been to enough to know they don't end here. There's either a private afterparty or a secret speakeasy nearby where these people get ridiculously drunk, when their real freakiness comes out. I've fallen down that rabbit hole a couple times, and I learned quickly, it was fun, but not quite for me.

And I definitely don't want Sunny getting involved with that, so I'll be keeping her close today.

Of course, once she starts the internship, I won't have any real control over her. She'll want to meet new people, try new things, and I should want that for her. I should encourage her to be adventurous. Sunny is not impulsive like I am. She'll keep things modest and safe without flying off the deep end like I did at her age.

Speaking of wild things I did, a familiar face across the room comes into view and sends my heart racing.

Diana York.

My best friend's wife. Correction: *Ex-best friend's ex-wife.*

Her eyes meet mine and she saunters over with a sly smile on her face. "Alexander Caldwell," she says in a sing-song tone. "Didn't think I'd see you here."

Diana is beautiful with her honey blonde hair and sharp cheekbones. I was always attracted to her, even for the ten years I knew her as Tyson's wife, but I only acted on it that one time in Mexico. She reached out to me a couple times after the divorce, but I couldn't bear to answer back. The memories were too painful, plus Diana isn't the type of woman to cling. Her marriage to Tyson was on the fritz anyway—everyone knew that, but I still lost everything regardless.

"Hello, Diana," I answer with a smile.

She comes in for a hug, and I wrap my hands around her shoulders.

"I heard you got yourself all settled down in the suburbs," she whispers, touching my cheek in a loving gesture. "I was glad to hear it."

"I'm actually here with my girlfriend," I say, pointing toward where Sunny is crowded by a few of the art-lovers I don't know.

Diana nods, knowingly. I assume before she says anything that she already saw plenty of pictures of us together.

"She's precious, Alexander. Keeping you in line, I hope."

With a small laugh, I nod. "She is."

Just then, a roar of laughter breaks out on the other side of the room, and we both glance in that direction to see the crowd around Sunny howling, her included, and I can't help but admire how she glows in this moment. She's in her element, far more than I've seen her in either my backyard or her mother's.

"Wanna grab a smoke?" Diana asks, pulling a pack out of her small purse.

I don't smoke anymore, but the idea of stepping outside to escape the bright lights and noise sounds good. "What the hell," I answer with a smile. We head for the back of the gallery, and I'm about to stop and tell Sunny where I'm going, but she seems to be having such a good time, I don't want to bother her. So, I slip outside with Diana instead.

When she hands me a cigarette and a light, I inhale, savoring how much it burns. It's been years since I last lit up, except for the occasional light up when I'm so drunk, I can't even feel what it's doing to my throat. It burns, and I resist the urge to cough as it assaults my lungs.

Sunny will probably hate the way these make me smell.

"You look good," Diana says with a soft smile. "Better than the last time I saw you."

"Thanks," I reply through a puff of smoke. "You do too."

"Your new girl reminds me of that model you dated a couple years back. The one we went to the movie premier with."

It takes me a moment to remember the face, but I know the girl's name was Esther.

"She was young, too," she teases me.

"No, she wasn't," I laugh. "She was at least twenty...something."

A sweet cackle escapes Diana's lips as she pulls another drag from her cigarette. "How old are you now?"

"Fuck you," I snap back as she giggles.

Diana stares at me for a few long moments with a hooded expression in her eyes.

"How long will this one last?" she asks with a gravelly texture in her voice.

I don't answer. It's like I'm suddenly seeing my own behavior from outside my body. Why am I standing out here with someone I very recently fucked when I should be inside proving to the woman I love, that I can be a loyal boyfriend?

I don't want to fuck Diana. The old me would have, but how long after Sunny leaves will I return to the old me? What if I come out during those six months and run into another beautiful old hookup?

"I should go," I say, ignoring her question.

"Alexander, I'm sorry," she mutters, but I walk inside anyway.

As we make our way back into the gallery, I feel Sunny's eyes on me. She looks concerned, biting her lip, and I hate myself for it. My stomach sours.

Leaving Diana, I walk straight over to Sunny.

"We just stepped out for a smoke," I say, taking her hand before she can ask.

"I didn't know you smoked," she scowls, smelling my fingers as she pulls them to her nose.

"I'm sorry," I whisper, leaning down to kiss her cheek. "I'll wash it off as soon as we get home."

Home. I want to take her home. Our home. Right now.

"They want to see the mural," she says, holding my hand and looking up at me hesitantly, and her words hit me like a punch. It's like she read my mind.

Honestly, I don't want the party at my house. The house is my sacred space, *our* space. It's where I leave all of this stuff behind.

"What do you think?" she says carefully. Her eyes have hope in them, and I know she wants to take pride in her work at this moment, and I'm only sorry she has to ask me first.

"I wouldn't deprive anyone of seeing it." I lean in and kiss her again. She links her hands around my neck and deepens the kiss.

"You will be rewarded," she hisses against my mouth. "But you really have to shower. You stink."

* * *

There are more people at the house than I expected. Sunny is in the pool with a few of the girls, including Valerie, who are all so liberated they think it's acceptable to swim in my suburban pool at eleven at night in nothing but their panties.

Thankfully, Sunny has plenty of swim suits here and is keeping herself covered. I can hardly look at the water with the four pairs of bare tits splashing around in there. Most of the guys are sitting around the patio, but a few of them are watching the girls in the pool because it doesn't matter how much you appreciate art, tits are tits and guys are guys.

Gino sits back and laughs with a thick joint between his fingers. I have a gnawing feeling in my gut and I just wish these people would leave. I've never felt more like a grumpy old man than I do right now. I walk to the bar to get another drink, hoping the bourbon will calm my nerves. I offer one to my tablemates, but they all brought their own beers in a small cooler.

"I love your girlfriend, Alexander. She's so adorable!" As I glance down in the pool, Valerie has her arms wrapped tight around Sunny, her small tits pressed up against my girlfriend, and the lazy smile on Sunny's face tells me she's either been drinking or taking hits off Gino's blunt.

I laugh at them and shoot Sunny a harsh glare that makes her giggle. She's going to be paying for this later.

As I mix my drink at the bar, I catch a glimpse of the painting. I see Sunny there. The girl doesn't look like her, but I see her in every stroke. Each day spent painting that wall and how my feelings for her progressed with each brush stroke.

Hearing the party behind me, I see Sunny and Valerie wrestling in the pool. This is how it's going to be for her at that program. Everyone will want her. Men, women. They will try to suck the youth and life right out of her. And in some sense, no matter if we try to stay together or not, she will stop being mine to some degree.

As I turn around, I nearly drop my crystal tumbler on the pool deck. Sunny's wet bikini top is sitting on the ground by my feet. My eyes travel over to where Valerie has her perched on her shoulders, playing chicken with another pair of girls. Every guy around the pool is cheering them on and practically drooling at the tit display.

As Sunny and Valerie spin toward me, I see her bare chest, those pink perky nipples for everyone to see, and something in me snaps.

"Sunny!" I bellow, picking up her top and throwing it at her.

She yelps as it lands on her shoulder with a *thwack*.

"Put it on," I grit through my clenched jaw. The party goes silent, and Sunny climbs down from Valerie's shoulders.

I see the stubbornness in her eyes. She wants to fight me, and refuses to put it on. She just loves to push me.

"It's getting late," Gino says behind me as he motions for Valerie to come with him. The party quickly moves to leave, but Sunny doesn't back down.

"I was having fun," she mutters.

I walk away from her and try to be a hospitable host, seeing everyone out and thanking them for coming.

When I finally walk out to the empty patio, Sunny is stomping around, putting away the trash and cleaning up the towels from the pool.

I'm still red hot, picturing her in that pool, knowing that if I hadn't stopped it, the party would have escalated. And I know exactly how it would have ended. Someone would start getting handsy, maybe one of the girls. It would turn into kissing. The guys would join. The party would move inside. No one would stop it before it turned into an all-out orgy on the living room floor, and she would wake up the next day not entirely sure who she slept with, how many people she let fuck her, or if what they did even really counted as fucking.

And it would go on for years. Again and again.

"I know you were just having fun, but as long as you're my girlfriend, you keep those tits covered unless I'm the one seeing them."

She doesn't answer, just keeps stomping around.

"I'm trying to keep you from making the same mistakes I did."

Spinning on her heels, she points a finger up at me. "Oh, like disappearing with your ex out the back to have a smoke? Did you seriously think that's okay?" she screams at me. "They told me she was your best friend's wife, and you fucked her last year and broke them up. I could see the look in their eyes when you left. They pitied me!"

Shame floods my senses as she yells.

"You're going to get a lot of looks like that, Sunny! You know what you're signing up for with me. I didn't do shit with Diana, and you fucking know it."

"Well, you know how I felt when I saw you walk in

227

together. But you won't even let me have a little fun? You think everyone is fucked up like you!"

"Do you understand that I'm just trying to protect you?"

"No, you're not. Right now, you're acting like my dad, abandoning me one moment, controlling me the next."

As she walks away, I snatch her up by the elbow and pull her against me. "I am not your dad, Sunny. Don't project your daddy issues on me, little girl."

Shoving away from me, she turns and slaps me across the face. In a swift movement, I grab her wrist, but I'm too hot, too wired that I don't know what I want to do next. The blood raging through my body for her drives me to wrap my arms around her and crush her mouth with mine. She fights me, twisting away until she's hanging in my arms, her back to my chest.

"You're too good for me, Sunny. Don't you see how fucked up I am?"

Her chest cracks in a sob. "I'm fucked up too, Alex."

"No, you're not. You're young, and you have your whole life ahead of you."

When she finally settles her weight and presses her back against me, I feel her fingers wind with mine. "What happens when we're at parties alone?"

I don't answer because I can't think of things like that.

"What happens when you get bored here, and your friends invite you out?" she whispers.

Pulling her face back toward me, I find her lips with mine, and I kiss her until she stops talking. These are questions that we can't answer because they will inevitably lead to one of two possibilities.

One: we lie and make promises we can't keep. I promise I won't get bored. She promises she won't let things get out of hand.

Or two: we see things for what they are. This thing between us is temporary. Too fragile to withstand the pressure.

So, I don't let her talk, and she doesn't fight me. When I lift her bikini top, exposing her tits, I palm the right one, squeezing it hard and thinking about the way the other men stared at her. She whimpers as I pinch the pink bud at the end.

"Do you care about me, Alex?" she breathes as my hands skate down to her thighs.

"You're all I fucking care about, rain cloud."

"Show me." With her head hanging back, her long braid almost touching her ass, my mind registers what she's asking me. Just to be sure I'm understanding her correctly, I grab the long braid and give it a forceful tug, making her cry out and arch her back even more, driving her ass into my hardening cock.

She wants me to be rough. It's not that I want to hurt her, but I want her to feel how intensely she makes me feel. How my blood boils for her. How the force of my thrusts matches the way she makes me feel every fucking day.

Looking down at her bikini bottoms, her round, supple ass in my hands, I pull the fabric up, revealing one bare cheek. With her braid still twisted around my hand, I rear back and land my palm hard against her ass. She gasps, and tears spring to my eyes.

I feel it. The pain, the excitement, the lust. I feel it all like her skin is mine.

Wrapping my fingers around her throat without squeezing, I pull her back so I can kiss her again.

"Tell me you're going," I say with my teeth next to her ear.

She moans in response, and I rear my hand back, landing another sharp sting against her ass.

"Tell me."

"I'm going," she cries.

"That's my girl." My hands run the length of her body, trying to memorize every inch. "I love you so much it hurts, Sunny."

"Show me," she gasps, and I feel her tears run over my fingers as they graze her lips.

Emotion pours out of every pore in my body as I yank down her bikini bottoms. It only takes one swipe of my zipper before my cock springs free from my pants, and I pull her back, gripping her hip bones and shoving myself inside in one rough thrust.

"Yes!" she cries out, and I wrap her up in my hands again, squeezing my fingers around her throat. Slamming into her again and again, I try to pour every ounce of my love for her into every slam of my cock in her tight little cunt.

"Harder," she moans, and I nearly break.

"I don't want to hurt you," I whisper against her shoulder, taking a bite of her precious flesh as I pick up my speed.

"I want you to." Her voice is strained, and I know it means she's close. Rearing my hand back again, I land an even harder smack against her ass, rubbing the sensitive skin after I do and driving in even rougher.

She collapses against the back of the couch, and I continue slamming myself home. Just before I feel her pussy muscles clench around me, knowing she's riding this wave of pleasure, I collapse my body on top of hers, inhaling the scent of her skin, knowing deep down that this is the last time I'll have her here like this.

The things we've admitted, the fears, the doubts, the new knowledge that even our love cannot withstand the pressure we will put it through, will break us. Whether I want to admit it or not, this thing between us is over, and there's nothing I can do to save it.

With that sobering realization, I come hard inside her.

Her body is lying limply over the couch. My poor, beautiful, broken Sunny. Before she can move away or start another fight, I scoop her up gently and carry her to our bed. Her face is streaked with tears, and I don't bother to clean anything as I crawl in next to her.

Neither of us says anything as she cries, and I hold her, stroking her back.

I want to tell her how much I love her or that we can make it work, but I know it's futile. Empty promises and false hope.

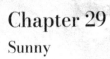

Chapter 29
Sunny

I sleep in Alexander's bed for the last time. I knew things were over before we went to the party, before he walked out with his ex, before we fought. The idea of staying, prolonging the pain of knowing what was coming felt only slightly worse than walking away from him.

Once I had to face the truth—that I wanted that internship more than I wanted anything before, I knew I had to accept losing him.

While he's out for his jog, I text Valerie, and she agrees to let me stay with her. I can't go back to the guest room or to my mom's. I can't be that close to him, and I didn't want my mom and my sister in my business.

Part of me stayed. A piece of my heart was infused in those paints that covered his wall, and as I took one last look at the mural on my way out, I saw my own transformation there. From the bright rays of the sun that shone down on that girl, I saw the way I'd changed this summer. Opening up to someone for the first time. No longer hiding behind this rain cloud. Giving my heart away and knowing that it was loved in return.

Alexander and I knew it was a risk to jump into this. The higher you jump the harder you fall, and I took this risk. As I laid in bed that night, I considered staying. I told myself we could try this. I could go to the internship for six months, a long-distance relationship, and we could come out of it stronger, but I knew the paranoia and the guilt would ruin us. It would hurt so much more than this. And by the way he reacted at the party, seeing me be the young, happy girl he wanted me to be...but doing it without him...it broke something in him, and I can't hold that on my shoulders.

As he walks in from his jog, he doesn't look at me. He just sees the bags by the door. I expect him to fight, and I keep waiting for him to try and stop me, but he doesn't.

"Where are you going to stay?" he asks.

"Valerie's," I whisper, staring at the floor.

"You know you can stay here," he mumbles, his back leaning against the wall opposite me.

"The internship starts in a couple weeks. I'll be fine."

As he stares at me, I tell myself that he has grown sick of me. He did this with all of the girls and it's just who Alexander is. Knowing that I was just like the rest of the girls actually made me feel better. It reminded me that I wasn't walking away from anything special. Just a sexy fling with the hottest bachelor in Pineridge. Any girl should be so lucky.

There is no real breakup conversation, but it was never a real relationship to begin with, was it? We were a summer fling, a phase and moment in time. I was Alexander's road to recovery and he was the support I needed to get out of my head. When I couldn't convince myself that I was worth it, Alex reminded me I was.

As my phone chimes with a text from Valerie that she's at the house to pick me up, I finally raise my eyes to reach his for the first time. He doesn't say anything, just crosses the space and pulls me into his arms.

"Leave this all behind, Sunny. Do you understand? Leave me, your mom, everything. Just go and don't look back." His words crack open something in my chest, and it feels as if I never truly stop bleeding out.

It takes me days to get out of bed. Valerie is an amazing host, offering me space and companionship when I need it. She makes me binge watch trashy reality shows with her, and she stays up with me all night, making me paint when all I want to do is cry.

I only check his social media a few times, and I don't know if I'm terrified to see him miserable or happy. There's nothing on any of his accounts, but on the third day, he posts a picture from the day at the cherry blossom festival. Neither of us are in the picture, and it's just a photo of a blossom. The caption reads *Blossom*. Just that. I don't know if he's just pointing out what is in the picture, or if it's a message to me. Is he telling me to move on and grow?

Either way, I look at the picture about a hundred times a day, touching the picture, like he can actually feel it.

The pain would go away. I keep telling myself that every day.

I love you so much it hurts.

Those words repeated in my head for days, and by the fourth day, I knew it wasn't healthy. To love someone so much was reckless. Someone was bound to get hurt.

On the fifth day, Valerie takes me to the city to get a

tour of the program facility. She had put in an official recommendation to the university, which meant I was basically a shoe-in. In true co-op style, the program was housed in a warehouse loft with a small living quarter above, big enough to house eight people with three to four in each room. It was cramped, cozy, but she said the energy was good. I looked forward to the company and the structure. Responsibilities were evenly doled out to every member, which left optimal time for art and exploration.

The program sounded like a dream, and as she and I sat at a small cafe, I tried to feel as excited as I wanted to feel. I would live and breathe nothing but art for six months. And that was a dream come true. The aching pain in the middle of my chest would subside, eventually.

On move in day, I take nothing but a duffel bag full of clothes, my new Bluetooth headphones, and the brushes Alexander bought me, even though I knew they needed replacing.

His large shirt, covered in paint, stays folded on the guest bed in Valerie's apartment. I almost packed it, but I knew it would only prolong the pain. I need to be rid of this ache as soon as I can.

By the first day of classes, everyone already knows who I am, and I'm pleasantly surprised that it's not because I was Alexander's too-young girlfriend, but because I was the *Sun-kissed Lust* artist.

"You never gave it a proper name," Valerie says in front of my new roommates. "So... We gave it one for you."

My roommates are all young, the oldest being in his mid-twenties. They all appear far more cultured and hip than me, but I brush off the immediate feeling of inadequacy. I imagine Alex standing next to me, introducing me as the wildly talented person, that I am. It helps.

I'll take the good things, I tell myself.

On the first night in the co-op, I cry silently into my pillow, not moving even one muscle in my face as the tears soak the sheets. It's the first time everything feels so irreversible. I can't just walk across the yard and crawl into his lap. His bed is miles away, and I should be in it.

This will go away.

It has to.

Chapter 30

Alexander

There's a blood stain in the grout of the pool house. I can't help but compare her mark on this world with mine. I have literally nothing better to do than sit on the floor with a toothbrush, trying to scrub the fucking blood out of the grout.

I've been out here since four in the morning, when I woke up with a dick as hard as stone from dreaming about her bent over my couch again. A far cry from the dreams I used to have about banging her in the filthy stall of a shitty club. I refused to palm my own dick after waking up. I want to feel the fucking pain because it's all I have left. When it doesn't hurt, I feel nothing, and I hate feeling nothing.

"Alex," a voice calls from the front door. Charlotte told me she'd be bringing me food today, but I wish she wouldn't bother. I didn't want to tell her about Sunny in the first place, but she figured it out by my tone over the phone. She said I sounded like night and day, and that metaphor is not lost on me.

The sun is fucking gone...in case it wasn't clear enough.

"Jesus," she mutters as she finds me on the floor. Her shoulders heave with a sigh, and she reaches out to help me up. "You look like shit."

"Thanks," I mutter.

"Want to talk about it?" she asks, walking back into the house. She starts pulling groceries out of the reusable shopping bags she carried in. I tried grocery shopping yesterday, but I walked in, took one look at the carts she used to ride on and the seaweed snacks by the counter, and I skipped the shopping and beelined for the overpriced Whole Foods bar instead. Apparently, they have a three-drink maximum, but if you're Alexander Caldwell and you flirt with the bartender enough, she'll serve you five.

"Not really," I answer, pulling the cookies she knows I love out of the bag and ripping open the box.

"I've never seen you this bad, Alex." There's a hint of a smile on her face, and it's making it very hard not to lose my shit.

I don't have an answer to that so I simply shrug, tossing a cookie into my mouth.

"Can you fix it?"

The idea of explaining it sounds exhausting, so I lean back on the stool and rest my head against the cool quartz countertop. "It's complicated, Char."

"Complicated is good, Alex."

"What the fuck is that supposed to mean?" I snap back, losing my patience.

"It means that every relationship you've suffered in the past had a pretty simple demise. You cheated on her, she cheated on you. You stopped calling or you lost interest. Complicated means there were more complex feelings involved, and I'm not gonna lie, Alex...this is what you needed."

"I needed to have my heart ripped out of my chest?"

Finally, Charlotte sits down on the stool opposite me. "I'm going to need more information. I have nothing but time, but first, you need a shower." She waves her hand in front of her, and I can't help but laugh. The most I'd really showered in four days was a couple cold dips in the pool to stave off the raging hard-ons.

"Fine. Make me something to eat, and I'll tell you about it when I get out."

The shower is exactly what I need. The hot water beats down on the stiff muscles in my neck and shoulders, further proof that I've been sleeping like shit.

When I come out, my sister finishes grilling a panini on my stove and passes me a plate that smells like roast beef and peppers, the first hot meal I've had in days. Over our lunch, I tell her the basic rundown, Sunny leaving for the internship, the conversations we had before the end, the fights, the silent but mutual acceptance that she needed to do this on her own.

After I'm done, I'm surprised to find my sister's eyes moist and red-rimmed. "What?" I blurt out, seeing the emotion on her face.

"I wanted this for you, that's all."

"I feel like a teenager," I sigh. "Lovesick and missing my girlfriend. It's pathetic."

"And you don't think she'll come back when the program is over?"

"I don't want her to, Charlotte. Sunny has her whole life ahead of her. She's going to get jobs all over the world. I'm forty-fucking-years old. She doesn't need me weighing her down."

"Alex," she says, putting her hand on my arm. "I'll admit, I was skeptical at first. I thought you were back at your same old tricks, getting in bed with a teenager. But when I came over and saw you two together...I'd never

239

seen you happier. And not just a superficial happy either. Baby, you were more yourself with her than you ever were without her."

It's hard to breathe. I know what she's saying is true, and I was happy with Sunny. But it doesn't make anything easier. She's not telling me anything I don't already know.

"I'll get over it," I mumble, moving crumbs around on my plate.

She laughs quietly. "No, darling. You won't."

Her words stay with me for the rest of the day. And something about the hot meal and hot shower has me feeling energized, more than usual. My mind is running a mile a minute, and I desperately need something to busy my hands so I glare at the stack of boxes in the corner of the living room. Putting on a little music on the Bluetooth speakers, I start opening them one by one.

As I start hanging pictures and arranging books on the shelves, I replay every moment with Sunny from the first encounter to the very end. I remember the first time I wanted to kiss her, when she came over and stared at that blank wall, and I remember the first time my lips finally touched hers.

A play-by-play runs through in my mind as I work from one room after another. By the time I finish unpacking the last box, working through the memory of her bent over the couch, knowing it was goodbye, I'm spent.

So spent, I fall asleep on the shag rug in the middle of the living room.

In my dreams, she's there, lying on top of me, her hands caressing my chest, my shoulders, my neck. She whispers against my skin.

"Show me."

And somewhere between dreaming and awake, I let my hand do what my body so desperately craves. With her name on my lips, I let the vision of her, riding me like the beautiful confident woman she is, carry me through until I'm calling out for her and spilling my seed all over my own hand.

After I clean myself up, I hit the showers again, crawl into my bed, feeling more at home than I have since I moved in. I'm finally surrounded by the things that make me, me and I think about what my sister said. I wasn't just happy when Sunny was around, I was free to be myself, and I know I never would have gotten there without her.

Chapter 31

Sunny

Four months later

The inspiration won't come. The more I stare at these paints, the less I feel like a true artist.

I've had a pretty amazing experience so far in the program, after the first few weeks of misery, but at the end of the first month, I started sleeping through the night. I stopped crying and started making friends.

I still missed him so much it hurt. He was always in my dreams, and whenever I started painting or sketching anything he was there. But it wasn't killing me anymore. Time was not going to heal this wound, but at least I grew used to the pain.

Our first showcase is this weekend, and we've each been given a commissioned area of the downtown square for their annual City Arts Festival to design and display however and whatever we want. I have a sketchbook full of ideas, but nothing feels powerful or important enough.

"Girl, just start painting," Hanna, my German roommate calls toward me while I stare at the spray paint cans at my feet. I've started to fall in love with spray paint. It was never my usual medium, but there's something about the toxic smell and way you can manipulate it that's led me to pick it up more than my brushes anymore. That and my acrylics still bring back too many memories.

If I pop open my paints, I smell them on his skin. I feel his lips on my back. I hear his voice in my ear. But he's not really there, so I don't bother teasing myself.

I didn't invite him to the festival. Of course, it's a free event to the public, so maybe he'll come anyway. Maybe he'll bring someone new. Maybe I'll see him strolling through the crowd, admiring the sidewalk chalk display with a supermodel on his arm and a look on his face like he doesn't even remember my name.

I did invite my mom, Cadence, and my dad. I haven't spoken to Dad since the fight, and I doubt he'll come, but I feel ready to finally put the pain and anger I hold toward him behind me. I'd like to act like a regular father and daughter now, unless he chooses not to show, at which point I will move on anyway.

Love cannot be replaced. The love someone denies you cannot be filled by someone else. Alexander gave me enough of it to make up for what my parents denied me, but it was never intended to. He didn't give me love to fill the empty cup. He gave me love to teach me how to stand on my own without it.

Those times he forced my chin up, made me look at what I'd accomplished, what I deserved...he built the legs I'm strong enough to stand on now. The rest of them were only concerned with knocking them out from underneath me, so I never had to look down on them.

I know Cadence is coming. I've spoken to her every day, and I get the feeling that watching me pursue my dream is inspiring her. I can't wait to see her face.

I hope my mother comes. I want to see her face outside of our backyard.

"You're going to run out of time, you hussy. Start painting." I've gotten used to Hanna's brash attitude and terms of endearment. I hated her at first. I was in so much pain and moping, but she was never gentle with telling me to snap out of it, stop crying and use my pain in my art. She is German through and through.

The other housemates have been kind and wonderful, but I didn't bond with them the way I did with Hanna.

"You're nervous because you think he'll come," she calls over to me from her spot of eight by eight, taped up along the wall. "Or you're nervous he won't come. Either way, use it and start fucking painting!"

"Both," I mumble as I pick up the seafoam green paint. If I paint something he'd like to see, I'll be disappointed when he doesn't show. If I don't paint something for him, I'll miss an opportunity to show him something of meaning if he comes.

"Come on, Sunny," she calls, and I laugh. Her painting isn't much more done than mine, and this is all we really have to finish this week, so I don't know why she's being such a pain in my ass.

Hearing her say my name makes me think of the first time she heard it and laughed at me. "You are anything but Sunny," she said, and it immediately made me bawl because it's what he said. It took me a couple more weeks before I opened up to her about that and told her what his nickname was for me. His little rain cloud.

I don't feel much like a rain cloud anymore. At least I'm not so down and sad anymore. I'm still sad, but I live with it. I work through it, and I used it to push me forward. Don't get me wrong, I'd kill to see him again. I'd crawl back to our bed if I could, and I don't foresee myself ready to move on to anyone else anytime soon. I can't even look at other guys right now, and I definitely underestimated the amount of partying that would go on here. But none of it interests me.

Part of me is still holding out for him. I know that. And I know that will go away with time, too.

The idea of the rain cloud nags at my mind, and I look down at my colors again. Without a sketch, I grab the gray paint and stare at the wall.

"Fuck it," I say and start the outline of a cloud on the wall. Within minutes, I have a full sketch in my head, and I have to move fast before it goes away. Whether he comes or not, I'll make sure he sees this. I think he'll be proud of it.

* * *

The day of the festival comes around, and I'm so busy running around, helping set everything up that I don't even register the nerves. It's the first nice weekend of the year, and it's finally warm enough for people to be outside so, the streets are instantly flooded. The wall of student submissions is just along the main drag, giving us a perfect view of the crowds. We're supposed to stand by our artwork all day, but the sun is blazing, and even with the cool breeze, I feel like I'm sweating my ass off. It's already crowded when I find my rain cloud and stand by it. Hanna is there next to me, taking hits off her vape pen every five minutes.

When I feel my phone buzzing, I know it's Cadence, so I fish it out and give her directions to where I'm standing. A moment later, I hear her shrieking as she bolts across the crowd and snatches me up into her arms. This is the first time Cadence and I have been apart in our entire lives. Even when I was at Alex's house, I still had her nearby, and I could see her when I wanted.

Suddenly seeing her for the first time in five months has me feeling emotional. I run toward her, meeting with a hug that knocks the breath out of us both. There's something to be said about having your sister around when you're feeling bad, but having her here when I'm feeling good might be my favorite.

"I'm so proud of you," she cries into my hair. When she pulls away, her face is wet with tears, and I marvel at just how gorgeous my sister is. While everything about me feels quiet, small, and meek, Cadence is fierce, loud, and fearless.

"This one is yours?" she asks as she steps forward, squeezing my hand in hers. I feel myself looking around for mom, but it becomes painfully obvious that she came alone.

She catches me looking. Biting her lip, she says, "She's at Passages. She didn't want me to tell you, but I thought you should know. If she was going to miss this, I knew you'd be happy to know it was for good reason."

It feels like a weight has been lifted off my shoulders. My mother going to rehab, and not using the smallest reason to bail, feels major. I want to ask more, but I can tell it's weighing on Cadence too much so I change the subject. I tell her all about my rain cloud, and she tries her best not to cry. Then she tells me about a hundred more times that she's proud of me.

"Is he coming?" she asks without looking at my face.

"I don't think so," I answer quietly. "I didn't invite him."

When I glance at her, I see her biting her lip, and I can tell she's holding something back. Of course, she lives behind him, and she can probably see just about everything he does. If she knew something about him, I could ask and she would tell me.

But that would only make things harder. If he's moved on, I don't even want to think about how bad that would hurt to hear, but also if she tells me that he's miserable, it will only make this pain I'm enduring last longer.

She must sense my hesitation because she looks at me. "How are you holding up?" And I know she's referring to him.

I shrug. "A little better every day."

"Breakups are hard, sis, but I have to admit. I didn't see this one coming. It took Alexander so long to find someone he was willing to give it all up for...I didn't think he'd ever let that go."

The wind leaves my lungs like her words ripped it out.

He let me go. All this time, I saw this as setting me free, but something about hearing her say it the way she did makes it sound like he sacrificed himself for me.

The whole time he was afraid he was pulling me down. Alexander held onto me so tight because I was the one thing holding him above water. And he let me go.

I'm suddenly desperate to know how he is. I should have called or texted or something to keep tabs on him, to make sure he's okay. He was always supposed to take care of me, but who's taking care of him?

But just as I'm about to ask, Hannah interrupts us by introducing herself to my sister. She offers to watch my spot, even though there's really nothing for me to do, so Cadence and I can go get some lunch together.

It's nice to have time to just update my sister on my new life at the co-op, everything I learned, and the jobs I'll have after it's over. Before I know it, we're saying goodbye, and I'm already desperate for this program to be over so I don't feel so separated from her anymore.

As the hours go by, I start to lose hope that Alex is coming. Why would he come? I didn't tell him I'd be here. This isn't his sort of scene anyway. It's stupid of me to not invite him and then expect him to show. Who does that?

The show starts to wrap up just as the sun peeks below the horizon, painting the sky in shades of orange and blue. I get caught up talking to a couple straggling through the festival when I see him approach.

I lose my voice mid-sentence. He's walking against the natural grain of the crowd toward me, in his jeans with a long-sleeve shirt and a lazy hoodie on over it. His beard has grown out, and it shows the white patches along his chin line. When my eyes lock on his, I lose my breath.

Watching him approach, my throat tightens and I wonder if he'll hug me. Will he just say hello and move on? Or will he sweep me up in his arms and carry me away? Part of the irrational brain hopes it's the latter.

Instead of wondering for long, it's me who closes the distance, stepping up to hug him as soon as he's close enough to touch. His arms fold around my midsection, squeezing me tighter than Cadence did, and we don't speak as we just hug each other for a long breathless minute.

He smells so familiar; it makes tears prick my eyes. Where his shoulders used to be narrower, he's built muscle, and his skin has lost its summer tan. It brings out the blue in his eyes I notice as he leans back.

"I'm sorry I'm late," he whispers to me, our mouths just inches apart.

"You're not late," I answer, letting myself get lost in his eyes. I'm not grappling with my choices anymore. He's here, and it feels amazing.

Just when I think he might kiss me, and I don't know how I would feel about that, he pulls away, looking at the wall behind me.

His eyes go wide, and he steps forward giving it the same look he gave the girl the first time I painted her. "Sunny…" he whispers.

"It's a rain cloud."

He answers me with a smile. "I know it is."

The rain cloud is really so much more than that though, and I watch as he stares at it, finding every small detail I hid in the design. The gray cloud rains, but instead of water, music falls from the gray orb. There's a tree sprouting, a spatter of color, cherry blossoms, a candle like from a birthday cake, a human heart, and a fire. It is everything we are and everything he made me. It's us. The single biggest thing in my life so far, and I knew he would see it eventually, but I'm so glad it's here where I can watch his reaction.

His hand touches my back softly, and I fight the urge to crawl into his arms again. He's quiet for a moment as he stares at the painting. Finally, he looks at me, his eyes lingering on my face like he's looking for something.

"Can I take you out for dinner?" he asks carefully, looking around.

My heart pitter patters harder in my chest. Dinner with Alex, sitting alone with him, to just be near him. I'd walk away from anything for that.

"Yeah. We're just about done anyway," I mumble, trying to act as nonchalant as possible.

"Are you sure?" His hand touches my elbow and I practically melt.

"I'm not in prison, Alex," I laugh, and he smiles, creating little wrinkles around his eyes.

After saying goodbye to Hanna, I meet Alexander on the sidewalk, and we walk together to a place in the city that apparently has the best chicken and waffles. Being around him feels natural, like we are still the same two people together, even if we've changed apart.

While we walk, he asks about the program and I tell him everything about the friends I've made and what I've learned. As we come up to the restaurant, he opens the door for me, and I walk past him, letting his eyes on my face send a warm rush of blood through my veins.

Sitting across from him at the small table, I can't take my eyes off his face. He's softer than before, like he's healthier, happier. Twisting my napkin in my fingers, I don't dare to let myself hope. I keep preparing myself to hear him say he's seeing someone, and I hope that when that happens, I hold a smile instead of bursting into tears which is what I want to do.

"How are you?" I finally ask when he lets me stop talking about myself. I twist the napkin between my fingers a little tighter.

He nods, holding a tight-lipped expression. "I'm okay," he answers.

"Just okay?" I can tell he's holding something back, and I'm not sure I want him to open up any more than that.

"Just okay. Some things are really good, but other things…" his eyes meet mine.

And I understand. There are parts of my life that are wonderful, new, and exciting, but beneath all of that, I'm miserable. It evens out to just okay.

My hand moves across the table and touches his hand. Immediately, his fingers are squeezing mine, and my body is on fire.

What now? Can we go back to what we had? Would it make all of this pointless?

We eat quickly, and he offers to walk me back to the co-op since it's dark now. We're silent again, but the energy is anything but easy and calm. My hand itches with the near-ness of his, and I'm dying to reach out and hold his.

Just as we pass a dark alley, I'm swept away from the sidewalk, and I meet his chest with a crash, stealing the breath from my lungs. I don't even bother gasping for air. All I care about is his lips, so when he leans down, I wind my arms around his neck and pull his mouth to mine.

We kiss each other hungrily, his body grinding against me like it's the first breath we've taken in months. He moans into my mouth as I devour his lips. I will never let him go; I tell myself. Now that he's back in my arms, there is no way I can let that go.

"God, I missed you," he breathes against my mouth, and I quickly reply with the same.

"I missed you, too." Our foreheads meet, and it's like the last four months don't exist anymore.

His hands are on my hips, then around my waist, holding me tighter than ever before. The questions swirling around my brain have quieted, but they are there, linger-ing, waiting.

"I don't have to go back just yet," I whisper against his lips. "As long as I'm back by breakfast."

A low growl hums from his chest as he pulls me tighter. "I... can't..." he says, and my shoulders deflate, a cold sweat sweeping over my body. He can't? Sensing my panic, he continues, "I made a promise..."

My body falls away from his. "A promise to who?" If there's someone else, I don't know what I'll do, but it's something I don't want to consider. I can't.

"A promise to...myself," he finishes, knitting his brow and looking down at me, waiting for me to understand.

And it takes a moment before I realize what he's saying. My eyes pop open and I grasp his arms tighter. "You haven't...?"

He shakes his head slowly. "In four months."

I have to bite my cheek to keep from smiling. A swelling pride engulfs my chest. Alexander Caldwell has voluntarily given up sex for four months as a promise to himself. Not me. Not his sister. Not anyone else. Just himself, and it feels like my heart is about to explode with pride.

When I can't fight the smile any longer, I launch myself back into his arms. "That's amazing, Alexander. I'm so proud of you."

"I don't want you to tell me if you've...you know," he stammers.

"Alex," I whisper. "I never stopped being yours."

His cheeks redden, and the corners of his lips turn up in a smile. Kissing me again, I let myself get lost in his nearness.

"Will you wait for me?" he breathes, taking his mouth to my neck, and it feels impossible. I don't want to wait another second for him, but I know this is what's best for him. After everything we've been through, this could be the thing that brings us back together.

"I will always wait for you."

Chapter 32

Sunny

I t's been two weeks since the art festival, the night I saw Alexander, and not a day has gone by that we haven't spoken. Every night he calls and we talk, his voice in my Bluetooth headphones while I paint.

The inspiration comes so much easier now. The paint runs out of my fingers with ideas, color and life on the canvas since that night.

We don't talk about the future. We don't even talk about the past. Mostly, we just talk about meaningless topics—our favorite memories as kids, things we were better at, what we would do if we could start it all again. It's like I'm learning him all over again, meeting the same man again, but knowing him differently. Falling in love with him again.

He keeps the dark things to himself, and I don't pry. Alexander talks now like he's healing, and I don't want to be the one to bring up the bad things, so we dodge topics like sex, love, and relationships. For me, he skips talking about my parents, the split, and how many times I've been smacked around by my mother. The conversations are superficial, but I see the light at the end of the tunnel. We're not as fucked up as we once were, and the future looks bright.

I only have six more weeks until I'm free. There haven't been talks of job prospects yet, but I feel them coming, and part of me is dreading them. What do I do if I'm offered something amazing far away from here? Do I ask him to come with? All I can really think about right now is going home, his home. Our home. My side of the bed that is still waiting for me.

Alexander and I built our lives together before we started our relationship. Before we allowed ourselves to start anything. And now I know that we should have waited until we worked out some of these things we need to work through. And part of me knows there are still so many landmines ready to ruin it all if we don't get through it before the program ends, and we truly begin.

He cuts our talk short one night, and I can tell he's feeling anxious. Normally, he's in such a good mood, light-hearted and easy to talk to, but tonight I can feel the rest-lessness in his voice. I want to tell him it's only six more weeks, but I don't know if he's unsettled because he misses me or he misses sex, and I don't think I want to know.

It's only 8:30 on a Friday night when he calls it a night. "I'll call you tomorrow," he mumbles across the phone line.

"Okay." What else can I say? We haven't defined the boundaries of our new relationship. How the hell am I supposed to know what I can say at this point, but I feel him struggling and I can't be there to help him.

I don't sleep well that night. Something is gnawing at me while I toss and turn, checking his Instagram like a stalker because I'm desperate to know if he's home or out. I finally doze off somewhere after one in the morning when my phone rings. His face is on the screen, and I panic, sitting up in my top bunk to answer it. The room is silent, but most of my roommates sleep with headphones in to block the sound of everyone else shifting, snoring, or coming in late from the studio.

"Alex?" I breathe.

Before I hear his voice, I hear the wind blowing. There is distant music—and I know he's out.

"I fucked up, Sunny." His voice is like gravel, deep and pained.

The blood drains from my face. "No," I answer, half-plea, half-statement. He wouldn't fuck up, not now, not after everything.

Suddenly, the room is stifling, and I have to get out. Climbing off the top bunk, I slip on my flip-flops, and I run out of the room, through the studio, to the street out front.

"Where are you?" I ask in a rush. I'll go to him. I'll fix it. I just need to see him.

"I thought I was ready to go out. I thought I could handle being out with my friends again. I missed that, Sunny. I missed having fun. I never missed that when you were here."

"Alexander, where are you? I'm on my way." I just start walking, without direction. Which is stupid in the middle of the night for a single young woman, but his voice is in my ear, and I have to push out the realization that Alexander fucked someone else. I just need to be near him. I *have* to fix this.

"I'm sitting on the roof of the Hyatt." There's a slur in his voice, and I know it means he's been drinking. My stomach rolls.

"Just talk to me. I'm coming to you."

"No, Sunny. I called because I want to talk to you. I need you to know everything about me. If we're going to do this...if you're coming home to me, then we need to get the heavy stuff out of the way. The really ugly stuff. You know it."

I do know it. But it doesn't mean I want to hear about him with anyone else, and my mind is not about to process what this means for us. Did he cheat on me? Are we technically together? I told him I was his...but would I take him back if he did? Pushing the heavy thoughts aside, I breathe a heavy sigh into the phone.

"Then talk to me." I stop at the stop light and look toward the city center. The Hyatt isn't the tallest building in Pineridge, but I can make out the lights of the sign. I could be there in fifteen minutes by car.

"Remember that blonde woman who came to the house? The one I fought with. It's her birthday. I thought I could handle it, and the drinks started pouring..."

"Alex." My voice is pleading with him. I don't know if I can hear this part.

"She and I have always had an easy physical relationship. I knew she was lonely, too. I knew coming out tonight would be bad, but I was so fucking bored at home. I missed you so goddamn much, that I couldn't stop myself."

Tears prick my eyes. Somewhere in the back of my throat, anger bubbles and I'm ready to scream. "What did you do?" I ask through grit teeth.

"I panicked, baby. I should have gone home, but I just thought some fresh air would help so I came up to the roof, and the fucking door locked on me. Now I'm stuck up here, sitting around an empty pool, and I thought about you."

I swallow, pacing back toward my apartment building, trying to piece together what he's saying. "Did you...break your promise, Alex?"

"No," he says with a hint of sadness in his tone. "But I

almost did, Sunny. I almost drank too much, promising to go home with her, like we do every year. I wanted to."

The air leaves my chest, and I drop onto the steps leading up to the front porch of the studio. "Alex," I breathe. "You scared the shit out of me."

It's quiet a moment, and I stare across the city again, imagining him up there. Knowing it's too far, much farther than when only our backyards separated us.

"Remember that night when I stood at my window, and I let you see me?"

I hear his heavy breath as if he's laughing on the other end of the line. "Of course, I do. I knew you were trouble even then."

"I wanted you, Alex. I wanted you to be my first because I trusted you."

"Do you still trust me?"

"Yes, I do," I answer, biting my lip. "I trust that your heart is good. That you know the mistakes you've made, and even then, I trusted that you would be different with me."

"The things I did in the past, Sunny. Those weren't mistakes. I was irresponsible because I could be. I broke girls' hearts. I was cruel on purpose, and the reasons I was so fucked up would only be excuses I don't deserve."

Only our breathing fills the line for a moment until he finally mumbles so quietly, I almost don't hear. "I don't deserve you either." And it feels like a sharp knife to my chest. How can he feel that way when I want him so badly? How do I take away this pain for him, opening the doors for our future?

Standing up, I walk up to where the patio chairs sit on the porch, and I bundle my legs up inside my large sweatshirt. Then, I brace myself for what I'm about to ask.

"Then tell me everything," I whisper into the phone.

"Say it all now and then let it all go. Allow yourself a fresh start, and if after I hear everything, I still think you deserve us, I'll come to the house after this is over."

There's a strangled sounding breath, and I know he's fighting tears on the line. After a minute, he starts talking. He starts with his teen years, growing up with such little supervision and too much money. How he threw away his college years partying, trying every drug he could get his hands on, and forming an unhealthy relationship with sex that evolved over the years.

He tells me about the business ventures he started and abandoned, how desperately he misses that life. How he feels he doesn't deserve an ounce of happiness anymore.

"Remember that girl from the gallery party? The one I went out back to smoke with?"

"Yes," I breathe, afraid to hear the rest of this story.

"She was married to my best friend for ten years, and during that trip to Mexico last year, I fucked her in the hot tub. I hurt the person who cared about me most, and for what? Sex?"

"Is that how you got that scar?"

"Can you blame him? He threw my ass into that coffee table, and I didn't even fight him. I knew I deserved it. That's when I knew I needed a change, Sunny. I couldn't live with myself anymore, so I sold my condo and moved into the house."

It was the most painful part of his story, and something about it, knowing what he'd put himself and the people he loved through pained me.

More than once through his two-hour long dialogue, he wept. It was a completely different Alexander than I knew, but I stuck through every word, wishing I could wrap my arms around him.

By the time he finished, we both watched the sky start

to lighten up on the eastern horizon. He didn't ask me anything as the conversation came to an end, and even if he had, I wouldn't have told him. This was about more than whether or not I still trusted him. The things he told me were hard to hear, and I could make excuses like he said. I could say he was a different person then or he had his own issues, but making excuses doesn't make it any easier to accept. He fucked up, and yes, in some ways, he was fucked up.

But I still trusted him.

We don't get to love people because they are perfect or because they've made every right decision. Love is not a reward for good behavior. Love is unconditional because the strongest love endures the hottest fire. And after tonight, knowing more than just the beautiful facade of a man I met in the pool house, I fell in love with him even more.

Before we hung up, I heard the security guards opening the door for him, and we said our goodbyes. He sounded lighter, like everything he had been carrying was weighing him down. But also because even if I wasn't with him, he knew he wasn't alone anymore.

Chapter 33
Sunny

There is no real graduation ceremony for the program. On the last night in the apartment, we threw a party and reminisced. Some of us are celebrating new jobs, and a lot are just celebrating an accomplishment.

Me? I'm just ready to get home.

Just before the party kicked off, Valerie pulled me aside to let me know there was an opening for a commissioned piece in Belize. It would only be a two-week job, but the expenses were paid for and the job was mine in a couple weeks if I wanted it.

"There will only be more after that," she said before leaning in for a hug.

I never fully answered her, but she basically said I had about a week to decide, though I shouldn't take the whole thing.

The whole thing keeps spinning around in my head as I ride home with Cadence. My few things are packed in a duffel bag in the back seat. Alexander and I have only spoken briefly since that night he spilled everything. I feel his distance now, and I don't know if it's because he's keeping himself away from me or if he wants to give me time to consider my next choice.

But I don't need time.

I'm going home with Cadence, but I won't be staying. That isn't my home anymore. Alexander is my home, and there is nothing stopping me from going to him. It's the most scared I've ever been in my entire life.

What if he broke his promise? What if he moved on? Has grown tired of me and no longer sees a future with me?

The girl who he met almost a year ago is a far cry from how I feel today, ready to take the biggest leap of my life. I'm going to ask him to go to Belize with me. I want him there, every step of the way, and if he says no, then I'll be turning the job down. I can't leave him again. As much as my pride wants me to pursue that job, my heart wants a future with Alexander more.

As we pull up to the house, I feel Cadence tense beside me. She's been quiet the whole way home, and I know she's up to something. I quietly pray it's not a surprise party. I'd hate to be rude, but I need to be alone with Alex today.

When she heaves a heavy sigh as we pull into the drive-way, I see my mother standing on the welcome mat. She's about twenty pounds lighter and her eyes are brighter, almost as bright as her smile.

"She didn't leave early if that's what you're wondering," Cadence says with a hesitant smile. "I think it really took this time."

My heart pumps wildly in my chest. Seeing my mother like this, so clearly is almost difficult to accept. When I step out of the car, she rushes toward me.

"Hi, baby," she squeaks, tears flowing freely down her cheeks.

"Hi, Mom," I reply, my voice cracking, and then I'm in her arms. She squeezes my body tight against hers, and I feel her heart hammering too.

I'm trying not to get my hopes up. I don't want to enjoy this version of Mom too much, for fear that it's just a phase and that she won't be around to stay. But today is all about taking leaps, so I decide to jump head first and wrap my arms around her, too.

When she feels me hugging her back, she sobs into my shoulder. And we just stand there like that for a long moment, not saying anything as we both cry. I don't know when my eyes started watering, but for the first time ever, I feel safe with my mom. Safe enough to cry for her.

Cadence takes my bags inside, and I meet my sister and mom around the kitchen island. Mom tells me all about her program and her new hobbies, which apparently include bread making. We laugh together as a family, and it's nice, but I'm still restless.

When it grows quiet, I look at the both of them. "I can't stay," I whisper, waiting to see the disappointment in my mother's eye.

Instead, there is understanding.

"We figured," Cadence answered with an easy laugh. "Mom's been taking him sourdough, and I think he's actually starting to warm up to her."

"It was the cinnamon rolls that got him," she smiles.

This is all too weird. I almost can't bear to even look too closely. What if it all goes away next time I look? Then, I remember how I felt when Alex bared his soul on the rooftop.

Love is not a reward.

I may not forgive my mom yet for everything that

happened, but I still love her. Before I walk out the back door and across the yard, I pull her into a tight hug, and I tell her so. It makes her cry again, but I don't start this time. I'm too anxious to get to his house. Be in his arms.

Leaving my sister and mother, I walk across the patio and backyard, almost feeling like I'm intruding. Is he expecting me? I'm sure he knows the program ended today, but I'm still afraid I'll catch him off guard.

He's not on the patio, but as I head toward the back of the house, something catches my eye in the pool house. With the doors wide open, he's standing with the mural at his back, facing me—like he's waiting for me.

I see his Adam's apple bob as his eyes land on mine. There's relief in his expression, and I don't hesitate, racing toward him and burying my face in his chest. His warm arms engulf me, squeezing my body impossibly tight.

Hungrily, my lips travel up to his mouth, kissing him fiercely. He sucks my lip between his teeth, nibbling enough to light a spark in my body. I really expected that we might actually say at least a few words to each other before we screwed each other straight into next week, but if he keeps kissing me like that, there is absolutely no chance of us waiting.

"Wait," he breathes against my cheek as he pulls away. "We can take our time."

Take our time? Six months for both of us and he wants to take his time? I feel like I'm crawling out of my skin. Reluctantly, I sink back on my heels, looking up at him. He still has the warm beard, and his temples have a few extra colorless strands. I run my hands through his hair, and for a moment, I try to feel a difference. Does knowing what I know about his past change how I feel about him? Am I completely sure about this?

When he smiles at me, the gentle wrinkles in his eyes

shining down on me, I know there isn't a shred of doubt. If anything, my love has only grown.

"You're home," he whispers, kissing my forehead, a hint of question in the hilt of his voice.

"I'm home," I echo, reassuring him. I'm home...for good.

I'll bring up Belize later. There's still time. For now, I just want to enjoy this moment.

"Come inside. I want you to meet someone."

He winds his fingers with mine and pulls me toward the house. I nearly dig my heels in, afraid of who this someone might be, but when I spot the brown striped cat rubbing against his leg as we walk through the door, my jaw drops.

"You got a cat?"

He picks up the animal, and the cat starts purring immediately, rubbing his head against Alexander's chin. It almost seems out of character for him, the man who holds everyone at a distance, falling into a pile of mush for a cat.

"After you left, he just started showing up, hanging around outside. So, I started feeding him, and then he just never left."

Leaning in with a smile, I pet the cat and he purrs against my hand. We never owned animals growing up, but already I can see the appeal. When the cat looks at me, I feel a bond with him. "What's his name?" I ask.

"George."

A laugh bursts from my lips. "That's a terrible name for a cat," I laugh.

Alexander shrugs. "It fits."

My smile stretches across my face as I stand flush against his body, the cat between us we both pet him, until George decides he's had enough and jumps away, finding a spot in the window to nap.

Alexander leans down and kisses me again, and my heart starts hammering in my chest again. When his hands cascade down my back and land on my waist, I press my hips into his. His body reacts immediately, and I can feel it.

"Can I make you dinner first?" he asks, pulling our lips away but keeping his forehead pressed against mine. I have to swallow down my disappointment. I was ready to move this conversation to the bedroom.

"Of course," I answer easily. As he walks away toward the kitchen, I follow him until I take a good look around the house.

It's so unfamiliar from the way I left it. Art hangs on every wall, pictures in frames around the living room. As I turn the corner into the hallway, I notice the office is fitted with a desk with a laptop and papers stacked along the surface.

I almost can't believe it's the same house. There isn't one box in sight.

"I unpacked," he laughs.

"I see that." I try to laugh in return, but the good feeling gets caught in my throat.

He busies himself in the kitchen, and I can't stop looking around his house. He's made it a home. I can see signs of him living here, happy here. Whatever he's working on in that office, it looks like he's deep into something, and although I'm anxious to hear about it, I'm also dreading hearing about whatever it is.

Alexander has finally settled down. His house is a home. He got a fucking cat.

And I want him to leave it all behind to chase me to Belize.

All through dinner, I try to hold my smile for him, but while I watch him cook, sitting at the counter, I can't stop weighing these options in my mind.

Turning down this job feels impossible.

Leaving him again...even more impossible.

But what choice do I have? It's not fair for me to ask him to uproot his life again, not when he's come so far. What if doing so would throw him back into his old behavior? What if the party scene in Belize brings out the old Alexander and ruins all of his progress?

I have a feeling that if I asked, he would undoubtedly say yes.

And I can't take that risk.

While he's busy stirring the pasta on the stove top, his back to me, I pull out my phone and shoot a quick text to Valerie. As soon as it's sent, I feel a weight lifted off my shoulders.

There will be other jobs. I can find fulfilling work here in Pineridge. Now there is absolutely nothing standing in the way between Alexander and me.

When we sit down to eat, we lift our sparkling waters in the air as a toast. "Alright, so tell me everything. Did you get any job offers yet?"

I knew this question was coming, and I won't lie to Alex, but I have to find a way around it.

"A couple, but I'm weighing my options."

"That's amazing," he says with a smile. "I'm so proud of you."

Looking at him, sitting across from me, happier than I've ever seen him, I feel myself falling all over again. "I'm proud of you, too."

"I haven't changed too much?" he asks with a wink as he leans back in his chair.

"You're still a cocky prick most of the time, right?"

His smile stretches. "Of course."

"Good," I answer with a grin.

The moment grows tense as he stares at me, and I feel

the heavy questions on his lips. "About that night, Sunny…"

"I'm glad you told me everything, Alex. But it didn't change anything for me."

He leans forward and takes my hand. "I don't deserve you. It just doesn't feel right…"

Still grappling with his troubled past, I see the struggle in his expression, and I can't bear to be this far away from him, so I close the distance and climb onto his lap, kissing his lips.

"You were so afraid you would ruin me, Alex. That I would come out of this worse for having been with you, but do you see how much you've changed me? I'm not afraid of anything anymore. I had no one in my corner, Alex. Then, I had you. You didn't make me worse, you made me better."

When his mouth finds mine, he kisses me with everything he has. The struggle is gone, and I give it all right back to him. This time, I don't let him stop as I kiss down his cheek to his neck, working the buttons on his shirt at the same time.

Suddenly, we're standing, and he's holding me with my legs wrapped around his waist. His hands are hard against my backside as he pulls me tight against him. Walking to the bedroom, I'm desperate for his body.

Slowly, he drops me to the bed, climbing over me. He lifts my shirt over my head, trailing kisses from my belly, up to my neck and then to my mouth. We are both starved for each other as the clothes start flying off our bodies until there is nothing left between us.

With his lips around my nipple and his fingers deep between my legs, I nearly come for the first time in six months, but he pulls away just as I almost crest the peak. I let out a cry as he moves away. Looking down at me, he smiles a wicked grin, knowing exactly what he's doing to me.

"Stop messing around, Alexander Caldwell."

"Promise you'll come with me," he says laying his body flat against mine. "Promise you'll wait."

Before I can promise him anything, my breath escapes my lips as he presses himself inside me, and I don't see how it will be possible for me to wait.

He lets out a long, delicious groan once he's as deep as he can go. The sweet sensation of him filling me, touching places inside of me that make me want to die for him, make his request seem impossible.

"I don't think you'll have to wait for long," he grunts against my lips as he pulls back and slams back into me, going as deep as he can go.

Finding his hands with mine, I intertwine our fingers and I keep his lips on my mouth as he moves, picking up his speed. Our breaths mingle through every gasp, and as I hold my body back, somehow trying *not* to come, I feel like his pleasure is mine.

I didn't know two people could be as close as we are at this moment.

My walls are coming down as he reaches deeper and deeper, faster and faster, and I'm not sure how I'll last much longer—until he gasps my name, and I breathe his in return.

Finally, we both let go.

Electricity erupts from my core, coursing through my body as my orgasm lasts and lasts. We're both gasping and quivering as our bodies finally relax. He kisses my lips, sensitive and swollen from the roughness of his beard. When his eyes find mine, we both relax into easy smiles.

Chapter 34

Alexander

George wakes me up around seven like he does every morning, walking across my chest and purring into my ear. But it's like as soon as he sees the petite girl lying next to me, he decides she's a better choice and crawls over to her. Can't say I blame him.

She stirs with a smile, petting the cat and looking at me with a sleepy grin.

"I have to feed him, but I'll be back. Don't move."

Leaning over, I kiss her quickly on the mouth and get out of bed to feed George, knowing he won't leave me alone until I do. Returning to the bed, I notice my phone buzzing, but I don't even bother to flip it over to see who's calling. Whoever it is, they can wait. Climbing back under the covers, I find Sunny's warm body completely naked and pull her over to me.

All I want to do is cover her body with my mouth, repeating what we did three times last night. I can't remember the last time I had stamina like that, but six months without sex can do a body good apparently.

I can't remember the last time I felt so good. And just not physically. My mind is clear, and I don't have the doubts and worries weighing on me like I did when I moved into this house. Every terrible thing I told myself when Sunny started staying here feels like a distant memory now. It's just her and me, and all the cards are on the table. There are no secrets between us anymore, and if she still wants me after she learned the truth, then I am freer than I've ever been before.

After some beautiful morning sex, Sunny jumps into the shower. I'm tempted to join her but morning runs are another one of my morning routines that I can't skip. Grabbing my phone, I plan on making my run short today so I can get back to her.

Putting my earbuds in, I start my playlist and take off out the front door. I'm only about a quarter of a mile in when the music is interrupted by a call. Glancing down at my watch, I see it's Valerie, so I hit the accept button.

"Morning, Valerie. What can I do for you?"

"Well, Sunny isn't answering her phone. I assume she's with you." She sounds almost irritated.

"She's back at the house. What's up?" I ask, eager for her to get to the point.

"Maybe you're the person to talk to anyway," she says only hesitating for a moment. "She texted me last night. She's turning down the Belize job, and I think it's a mistake, Alex."

I stop running, my heart hammering in my chest. "What Belize job?" I ask.

"It's not my place to tell you, I know that."

"What Belize job?" I echo, growing hot.

"It's a commissioned piece. It's a big deal, Alexander, and I just hate to see her pass it up."

My face starts to feel clammy. "I'll talk to her, Valerie."

My voice is clipped as I hang up on the woman, turning to run back to the house.

Why wouldn't she tell me about that opportunity? That weightlessness I felt this morning is now gone because I have to worry about Sunny keeping secrets from me. Was she really afraid I would hold her back from this?

No. But if she thought it was between me and this job, she'd pick me.

What kind of man would I be if I let her do that?

Rushing back into the house, I meet her in the kitchen. She's making coffee in nothing but one of my T-shirts. There is still a red tint to her cheeks from last night and this morning. Not to mention the sight of her back in my home, doing these everyday things that should make me feel so good have me feeling like a selfish asshole. Because I want her to stay. I don't want her going to Belize, but once again, I'm forced into this corner.

"That was fast," she says with a smile, and I can't bring myself to be angry. Sure, I want to yell at her. Inside, I'm seething. I need her to be honest. I need everything between us to be transparent so that every single decision we make, we make together.

But I'm at a loss, and deep down, I'm scared as hell. What if I yell, and she leaves? What if I have to do what I did six months ago and push her away? I don't know if I can go through that again.

Letting the fear take over, I approach her and pull her small shoulders into a tight hug. Clutching her body in my hands, I press my face against her neck.

"Alex, what is it?" she gasps.

"I told you everything, Sunny. I didn't leave a single thing out. I need you to do the same."

Holding my hair between her fingers, she whispers. "I am…" It's obvious she's holding back.

"I don't know if you're trying to protect me or if you're trying to protect us, but we have no future if you keep me out of your life."

"Valerie told you." Her voice is quiet as she slumps against my arms.

"Belize, Sunny. You turned down Belize for what...this?" I say gesturing around to the house. "If I push you away, would you go? If I told you I didn't love you anymore, would it change your mind?"

She squeezes me tighter. "I wouldn't believe you."

"Then, take the job and don't force my hand." It pains me to say it. It actually hurts my chest to say those words, knowing that our time is limited, and this will keep happening over and over again.

"I won't leave you."

My blood boils. I hate myself for wanting her to stay. I hate that she wants to give up her whole future for me, and I hate that I love her so fucking much I have to endure this pain. Taking her face in my hands, I force her to look at me.

"Then, I'm coming with you."

With her hands clasped around my shirt and in my hair, I watch the tears pool in her eyes. "But what about the house?"

"Fuck the house, Sunny. It's just a house."

My chest tightens, keeping her face just inches from mine. It feels too good to be true. Too perfect to accept.

"But you've made so much progress this year, Alex. You've built a life here. I can't take that away."

Taking her lips in mine, I let her feel how serious I am. Could all my years of throwing my life away really come to this? Having everything? Having something better than perfection?

"It's nothing without you," I speak against her lips.

"What about George?" she cries, tears streaming.

"We'll bring him with," I laugh. "He'll love it there. And then after Belize, we'll go to the next place, and the next place. And as long as you're there, I'm there."

As she sinks into my arms, I try to process how this happened. And why the fuck I ever fought it. Sunny may be younger than me, but I wasted most of my life waiting for happiness to find me. I just never expected I would find it right next door.

Epilogue

Sunny

little over a year later…

"God, it's so good to be home," I moan, rolling over to wrap my arms around his torso. He's already awake and has been for over an hour. He's always up before me, answering emails on his phone and putting out fires before he's even had his coffee.

"Yes, it is," he mumbles, putting his phone down on the stand and rolling me over to trace kisses down my neck.

Wrapping my legs around his waist, I try to ease him into place. I love how he's always ready to go every morning.

"Why, Mrs. Caldwell," he groans, shifting his body to meet mine.

"Promise me we'll start every day like this," I hum as he grinds his hips against me.

"I think as long as you stay on the pill, that won't be a problem." He peels my clothes off slowly, and I silently think about him filling me with his seed. How eagerly I would trade in the luxury of morning sex for the chance to carry a little piece of him inside of me. But I promised him at least five years. So, for now I'll enjoy my orgasms before 9:00am.

As he fills the space between my legs, I look up at him and think about the first time I saw him, standing across the yard. I take myself back to the early days of our forbidden love, when the idea of being together tore us apart. I relive the moments that led up to this, when we fell in love, fell apart, and found each other again.

He settles his weight on my body, burying his face in my neck and wrapping his arms around me so that we are entangled and practically one. Our bodies move in a sensual rhythm until his ecstasy is mine and mine is his.

After we've both finished, I trace my fingers along the skin of his back. Neither of us move for a long time.

"I love you," he murmurs against my cheek.

Then, he places a kiss on my head and rolls over until he's sitting on the edge of the bed, facing away from me. "It's strange to be back here," he says, staring down at the ring on his finger.

"You worried?" I ask, reaching out and holding his hand in mine. I was afraid that returning home would be difficult for him. This town holds too many difficult memories for him, of things he's done and who he used to be. For so long, Alex lived up to people's expectations of him, mostly when they underestimated him. If he's back here, will he fall into that same old routine?

We talked a lot about settling down somewhere else. With every place we visited and talked about staying, the decision just kept coming back to this house. This is our home, where our love was born.

When he looks back at me, the morning sun bright behind him, I take a mental picture of how beautiful he is in this moment. With a glowing tan and a thick beard, he doesn't look like the defeated man I met a year ago. He's aged, comfortable in his own skin like he never was before.

"Not worried at all, rain cloud."

His phone rings, but he ignores it as he leans down to press his lips to mine.

"You can answer that," I whisper because I can tell he wants to. We're supposed to be on vacation from work, but Alexander loves his work. I see the way it fulfills him and how it's built back a piece of him that was broken.

"Thank you," he murmurs against my mouth before he jumps up and grabs his phone from the nightstand.

"Tell Joachim this is technically our honeymoon," I call as Alex disappears into the en-suite bathroom.

"He knows," Alex laughs. "I'm the one bugging him."

George jumps onto the bed and cuddles with me, purring by my head while he waits patiently for his breakfast.

Before Alex emerges from the bathroom in his running clothes, I climb out of bed and put on a robe, carrying George in my arms. The view from my bedroom window, the one that crosses the yard to my old house, stops me. The large picture window overlooks our pool, the pool house, and the yard that is now owned by a young family with three little ones, who all look like they're eagerly awaiting their chance to dive into the water.

In the dead of summer, I bet they're out there every morning. Alexander and I have only been home for a week now, and not a day has gone by that I haven't heard them out there.

We decided to keep the house during our year abroad. Cadence happily looked after the place while we were gone. Mom decided to sell the house not long after we left anyway, so my sister took the opportunity to live on her own until she saved up enough for her own place.

She got to watch George for us, too.

Carrying the cat out to the kitchen, I feed him first, then start on the coffee. Reaching for the mugs, the glint of my diamond setting catches the sun, and I pause, looking at the ring on my finger.

Six months ago, while I was finishing up a job in Australia, he proposed. Two weeks later, we said our vows on the beach in Hawaii. My mom and Cadence were there. His sister, Charlotte, and his new best friend and business partner that he met in Belize flew out. Just the six of us with a minister on a windy Saturday. My dress wasn't even white, but I didn't care. Neither of us did. We just wanted to make that promise and start our lives.

Since that day, it's been a whirlwind. He launched his business, a marketing agency geared toward pairing young artists with major brands. I took on my biggest job to date, a collaborative piece with Valerie and Gino in New York, and we were so busy working and traveling that we never took a minute to celebrate married life or enjoy a honeymoon.

So, we made this homecoming our honeymoon. No one is allowed to bother us for a whole week. With my birthday tomorrow, we made big plans to do absolutely nothing but sit around the pool and enjoy each other all day long. Being my twenty-first birthday, everyone including Hanna and Valerie are bugging the shit out of me to go out with them, but I keep putting them off. Call me old fashioned, but there's absolutely nothing in a bar that sounds better than my new husband at home on the couch.

Alexander weaves his arms around my waist and kisses my neck. He settles in, taking a deep breath as we just hold each other, my body pressed between his and the countertop.

"You sure you don't want a party tomorrow?" he asks. Always so concerned I'm missing out on something, which only makes me laugh. The last year has been so busy, a constant adventure, that I'll need at least six months to recover. I laugh, squeezing his arms a little tighter.

"I'm very sure."

He kisses my head again and snatches his earbuds and phone off the counter.

Just before he turns toward the door, our eyes meet, and he seems to lose himself in my eyes. I wonder if he ever feels this thing between us as intensely as I do. When my heart felt so empty, he was there, not to fill it with his own love, but to teach me how to fill it with my own.

Suddenly, he tosses his earbuds on the counter. "I'll run later." With that, he hoists me up onto his shoulder, and I let out a yelp as he carries me out to the pool. Luckily, the trees are in full bloom giving us enough privacy from the neighbors as he tosses my barely naked body into the water, following closely behind. The only watching eyes are from the brightly colored mural on the wall of the pool house.

Want to see Alexander & Sunny in five years?

Get the bonus epilogue here!

Read Sunny's sister, Cadence, in her story, Beautiful Sinner: geni.us/BeautifulSinner

* * *

Keep scrolling for signed paperbacks and other stories from this author!

Bonus Epilogue
Alexander

F ive years later

It's nearly midnight, and I know she can't sleep. Neither can I. As my wife stirs next to me, I quietly climb out of bed and pad down the hallway toward the patio door. It's a warm spring, warm enough to sit outside at midnight in nothing but my boxer shorts.

I'm turning forty-six tomorrow, and the uncertainty of our future has me feeling more sleepless than relaxed these days. Everything was going so nicely for the first five years of our marriage, but now...I don't know what to expect. Part of me wants these days to go by faster, but another part longs for the days when I had control. When I had my beautiful wife and nothing but time to savor every second with her.

I feel like I'm crawling out of my skin, so I dive into the deep end, coming up and seeing a light turn on in the kitchen. She stares at me from across the way, and instant shame floods my senses. She's worried about me. Worried how I will handle all this. Deep down she might even be worried I'll bolt.

As she walks out into the darkness, my gaze lingers on her perfect ankles and travels up her legs to the swelling mound growing where her flat stomach used to be. She's worried her body will change too much, that I won't find her attractive anymore, but as she dangles her legs in the water, I swim up to her, unable to keep my hands off her soft hips.

I love our midnight swims because it's the only time she's comfortable coming out in nothing but her panties. Her swollen breasts are there for me to caress. I can't get enough of her changing body. I know it won't stay this way, but I'm along for the whole ride.

"It's after midnight," she whispers as I scoot her bottom to the edge of the pool so I kiss her inner thighs. "Happy birthday."

"Got my birthday present right here," I moan against the warm fabric between her legs.

Leaning back on her hands, she lets out a gentle hum of pleasure. But just as I move back in for another kiss, I feel something move against my hand.

Both of us jolting, I stare at her face with wide eyes.

"Did you feel that?" she gasps.

"Yes," I stammer, holding my palms against the tight skin of her belly. Up until now, only Sunny has felt our little girl kick. I seem to miss it every time she says she's active. Every step of the way through this pregnancy, I keep waiting for the moment when it feels real. The blue line on the stick, the heartbeat at the doctor's office, the first ultrasound. When I asked Joachim if this was normal, he just told me that until you hold that baby, nothing feels real. And nothing will ever be the same after that moment.

I can't wait.

But I'm also fucking terrified.

What kind of father will I be after the mistakes I've made? What if she ends up like me—reckless and wild? What do I do when she inevitably finds out about my life before her?

These questions swirl around my head with every passing day.

"You have that worry in your eyes again," Sunny whispers, running her nails along my scalp to calm me down.

When I look up at Sunny, I remember the pain she endured because of her parents' neglect, and I promise myself (for the four-thousandth time) that I will never let this child feel that way. If I can do that much, surely I won't be a total failure as a parent.

"Aren't you scared, rain cloud?"

"About giving birth? Sure. Everything else…we'll get through it together, Alex."

As I rest my head against the warm flesh of her thigh, I can't imagine loving anyone the way I love Sunny. And watching her grow with my baby, my heart has only swelled. Some days I'm afraid I'll wake up and learn it was all too good to be true. How could a guy like me expect to be so lucky?

I spent so long making the worst decisions, hoping to fill a void with all of the worst things possible. When Sunny walked into my life, she didn't just fill the void, she became my life. And for five years, it was just us.

Now, our lives are about to grow.

"I hope she has your eyes," I say, still hanging onto Sunny's lap.

Holding my hands and lips against her belly, I feel the

movement again. It's like Sunny's insides are rearranging themselves as our daughter shifts around in her cramped space.

"She can hear your voice," Sunny whispers.

Looking back at her belly, I lean in with my lips against her skin. "Hello, Isabel Rain."

Again, there's a thumping against my palms. I know I should feel ridiculous, but when I look up and see Sunny's eyes full and wet, I don't give a shit how it looks. I lean in and tell our baby that I love her, holding my wife as close as possible.

In just twelve more weeks, I'll be a father, starting a whole new phase of my life at such a late age. After the time I wasted and mistakes I've made, I'll take every single second of this luck I've been handed. And I will never waste another second for as long as I live.

Thank you for reading *Beautiful Monster*.

I never meant to write this book, but these characters stole my time and attention until I told their story. I loved every minute, even when I wanted to tear my hair out just trying to get it right.

If you loved Alexander and Sunny, please consider leaving your opinion for future readers to see. Click here to review.

This book was a team effort, and it wouldn't be right if I didn't acknowledge those who helped me in this process.

My beta readers: Adrian, Suzanne, Kari, Erica, Jenn, Rachel.

My editor: Nikki Holt Sexton

My cover designer: Barb Hoeter of Coverinked Designs

My graphic design artist: Amanda Shepard of Shepard Originals

My PR company: Give Me Books Promotions

And last but not least, the BEAUTIFUL members of Sara's Sweets, who are too many to name. Every day, I log in to that group because you lift me up. Thank you.

muah

Also by Sara Cate

Salacious Players' Club

Praise

Eyes on Me

Give Me More

Mercy

Highest Bidder

Madame

The Goode Brothers series

The Anti-hero

The Home Wrecker - coming in 2024

The Heart Breaker - coming in 2024

The Prodigal Son - coming in 2024

Age-gap romance

Beautiful Monster

Beautiful Sinner

Wilde Boys duet

Gravity

Freefall

Black Heart Duet

Four

Five

Cocky Hero Club

Handsome Devil

Bully romance

Burn for Me

Wicked Hearts Series

Delicate

Dangerous

Defiant

About Sara Cate

Sara Cate writes forbidden romance with lots of angst, a little age gap, and heaps of steam. Living in Arizona with her husband and kids, Sara spends most of her time reading, writing, or baking.

You can find more information about her at
    www.saracatebooks.com

Printed in the USA
CPSIA information can be obtained
at www.ICGtesting.com
CBHW031408031024
15316CB00028B/218